SILVER HAWK

A Warrior's Pride

By: Alice Miller

Dedicated to the Indigenous Youth
Of many Nations...

You carry the hopes and visions of your people.
Take them into the future with honor.

For: Annalisa, Miguelito, Michael, Jonathan, Sara,
Rosalita, Lilly & Ethan.

Chapter One

"You're brother's weird," Tommy Eagle Chaser said. "He's always staring at people."

"He's not weird," Wolf said. He bounced the basketball on the asphalt. "He's just been through a lot of stuff." He looked over at Cheetah sitting alone in the wooden bleachers. His brother was staring straight ahead at nothing in particular, just staring. Wolf sighed. "Let's get back to the game," he suggested.

"No man," Steve Battise added, "he's weird. Look, Suzy's coming by. Watch him. He doesn't look or lean back trying to look good. He doesn't say hello to her…he just stares like he doesn't even see her."

Wolf began to bounce the ball at a regular pounding beat, trying to drown out their words. He'd heard them before. Tommy always started it then everyone else joined in.

"Hey Suzy," Tommy said, winking at her.

Suzy Takes-The-Bear scowled and walked the other way.

They laughed, loud and whistled after her.

"Look," Tommy said, glancing at Cheetah. "Look at him. He doesn't even move. Is he breathing?"

They laughed.

"Maybe he's not interested in…you know, Suzy," Steve said, snickering. "Maybe he's more interested in Jack." Steve pointed to Jack Dann who was stumbling drunk down the road.

Wolf caught the ball in his hands and looked directly at Steve. "You better shut your mouth," he warned in a low tone.

"Hey, I read the papers, ok? Maybe all that wasn't forced on him," Steve said. "Maybe he liked it."

Wolf dropped the ball and shoved into Steve's chest. They grappled and hit the ground. Wolf drew back his fist and swung hard into Steve's face. They rolled and Steve pinned him. Suddenly, everything stopped. No one yelled 'kick his ass'. No one laughed and they barely breathed. Steve's clenched fist was coming but it stopped and hung suspended in mid-air. Wolf shoved Steve off of him and got to his feet. Everyone was staring in the direction where his brother had been sitting. Wolf looked over and saw that Cheetah wasn't sitting anymore. Cheetah was standing in the bleachers with his chin slightly lifted and his head tilted a little to one side. It was as if he'd had been waiting for Steve to strike.

"He's a freak," Steve scowled, stalking off the court.

Everyone nodded, mumbled in agreement, and went with him.

Wolf sighed and began to bounce the ball at a regular pounding beat. He saw his brother out of the corner of his eye, but didn't acknowledge him. The ball hit the asphalt and back to his hand again, again, again…until two scarred hands caught it.

"I told you not to defend me," Cheetah said. "I don't care what they say. I told you that, eh?"

Wolf raised his eyes to meet his brother's intense gaze. "Do you know what they're saying?"

"It doesn't matter."

Wolf gave a frustrated sigh. He took his hands away and

left Cheetah holding the ball. He shook his head, muttering under his breath.

"What's wrong?" Cheetah asked him. "I told you it would be like this."

Wolf looked at his brother, standing there wearing the long black trench coat and street boots. Cheetah wore black pants and either a white or black muscle T-shirt and rarely dressed in anything else. He'd been running the streets with Los Caballeros in New York but here, his heavy Spanish accent sounded strange. "You don't even try," Wolf said.

"Try to do what, eh?" Cheetah asked, tucking the ball under his arm.

"Fit in," Wolf said. "We've been home for a week. You haven't talked to anyone all you do is sit and..." His voice trailed off in frustration. "Never mind," he said, walking away.

"Sit and what?" Cheetah asked, walking beside him. "You know I can't play basketball. I don't know how."

"I know that," Wolf said. He looked at Cheetah, who was his identical twin but he'd discovered there were never two people more unalike. "You stare at people."

Cheetah smirked. "What?" he asked.

"You stare at people and it..."

"Wolf," Cheetah interrupted, "I'm not staring at anyone, eh? I've noticed a lot of paranoia from your friends when I come around. Es that what you're talking about?"

"They're not paranoid," Wolf said, although he knew they were.

"Es called intimidation," Cheetah told him, "and es not my fault. I'm not trying to make it happen." He gave Wolf the ball. "I'll tell you what, I won't come around."

"Cheetah..."

5

"When my money comes," Cheetah said, "I'll go."

"Why can't you try to fit in?"

"How?" Cheetah asked, emphatically. "I don't even know what you're talking about."

"You stand out," Wolf said. "Everyone notices you but it's for the wrong things."

Cheetah huffed out a frustrated breath and turned his face away.

"It's just...weird," Wolf said. Cheetah turned his head slowly to look at him. Wolf wished he hadn't said it. "I mean..." he began.

"I know what you mean," Cheetah said. "I heard them and now I'm hearing you say their words. Es that what I have to do here to fit in? I'm not a copy of anyone else. I've always been different or eh...weird, if you remember right. I can't stop people from whispering or staring. I never could."

Wolf watched his brother stalk away from him. The wind picked up the tail of Cheetah's trench coat as he walked down over the small hill with a slight limp. He'd hurt his leg in the last fight he'd been in and it didn't seem to be getting better. He'd grown up in the city and nothing about him was ordinary. But Cheetah was right, Wolf thought, he'd never been ordinary. Even before their father went to prison when they were four years old, living together on the rez, the elders pegged Cheetah for someone an entire prophecy surrounded. They whispered and stared at him then, too. They said he had lived before. He had returned from the past because of *Wanagi Wacipi*, the Ghost Dance, and he was a warrior. Cheetah was a warrior, Wolf thought as he walked behind his brother, but he was a warrior of the streets. When their dad killed Jake Many Horses and mom took Cheetah to live in the city, the whole prophecy slipped and fell.

By the time Wolf got to the house, Cheetah was in the kitchen cooking supper. It was another thing about him that didn't fit what people had expected of him. He liked to cook. "I'm sorry," Wolf said, leaning on the frame of the doorway.

"About what? Es not your fault," Cheetah said. He took the pot to the sink and turned on the water to fill it. "I'm making spaghetti. Do you like that?"

"Yeah," Wolf said. He paused. "I don't want you to go anywhere."

"I don't know what to do here," Cheetah told him. "Papa got a job working construction. Maybe I'll do that, eh?"

"You don't need a job," Wolf said. "You have money." A lot of money, Wolf thought silently.

"Es not my money and I don't want it," Cheetah said, carrying the pot back to the stove. "I have to find something to do or I'll go crazy…or eh…crazier than I already am." He lit the gas stove and added, "Es what I hear anyway."

Wolf sighed.

"I'm not going back to school," Cheetah said. "That would be asking for trouble every day. You should finish. Get that scholarship and play college ball." He stirred the sauce, added another seasoning and tasted it. "How is this supposed to taste?" he asked Wolf. "Here, you try it." He looked at Wolf. His brother was staring at the floor again. "What's the matter now?" Cheetah asked, "Am I being too weird in the house? There's nobody here. I think es okay to be weird in your own house."

"I'm not going back to school," Wolf said.

"Why not?"

Wolf shrugged. He walked into the living room and sat down on the couch. He leaned his head back and stared up at the cracks in the ceiling. Why not? Yeah, why not go to school and hear this stuff all day long? It was bad enough as it was.

Stands Proud came through the door and found Wolf upset

and sitting on the couch and Cheetah was in the kitchen cooking supper. Every day was a repeat of the one before. "What's wrong now?" he asked.

"Nothing," Wolf said quietly.

"Oh, same thing as yesterday," Stands Proud said. "Big surprise." He went into the kitchen. "Hey son," he said to Cheetah.

"How was work?" Cheetah asked.

"Lousy," Stands Proud said. He sat down at the table. "Did you go to the doctor about your leg?"

"No," Cheetah said. "Not yet."

"Are you waiting for a special holiday? The new moon? A full moon?" Stands Proud asked. "Your next life time?"

Cheetah smirked. "None of those," he said. He put the spaghetti on the plates and got the garlic bread out of the oven. He put everything on the table. "Wolf, come eat," he called out. He looked at Stands Proud. "I'm waiting for an appointment. I called the day after we got here and I called on Wednesday too. Also, I called this morning."

"What did they say?" Stands Proud inquired.

"I get as far as telling them my name," Cheetah said, "and they say es not convenient for the doctor to see me today. Call again."

Stands Proud sighed heavily. He knew Cheetah would have a hard time when he came back to the rez but this was out of line. "Did you try the doctors in Rapid City?" he asked.

"Same thing," Cheetah said, "only they didn't say call back." He sat down at the table and looked up as Wolf came into the room. Wolf walked with his shoulders hunched forward and his chin down. He'd had a lost look to him ever since they had come back from the city. As he pulled a chair out and plopped into it, Cheetah felt the guilt washing over him like a constant rain. "I'm sorry," he said but Wolf ignored him. "I'm sorry you got mixed up in my life, eh?" Cheetah said in a louder voice.

"He's not mixed up in your life," Stands Proud said, leaning both arms on the table. "You're brothers."

Cheetah glanced at his father. "Es not going to work out."

"What isn't?" Stands Proud asked.

"Me," Cheetah said, "living here on the rez." He'd left with his mother when he was five and lived in New York for thirteen years. After everything happened, coming home was harder than he thought it would be.

"You've only been here a week. Give it a chance," Stands Proud said. He glanced at Wolf, the older of the two. "No one wants you to go anywhere."

"Eh you're wrong about that Papa," Cheetah said, getting up to get a glass of water. He winced as the pain shot through his leg and waited until he could move it.

"I'll take the day off tomorrow," Stands Proud said, "and we'll get that leg looked at."

"*Gracias,*" Cheetah said, hobbling over to the sink, "but I've been doing things on my own for a long time. I think I can go to the doctors alone. I'll go to the clinic."

Stands Proud sighed heavily and looked up at him as he came back to the table. "But you have money and those doctors in town should take it," he insisted. "The clinic is crowded and you'll be there all day."

"Eh well," Cheetah said, sitting down. "The doctors in town don't want my money or me sitting in their waiting room. I'm not doing anything else. All I've been doing is sitting around being weird and staring at people…"

Wolf got up from the table and walked through the living

9

room. He grabbed his coat on the way out of the house and slammed the door shut.

"What's wrong with him?" Stands Proud asked.

"Eh…" Cheetah said slowly, "his friends are giving him a hard time because of me. You know what es going on," he said. "Es not any different than before. I don't have a problem with being different from them but he does. A lot of people do."

"A lot of people understand too," Stands Proud said.

"Who does?"

"I do," Stands Proud said, "Your Aunt Jolene, Pete, Henry and…"

"They're family," Cheetah said. "They have to say they understand me. I'm the reservation freak, eh? They only claim me because they have to. If any one of them saw me on Salcida Avenue they would try to get away as fast as they could."

"You're not a freak," Stands Proud said. He set the fork down on the table and sighed. He rubbed a hand over his face. He was tired and it had been a long day.

"I'm not normal, eh?" Cheetah told him. "Normal is someone who's been here all their life, a person who doesn't have a hundred and fifty years of memories floating around in their head. Papa, I haven't been normal from the day I was born and I'm okay with that but no one else is, especially Wolf."

Stands Proud released an aggravated sigh. "There was only one person who could have told me what to do about this," he said, "and I killed him."

Cheetah smirked at his father's turmoil. "You should have let him finish telling the prophecy before you strangled him."

"I didn't like the first part much, obviously," Stands Proud said, "and I didn't think I wanted to hear the end of it. Now I think about it every day. I don't want you to leave here just because it's hard. Nothing is ever easy. You're supposed to be here. You know that," Stands Proud said, "everyone else will have to accept it."

"What about Wolf?" Cheetah asked.

"He should be more understanding," Stands Proud said. "He knows what you've been through."

"Everyone knows, eh? They're walking around saying I liked what Antonio and those men did. Maybe I could change that if I got a girl friend but I don't want one. Marisa was…" He stared hard at the table and everything before him was clouded with tears again. He saw her lying in the alley, with the blood on her chest, as clearly as he had that night. He could still hear the sound of his own voice apologizing to her and crying. Cheetah got up from the table. "Excuse me," he said. Angrily, he forced his leg to move.

Stands Proud didn't have to look. He knew what was going to happen. He wasn't a seer but the same scene played out every night this week. Cheetah had gone down the hallway, into the bathroom, and lost what little food he'd managed to eat. And mechanically, trying not to feel the pain, Stands Proud arose from the table and went to Cheetah's bedroom where he found his son sitting in the dark. Cheetah used to hate the dark. He feared it. Now, he lived inside of it. "Son..?" Stands Proud said, leaning with one hand on the frame of the door way.

"Es all right Papa," Cheetah said softly, with the darkness of night surrounding him. "Es all right."

Stands Proud knew it wasn't.

Chapter Two

The waiting room was crowded and there was no where to sit. Cheetah leaned against the wall in the corner, trying to stay out of everyone's way, and he waited. He learned not to look at the clock. Instead, he watched the people. Some of them he vaguely remembered from when he was little. Buddy was holding his head where someone or something had left a gash an inch long. Jim's face was troubled with deep concern but Cheetah couldn't see what was wrong with him. Cheetah watched his aunts, Jolene and Martha, waiting on people and taking them to the back room. They'd seen him and took a few seconds to say hello but they were too busy to say anything else.

The door opened and a woman came in, her eyes cast downward. Her face was bruised, colored purple, blue and black. There was a cut on her forehead and blood running down the side of her head but she seemed not to notice. She moved slowly, shuffling her feet to an empty space by the window where she could look outside.

Cheetah watched as the tears streamed over her face. He recognized the pain. He knew that look in her eyes, the slowness of her walk and the way she stared outside. He took the bandana out of his coat pocket, wet it under the water fountain and limped across the floor. He stood beside her for a few moments, waiting. He knew not to approach her too fast. When she glanced at him and moved a few inches away, recoiling from his presence, he wasn't surprised or offended. Ever so slowly, he raised his hand and offered the wet bandana, holding his hand out toward her. His throat ached and his chest tightened as his action caused more tears to flow from her eyes. Cheetah held his breath as her hand, trembling, came upward and her cut, swollen fingers, closed slowly over the cloth. He stood still and let her take all the time she needed to accept something from him. When she managed to steal the bandana away, he stood ready at her side. She covered her face, wiping the blood away and she began to cry harder. She fell against his chest because he was the only one there and

Cheetah wrapped his arms around her, feeling the violent sobs shaking into him.

The door opened and two Tribal Police came inside looking for her and finding him. They pulled them apart, shoved her back out the door but they hesitated before grabbing him.

"Come outside," Officer Kent Shortwing said.

"Why?" Cheetah asked. A hand slammed down on his shoulder and it shut his entire body down. He turned off the instant reaction to fight. He swallowed more rage and started forward. Cheetah hobbled to the door.

The people in the waiting room stared, as if they'd been expecting this all morning. That was Stands Proud's boy, the gang leader from the city. He'd done all the drugs on the planet and was probably still on a few. The papers said he'd been involved with a mob boss. There were six articles printed telling the story of how he was whipped and beaten. The stories said he was repeatedly raped by a group of men and they wondered if he was gay. No one said it to his face because he was supposed to be a hell of a fighter, a master of martial arts, but they whispered and they stared when he was taken away.

Cheetah stumbled out the door, catching the railing and trying not to fall.

"I don't know him!" the woman screamed and cried.

"I don't know her," Cheetah offered but the Tribal cop shoved into him and his left leg buckled. He felt himself going down but his arm caught and hung onto the rail. His body had collapsed but he didn't fall.

The Tribal cop hauled him to his feet and dragged him over to the car. "Where were you about an hour ago?" he asked.

"In there," Cheetah told him, pointing to the Indian Health Clinic. "I've been here since this morning, eh?" The cop studied him, hands on his hips, in an accusing manner. "My Aunt Jolene works here. Martha does too. You can ask them," he said. He glanced at the woman, sitting in the back seat of the police car. "I was just being nice to her," Cheetah said.

"Stay right there," the Officer Shortwing told him, "and don't you move." He called out to his partner, "Harold, watch him."

Cheetah sighed as the younger Officer came up and stood a foot away from him, with his hand resting on his gun. "I didn't do anything," Cheetah said, in a raspy voice. He waited in silence because the Officer stared at him, as if he was daring Cheetah to move.

Officer Shortwing came down the steps. "You're lucky this time," he told the young man. "He's telling the truth Harold. Everybody said he was in there," he said to the other Officer. He looked directly at the young man. "I knew we'd meet sooner or later," he said. "I wasn't here when they brought you in for that trial but I'm here now."

Cheetah turned his head and looked away.

"If I'd been here," Officer Shortwing stated, "you wouldn't have been able to run off like you did."

"I was cleared of all the charges," Cheetah said.

"That's what they tell me," Officer Shortwing said. "I sent to New York and I have everything on you in a nice, neat file. If you're inclined to add more to it, I want you to know you'll find it harder to get away with things on this reservation. Do you understand me?"

"Es perfectly clear," Cheetah said, looking straight into his eyes. He watched the man's confidence waver and Officer Shortwing's eyes flickered. "But I got away with nothing," he told the man, "and I pay every day for things I didn't do."

Officer Shortwing held his silence and stood firm.

"Can I go now?" Cheetah asked quietly.

"Stay out of trouble," Officer Shortwing advised him. "I've got your name on that back seat."

Cheetah nodded and walked away. He glanced at the woman in the car. Her head was down and the bandana was pressed to her face. She looked up from behind it and said she was sorry. "Es all right," he said. "Es all right." He watched the Tribal police car turn around and head down the road.

When he went back inside, Aunt Jolene was waiting at the door. She gave him a look of understanding but quickly guided him to the back room.

"We better get you taken care of," she said gently, "so you can go back home and rest."

"*Gracias,*" Cheetah said, knowing they were trying to get rid of him.

"The doctor will be right in," she said. "How's your dad doing?"

"He's ok. He's working a lot," Cheetah said. "I think it keeps his mind off things."

Aunt Jolene nodded. "Ok, take your stuff off and you can put it here. I'll get Dr. Mark."

Cheetah nodded. He took off his coat and laid it on the chair. It didn't take long before he was undressed and sitting in his boxers, waiting again. He stared at the posters on the wall. The door creaked open and Cheetah jumped, startled.

"Hey, how are you?" Dr. Mark asked. "You're Cheetah? Jolene and Martha's nephew?"

"Es right," Cheetah said, raising his brows. Was there someone who didn't know who he was?

Dr. Mark was reading the clipboard. "There's nothing on here except a name. Why is that?" he asked. He raised his gaze to the young man sitting on the table. "Hol-lee!" he exclaimed, looking at all the scars. "You're Silver Hawk," he announced.

Cheetah sighed.

Dr. Mark looked at all the scars. "When there's something wrong with you, how do you find it?"

Cheetah smirked. "It comes down to what's old and what's new," he said.

"I heard you had some scars," Dr. Mark said, "but you're like an abstract painting on a canvas here. How many are there?"

"I don't know," Cheetah said, honestly.

"Well," Dr. Mark said, leaning on the table and looking at him. "What's new?"

"Es my left leg," Cheetah said. He winced and lifted it up onto the table. The huge bruise on his thigh hadn't faded and the slight bump hadn't gone away either.

"What happened?"

"I went into a high side sweep during a fight and my opponent slammed his forearm onto my thigh," Cheetah explained.

"What's a high side sweep?" Dr. Mark asked, examining the bruise.

As soon as the doctor's hand touched him, Cheetah felt his mouth grow dry. There was a familiar ringing in his ears and his heart pounded. He grabbed the doctor's wrist.

Dr. Mark looked at the young man's face and saw fear. "I won't hurt you Cheetah," he said quietly.

"I know."

"You're hurting me," Dr. Mark said calmly. The skin where the kid grabbed him was whitening and a tingling sensation had already started.

"I...I'm sorry," Cheetah said and he opened his finger's,

slowly pulling his hand away.

"You don't like to be touched," Dr. Mark said.

"No."

Dr. Mark looked at the rest of the leg. "It looks like you've injured a tendon. Have you ever had trouble with this leg before?"

"No but the other one was broken," Cheetah said, "in three pieces."

"Must've been a hell of a fall," Dr. Mark said.

"I didn't fall."

"How did you break it?"

"I didn't," Cheetah said, looking away. "Someone else broke it with a lead pipe."

"How long ago was that?" Dr. Mark asked.

"I was fifteen," Cheetah said, "it was three years ago."

"It didn't quite set right," Dr. Mark said, noticing a slight bend in Cheetah's calf. "So…what's a high side sweep? You didn't tell me."

"Es a kick…eh…as high as your shoulder, coming sideways."

"You're leg was fully extended then?"

"*Si* and I was in the air," Cheetah told him. "When he hit me, the pain was so bad I…I fell flat on the floor. It was a couple of weeks ago and it was ok for a few days but the pain set in and I can't get rid of it."

"It sounds like a tendon," Dr. Mark said. "There's not much you can do for that. Stay off your feet, elevate the leg with ice and rest." He paused. "I read in a paper that you're a master of martial arts. Is that true?"

"*Si.*"

"You've been fighting for quite a while then," Dr. Mark said. "Did you ever pull a muscle or tendon in this leg before?"

Cheetah stared at him. "I…I don't know. Maybe."

"I guess with all of those past wounds it would be hard to remember a specific injury that caused you pain, wouldn't it?" Dr. Mark said. "What I'm thinking is…you might have torn the tendon or it could have pulled away from the bone. We'll give some time," he said. "If it's no better, come back in. I'll write a prescription for the pain…"

"No, no es okay."

"This has nothing to do with being brave," Dr. Mark said. "You've got your battle scars."

"Es not that," Cheetah said quietly. "I…I don't want the drugs."

"I have non-narcotic pain medicine," Dr. Mark said. "I'll give you some of that. Ok?"

"Ok," Cheetah said. He slid down off the table and started to get dressed. He felt the doctor watching him and he stopped. "What do you want?" Cheetah said. "Ask the question."

"Can I see the tattoo?" Dr. Mark asked. He'd been trying to get a look at it but the kid's long hair was over his chest and covering it. "I read about it in the paper. They said it's very rare. I studied street gangs when I was in college."

Cheetah turned to face him and moved his hair back and over his shoulder. "Es called the Mark of a Caballero Warlord but es no good anymore. You can see es been crossed out."

"It's a very intricate Spanish design, isn't it?" Dr. Mark said. "What do the words mean?"

"*Honro y orgullo* means honor and pride," Cheetah said quietly, "and *El Caudillo de Los Caballeros* means…the Warlord of the Gentlemen."

"I've heard it's very difficult to get out of a gang," Dr. Mark said hesitantly. "Were you jumped out?"

"No," Cheetah said. "The mark was crossed out and I was let go."

"That's virtually unheard of," Dr. Mark said.

"Es never happened before in my neighborhood, if that's what you mean," Cheetah said. "I had the position for four years…most Warlords' are dead in a year. I earned a lot of respect on the street."

"Do you miss it?"

"Every second of every day," Cheetah told him, "but I had to come home." Cheetah dressed and put his coat on. The doctor was still there and he had a waiting room full of people. "What?" Cheetah asked.

"I…noticed a very unusual scar on your side," Dr. Mark said. "It's not like anything I've ever seen before."

Cheetah grinned. "I was born with that one," he said. His gaze met and held the doctor's. "Es from a long, long time ago."

Dr. Mark glanced toward the door, then back at the young man. "You mean… from your…previous life time?"

"Yes," Cheetah said. "It was from a Springfield Carbine." He started toward the door. "Greasy Grass River fight."

"Bighorn?"

"Yeah," Cheetah said. He laughed. "But don't tell my brother I told you that because he is mad at me for being weird." He winked at the doctor and left the room.

Dr. Mark brought in the next patient and began the examination. Looking out the window, he caught sight of Silver Hawk leaving the clinic. The young man hobbled down the steps with the prescription paper in his hand. Dr. Mark watched as the kid crumpled it up and threw it away.

Chapter Three

The evening sun was setting beyond the hills as Cheetah walked home. Walking, even though it was cold, was the one thing that gave him peace of mind. Especially here, he thought. He'd had memories of the Black Hills, the vast prairie lands and the way the sky looked in the early spring ever since he could remember. The arrival of spring was always celebrated after a long cold winter. Cheetah saw the group of boys standing in front of the Trading Post, sharing a bottle in a brown paper bag. They waved it around, jeered and laughed at him but Cheetah kept walking. He groaned when he noticed they'd left the porch and started to follow him down the road.

"Hey fag," one of them said.

Cheetah walked along and ignored their taunting remarks. It was annoying and it had ruined his peaceful walk but aside from that, he didn't care what they were doing. He felt something hit the back of his coat. He wondered what it was. It must've been amusing because they laughed harder. He was coming to the part of his walk where he would be passing by the basketball court where Wolf and his friends would be finishing up a game and harassing Suzy Take-The-Bear. Cheetah didn't want to lead this parade by his brother. He turned around. There were six of them. He'd guessed right. All of them had talked and he'd counted the voices. He paid attention to where and how they stepped on the gravel road. They fell silent, staring at him, and stood dressed in similar clothes. They wore baggie jeans, shirts and their hats were on backwards. They were wearing similar colors, blue and white. "What do you want?" he asked calmly.

"So you're the tough gangsta from New York?" one of them snickered.

"No," Cheetah said. "I was *El Caudillo de Los Caballeros* from Salcida. I'm not anymore. What do you want?"

"We want to know if you're a fag," a voice from behind the others said. "You sound like one."

The other boys laughed.

"Step out here," Cheetah said, "where I can see you. Don't hide." He watched as a boy came out from the shadows. "You're the one with the gun, yes? A gang this size, here on the rez, I'm guessing you have it."

"So…are you a fag?" the boy asked menacingly, coming closer.

"What es your name?" Cheetah asked him.

"Luke Eagle Chaser," the boy said, raising his chin.

"Ah…your brother plays basketball with Wolf," Cheetah said. "Let me tell you something Luke. I've been shot four times and I've been in more fights than I can count. I've only been taken down three times in nine years. I'm guessing you're annoying me because you want me to fight?" Cheetah asked him. He paused and when the boy didn't answer he snatched the gun from the waistband of Luke's jeans. He put the gun in Luke's hand and aimed it at his own heart. "Here, this will make it easier. If you're going to do it," Cheetah said, "do it right. Don't just carry it as a back up for your mouth."

Luke stared hard into his eyes, refusing to back down.

"What are you waiting for, eh?" Cheetah said. "Let's get this done. Otherwise, I have to go home and cook supper."

Someone behind Luke snickered.

Cheetah looked over Luke's shoulder. "You have a problem with me cooking in a kitchen, eh? Es generally how I feed myself. I don't know how you do it." He returned his gaze to Luke's. "Are you still here, eh?" he asked. He rolled his eyes and sneered. "You're not going to shoot me," he said. He turned around and started to walk away.

"It must be true," Luke announced. "He didn't answer the question."

Cheetah stopped and sighed.

"Yeah," another one said. "He's a fag."

"You're the one who's a little fag," Jack Dann's slurred voice said. "Put that damn gun away before you shoot yourself."

Cheetah turned around. Jack Dann was a little older than he was and a little taller. He was wearing a dusty worn out pair of jeans and 'Fry Bread Power' T-shirt. He was wavering back and forth in front of Luke, holding a bottle of cheap wine.

"What's going on Luke?" Tommy Eagle Chaser called from the hillside.

"Ah shit," Cheetah muttered as Wolf and the rest of his friends appeared beside Tommy.

"The fags are giving us a hard time down here," Luke called back. He smiled at Cheetah.

"I ain't no fag." Jack growled, shoving Luke.

Tommy Eagle Chaser came down the hill side, followed by most of his friends. Wolf stood at the top of the hill with the basketball under his arm.

Cheetah backed up as Tommy came straight at him.

"Are you messing with my brother fag?" he demanded. "You'd better leave him alone."

"I'm not bothering anyone," Cheetah told him.

"Oh, so you can talk," Tommy said snidely.

Cheetah backed up a few more feet and turned around. He didn't care what they did. He was leaving. He saw the lights from the Tribal police car and he stopped. "Damn it," he said. He looked back to see everyone else running.

"You again?" Officer Shortwing said, getting out of the car. He grabbed Cheetah by the collar of his coat and shoved him against the car.

"I didn't do anything!" Cheetah yelled angrily. He felt the man's hands going over his body, searching him. "Damn it I…" He felt a hard knock to the back of his head and he was shoved into the backseat of the patrol car. He waited until Shortwing got in behind the wheel. "Why are you taking me in, eh?" Cheetah demanded.

"Resisting arrest and eluding the police," Officer Shortwing said. "Congratulations, you just won a week in the Tribal jail."

"I didn't…" Cheetah began. His seething rage silenced him. He looked out the window to see Wolf standing by the side of the road, with the ball still under his arm.

"This isn't New York," Shortwing said.

"No shit," Cheetah replied.

Officer Kent Shortwing looked in the rear view mirror. "There's no place to hide out here, is there?"

"I can't run," Cheetah muttered. He tried to lean his head back but it ached. "What did you hit me with?" he asked.

"If you hadn't attempted to resist…"

"I didn't resist anything," Cheetah said roughly. "If I had, you would be lying on the ground back there trying to remember what direction to stand up in."

"Are you threatening me?"

"No, I'm saying if I had, you would. Es not a threat. Es a 'what if' type of thing," Cheetah told him. "Damn it," he muttered. "I don't want to do a week in jail for nothing."

"It's not for nothing," Shortwing replied. "I warned you."

"Es soon as I can," Cheetah said tiredly, "I'm getting the hell off this reservation."

"Mission accomplished," Shortwing announced.

"Yeah," Cheetah agreed, glaring at the man. "Es right. I'm gone."

Chapter Four

When Stands Proud found out Cheetah was in the Tribal jail, he went down to try and get him out. He didn't have any luck. He knew he wouldn't be able to do it. Shortwing was a prick and they'd hated each other for a long time. The rest of the Tribal cops were okay. They looked after the people and picked up a few drunks so they wouldn't hurt themselves or anyone else but Shortwing thought he was F.B.I.

"No luck?" Turtle asked, hobbling up to Stands Proud.

"No," Stands Proud replied. "They won't give him to me."

"He didn't do nothin'."

"How do you know?" Stands Proud asked. "Everybody knows you sit in your trailer all day eating Frito's and drinking beer."

"People come by," Turtle said.

"Are you still dealing?" Stands Proud asked.

"Nope," Turtle said. "I found a new occupation. I'm all spiritual now."

"Shit," Stands Proud said with a slow sneer.

"That's how I know," Turtle told him, "your wild cat didn't do nothin'. I've been working with Jack Dann, trying to get him on the path…"

"Jack? On the path?" Stands Proud threw his head back and laughed. He patted Turtle's back. "Well, good luck with that," he said sarcastically.

"Stands Proud, you better let that wild cat go," Turtle advised.

"What are you talking about?"

"Those boys followed him for nearly a mile calling him a

fag," Turtle said. "Jack was watching the whole thing. They threw stuff at him and Luke spit on him." He carefully left out the part about Luke's gun.

Stands Proud sighed heavily.

"Tommy come down off the court and yelled in his face," Turtle said, "an' he still didn't do nothin'. That's when old Shortwing showed up. Everybody flew but your boy can't run." Turtle saw the hurt in Stands Proud's eyes. "I'm sorry bro. I know who he is and you know it too. The elders still believe all this will come around in the right direction some how but I can't see it."

"He'll probably leave," Stands Proud said, defeated. "That money from Tassiano is due in any day now. He's had his money from the fighting matches all along but I think he wants to settle things with that attorney first."

"How much money was that inheritance again?" Turtle asked.

"Five hundred million."

"Shit," Turtle said. He let out a low whistle. "He's gone."

"Yeah," Stands Proud said, "I guess you're right." He looked around. "Why the hell would he stay here?" He shivered from the cold Dakota wind and looked around. The excitement was over for these five minutes. In another minute or two somebody would be fighting, a car would roll over; someone would die of alcohol poisoning but some how life would go on.

"Why do we stay here?" Turtle asked.

Stands Proud sighed.

"Because," Cheetah's voice said from behind them, "they put you here."

Stands Proud turned around. His son had a bruise on his cheek. "What happened?" he asked. He gently moved Cheetah into a shadow on the side of the road. "How did you get out?" he whispered hoarsely.

"He hit me in the face," Cheetah said, "and I can't take that anymore."

"Did…did…did you kill him?" Turtle asked.

Cheetah gave Turtle a strange look. "What's the matter with you? Why would you think I'd kill someone for hitting me in the face?"

Turtle shrugged. "I don't know."

"I put him in the cell," Cheetah said, trying not to smirk, "and I let everyone else go."

Stands Proud laughed, hard.

"Hoka heyyyyyy," Turtle said. "Good one wild cat. We better get out of here. Let's go to my place. Shortwing is scared of my dogs. He can't get near the trailer."

"I'm coming," Jack said, appearing out of nowhere.

They went up over the hill and through the snow. Stands Proud helped his son, trying to ease the pain of his leg. It didn't matter if Cheetah was going slowly, Turtle was too. Come to think of it, Stands Proud realized, Jack was drunk and stumbling never amounted to much. "Warriors," he said aloud.

"What?" Cheetah asked.

"Warriors," Stands Proud said. "Look at us. We couldn't take over a one man gas station in the middle of nowhere."

"Sure we could," Jack slurred. "Do you want to?"

Cheetah laughed.

"Good to see you smiling Hawk," Jack said, reaching over and messing up his hair.

"Boy, you can smile now," Turtle said, "but Shortwing is going to be on you night and day."

"He has to get out of the cell first," Jack said.

"Eh well," Cheetah said, grinning. "It might be a while." He held up the ring of jail keys. "They'll have to get someone to cut the bars, I guess."

Stands Proud laughed.

"Hey…" Jack said in a slow stunned voice. "Who's that up there?" He pointed to the water tower.

Cheetah looked up. He didn't know the kid but this didn't look good to him.

"He's going to jump," Jack said.

They started walking over to the tower.

"Hey man!" Turtle yelled. "It ain't that bad! Come on down here!" The kid looked at him and the light from the tower lit up his face. "Shit. That's Ricky. That's Martha Burnt-The-Wagon's grandson. He ain't but twelve years old. Hey boy!" Turtle yelled. "Don't do it boy!" He hobbled toward the tower and fell onto his knees in the snow. "Come on boy! How we gonna win if everybody keeps dyin?"

"I can't get'm," Jack said, with a sad realization. "I..I can't go up there."

"I can," Cheetah said, limping toward the tower.

Stands Proud sucked in a breath and shuddered as he exhaled. He watched as Cheetah started up the tower but slipped because of his leg. Turtle was yelling his fool head off and Jack had started to cry. Stands Proud wondered why he was standing still. He ran over to the tower and started up behind Cheetah. "Go!" he yelled. "I'm behind you! I'll catch you if you fall!"

"*Muchas gracias!*" Cheetah called out, as the wind blew harder against him. "But I'm not going to fall! Be careful! There es ice!"

Stands Proud slipped but hung on. He scrambled to get

his feet right. He looked up at his son, climbing higher. "How the hell are you doing that?" he called out. "Be careful with your leg!"

"I am!" Cheetah called out but it hurt like hell and he didn't know if he could make it to the top. He grimaced and pulled with his arms, using his left leg for strength and to brace his body upright. He got to the top where the boy was. Cheetah could see the kid was crying. "Hey…hey you," he said gently.

Ricky glanced at him.

"What's the matter?" Cheetah asked. "What are you doing up here?"

Ricky looked down over the edge.

"Are you going to jump?" Cheetah asked him. "Es this a good place?" he asked, scooting over closer to the kid. "I've been kind of suicidal myself lately. I tried to kill myself four times this year." Cheetah looked over the edge. "Eh…I don't know. This *might* work. You could land at the bottom, get paralyzed and still be alive."

"It's high enough," Ricky said, sniffling.

"Are you sure?" Cheetah asked. "Maybe I'll jump with you."

Stands Proud hung onto the ladder on the side of the tower. He listened to the howling wind, the sound of his son's voice and the boy giving him a hard time.

"I don't want to die with you," Ricky said. "You're crazy."

"Hey, you don't know me, ok?" Cheetah said.

"I know you."

"Do you?"

"Everybody knows you," Ricky said. "You're that fag from New York."

"I'm not gay," Cheetah said. "I had a girl friend. She was everything to me. I didn't know how much I could love someone."

Ricky sniffed. "She leave you?"

"Yeah," Cheetah said quietly. "She left me."

"Why? Cause your crazy?"

"No es not why," Cheetah said. "Someone shot her. They killed her and now she's gone. Gone es forever, Ricky."

"So?" Ricky said toughly. "I got nothin' here anyway. I got no money. I got nothin'"

"Money?" Cheetah asked. "Money will fix this? Here. Here's a fifty. I'll get you more. Come on. Let's go down."

"It's not just money." Ricky wiped his face with the sleeve of his flannel shirt. He took the fifty dollar bill and shoved it in his pocket. He was shaking. "I can't....I can't find my mom. I live with my grandma but my mom is gone. I think she's over in White Clay but I can't find her. I tried..."

"Where is White Clay?" Cheetah asked.

"It's a place where everybody drinks and gets high," Ricky said.

"I can find her," Cheetah said.

Ricky turned to look at him. "You're lying."

"Listen, I might be crazy and who could blame me if I am at this point," Cheetah said, "but I'm from the streets. I just got here from New York. I had the biggest gang on the East coast, eh? I knew where they were." Cheetah paused. "Chico...if I can't find her, she es not to be found. But I will try."

"You promise?" Ricky asked.

"I swear it," Cheetah said. "We'll start looking tomorrow. Ok?"

"Honest?"

"I never lie Ricky," Cheetah told him. "I'll help you but you have to stay alive, eh?"

"You said you wanted to die," Ricky accused. He sniffed again.

"I'm crazy," Cheetah retorted. "Remember?" He thought he saw a small grin on the kid's face. He held out his hand. "Come on, I'll get you down." When the boy's hand grasped his, Cheetah closed his eyes and held on. "Ok," he said. "Let's go."

Stands Proud breathed a sigh of relief and started down the ladder. Below him people from the rez had started to gather. It was the next exciting episode on the rez. "Are you all right?" Stands Proud called out to Cheetah.

"I'm fine Papa, go down." Cheetah got onto the ladder and put Ricky between himself and the tower. "Ok chico, we're going down together, eh?" He started down slowly. "But if you decide to die again, you call me and we'll go up together."

"You are crazy," Ricky said.

"No, no I'm just tired, Ricky," he said.

"What was your girl friend's name?"

"Marisa."

"My mom's name is Betty."

"We'll find her," Cheetah said. "We'll try very hard, ok?"

"Ok."

Cheetah slipped and Ricky gasped. Cheetah struggled to get his leg in the right place. "Es ok Ricky," he said. "I got you. I have a bad leg now but I can get you down from here."

"What happened to your leg?"

"I hurt it in a fight."

"A street fight?"

"No, underground fighting es eh...different," Cheetah said. He looked down. Stands Proud was on the ground. "We don't have far to go now," he said. "Don't go up there anymore. Next time, I might not be able to come get you."

"Ok," Ricky said. He jumped two feet and landed on the ground. His grandma came running and wrapped her arms around him, crying.

Cheetah hung onto the bars and took a few breaths. He turned to put his left leg down and it came down hard. He had to use his hand to push his right leg forward. He fell against Stands Proud. "Ah shit," he said.

Stands Proud hung onto him. "Can you stand?"

"I think so," Cheetah breathed out. Martha Burnt-The-Wagon stood up in front of him and put her arms around his shoulders. "Es all right," he said. "Es all right. He's ok. I'm going to help him find his mom."

Martha looked at him. "What did he tell you?"

"He said she was in White Clay and he couldn't find her," Cheetah said, looking down at Ricky.

"Ricky," Martha said. "Ricky, honey." She went down on her knees and wiped the boys face with her hand. "Ricky, baby, you know that's not true." Martha looked up at Cheetah. "Betty...Betty was sick. She was real sick. The doctors tried..." She shook her head.

Cheetah closed his eyes and turned his head to the side trying not to hear her words. His own mother had passed away a short time ago and he missed her very much. He moved away from them, wanting to run but knowing he couldn't.

"Ricky...you can't find her. She's gone baby."

"Gone is forever," Ricky said.

"Yes baby," Martha said. "I'm sorry."

Cheetah felt the icy air coming and going from his chest. Stands Proud was saying something to him but he couldn't hear it. He saw his father's lips moving and the other people came closer and they were talking to him. It was all a blur. He felt separated from them, as if he were encased in glass. He pushed someone away and limped through the snow.

Down below the tower, he saw flashing lights. Cheetah turned and started going the other way. He was headed for the darkness when a hand came down on his shoulder. Cheetah turned and threw a fierce punch, slamming his forearm into a face. He saw Jack Dann stumble backward with blood coming out of his nose.

"Shit!" Jack said, holding his nose and looking at him.

Cheetah didn't say anything. He stared at the ground and began to shake.

"Maybe I shouldn't have come up behind you," Jack said, in a muffled voice.

"I'm sorry. Just...go away," Cheetah said quietly, "and leave me alone."

"You're too alone as it is," Jack said. He looked over his shoulder at the crowd of people. They were leaving. "I told Stands Proud I'd make sure you got home. He worries a lot about you."

Cheetah nodded. "I know."

"Come on," Jack said. "Fuck I got to get my head straight. I can't do this shit anymore."

"What's the matter?" Cheetah asked him.

"I think I'm sobering up," Jack said, blinking his eyes. "Holy shit! The world is still here."

Cheetah smirked.

"I've been drunk for the last seven years," Jack said, looking around. "Hey, look. Stars! A moon!"

Cheetah laughed and watched Jack jumping around in the snow.

"Wow," Jack said. "This is an interesting feeling."

"And they say I'm crazy," Cheetah said. He started toward home.

"There's nothing wrong with being crazy," Jack said. "I'll take that any day over being normal."

"Why?" Cheetah asked.

"Boring," Jack said. "Normal is boring." He walked with Cheetah and made sure he made it to Stands Proud's place. It was the first responsible thing he'd done in years. When they arrived he nodded and approved of the way it made him feel. "Will you be ok now?" he asked.

"Yeah," Cheetah said, going over to the door. *"Gracias."*

"No, thank you," Jack said. "You've given me the world, a sober world, and I thank you."

Cheetah rolled his eyes. "I didn't give you…"

"When I realized I couldn't save that kid," Jack told him, "I felt like shit. I watched you, the way I've been watching you around here, and I saw you go up there…even with that leg. Nothing stops you. You just go. It's what my grandfather used to talk about when I was a kid. The old ways, the old warriors….charging in and stopping at nothing. You're like that but I guess you're supposed to be."

"I'm like that because I've never been allowed to stop Jack, es all. I've never been allowed to quit," Cheetah told him. "I'm crazy like that, es all." He turned, opened the door and went into the house.

Chapter Five

For the next few days, Cheetah was on the couch with his leg elevated and packed in ice. He got up occasionally but not often. He never sat still before. He had always been moving, training to fight or walking the Caballero territory. The bruise was starting to fade and the lump had gone down. He didn't think the tendon was torn because the pain was going away. When he saw it was close to the time for Wolf and Stands Proud to come home, he got up and went into the kitchen to cook.

Jack came by the kitchen window, tapped on it and walked around to the front door. "Hey," he said, coming inside.

"Hey Jack," Cheetah said. He put the chicken in the oven. "How es everything?"

"They're all talking about what you did for Ricky," Jack said, "but the Eagle Chasers are still running their mouths." He sat down at the table. "How's the leg?"

"Better," Cheetah said.

"Good," Jack said. He tapped his fingers on the table, nervously.

"What's the matter?"

"Nothing."

"You seem worried about something," Cheetah said, glancing at him. He opened the refrigerator.

"I...uh...I'm not going to come around so much," Jack said, "I don't think."

"Why?" Cheetah asked. He closed the refrigerator door and turned to look at Jack.

"I got a job over in Rapid City, by the time I get back and..."

"Never mind," Cheetah said. "I know why." He knew the Eagle Chasers were still talking about him. When Jack started hanging out in the house, the rumors grew out of control. "Es all right," he said. "I understand."

"Listen, it looks like…"

"Hey, you can go now if you want," Cheetah told him. He stood at the sink and put the coffee into the basket, poured the water in and turned the coffee maker on. He wasn't surprised when he heard the legs of the chair scrape against the wooden floor.

"I'll talk to you later, ok?"

"Okay," Cheetah said, without turning around. He sighed and set the timer on the oven. He had about an hour before the chicken would be done. He reached up and took the check out of the canister. The money had come in days ago but he hadn't said anything. Cheetah took the check, put on his jacket and went outside.

The days were getting warmer and the snow was melting. He could smell the green earth waking up and coming back to life. Cheetah walked along the road and went into the Tribal Office. Shirley greeted him as he came through the door.

"Is my grandfather here?" Cheetah asked.

"He's in the back with the rest of the council," Shirley said. "They're having a quarterly meeting."

Cheetah nodded and went into the back office. Shirley started to get up to try and change his mind but she was too slow. He went down the hall and into the office with the older men. They gave him an odd look then they looked at Jonathan Argent, his grandfather. Cheetah walked over to where his grandfather was sitting, took a pen from the table, turned the check over and signed it. Quietly, he pushed it across the table and left it in front of him.

"What's this?" Jonathan asked.

Cheetah didn't say anything. He turned and left the room. He'd just given away over five hundred million dollars but he didn't want the money anyway. He still had his fighting money that he'd earned and that was enough for him. He was half way down the road when he heard his grandfather calling him from the porch of the Tribal Office.

When he got to the house, the phone kept ringing. Cheetah didn't answer it but when Stands Proud came in, he did.

"I don't know," Stands Proud said, quietly. "I'll talk to him."

Cheetah took the chicken out of the oven and set the table. There was a few minutes of conversation and Stands Proud hung up the phone. "I gave it away because they've been telling me I'm here to help my people. Eh well…that will help them, no?" He paused. "I'm free and clear of the whole damn thing now, prophecy fulfilled."

Stands Proud watched as Cheetah poured iced tea into the glasses and moved mechanically around the table. "If that's what you want," he said.

"It is," Cheetah said. "I'm leaving here."

"Son…"

"Don't try to talk me out of it, eh?" Cheetah told him. "I never liked being on a reservation and I don't like it now. I'm tired of the talk, the whispering and the staring. Es like being watched by Tassiano's men all over again. I can't move without someone reporting it to someone else."

"I talked to Jack," Stands Proud said, walking into the kitchen.

Cheetah paused for a moment before he put the iced tea back into the refrigerator. "He was here," Cheetah said.

"I know," Stands Proud said.

"There es nothing I can do about what they're saying," Cheetah told him. "It only gets worse every day. My leg es getting better and if someone says or does the wrong thing I might fight…and it would be bad. I'm going before that happens."

"Where?" Stands Proud asked.

"I don't know," Cheetah said quietly. "I haven't decided."

Stands Proud released a heavy sigh. He folded his arms over his chest and leaned against the frame of the door. "I don't think you're well enough to leave here," he said, forcing the words to come out.

"My leg will be ok," Cheetah said.

"I'm not talking about your leg," Stands Proud said. Wolf was late getting home and he was glad. "You hardly sleep at all. I hear you walking around the house at night," he said gently. "You haven't been able to keep food down and when you do sleep…"

Cheetah looked at him. "What?"

"You don't know?" Stands Proud asked.

Cheetah knew. He didn't want to talk about it.

"You're having terrible nightmares," Stands Proud said, "and a few times…you screamed so loud I…" Cheetah turned away from him. Stands Proud knew he would. "It's understandable with the hell you went through but I'm not sure you should go off by yourself."

"You think…I'm crazy," Cheetah said slowly, raising his gaze to meet Stands Proud. "You're buying into it, eh? Or maybe that's what you've always thought about your weird son."

"That's not what I…" Stands Proud's words halted. "Son…" he tried again.

"I'm not crazy!" Cheetah yelled, storming past him. He

went down the hall and slammed the bedroom door shut.

"I never said you were crazy," Stands Proud said, standing on the other side of the door. He waited for a response but knew he wasn't going to get one.

Cheetah paced inside his bedroom, back and forth across the floor. It was bad enough that Wolf thought he was weird. It was worse when everyone else believed he was gay and that he liked what those men had done to him, as if he wanted it. Now Stands Proud thought he was crazy. They knew who he was and it didn't matter. They whispered and stared. They seemed excited about the prophecy at his trial and now that he was home, they said he was odd, strange and not like anyone else. Wasn't he supposed to be? At least in the city, they knew him and accepted him for what he was. But now that was gone. He'd given it up. In all the years of pain Tassiano had given him, Cheetah never felt anything as bad as the night Miguel crossed out the mark on his chest. He'd lost everything he loved. Mamita, Marisa and Los Caballeros were gone.

Cheetah stopped pacing and stared at the wooden box in the corner of his room. He'd put it in the corner, covered it and put a lamp on it when he'd moved into the house. He walked over to the box and hunkered down beside it. Cheetah moved the lamp, uncovered it and opened the lid. Inside the box were weapons Tassiano had given him as gifts and he knew how to use them all. Cheetah reached down into the box and took out the automatic handgun. He found the clip. He carefully closed the box, covered it and put the lamp back where it had been.

Cheetah knew what he was going to do. He knew exactly how and where he was going to do it. He had no feeling of sadness. There was no pain. And this time, no one would be able to save him. He would not fail. He put on a jacket, in a calculated manner, which would make it easy to conceal the gun and left his bedroom.

"Where are you going?" Stands Proud asked. His voice

was hoarse and pleading with his son at the same time. "Son?"

"Out," Cheetah said. He pushed open the door and stepped onto the porch. When he saw the purple low rider sitting there, he stopped and stared at it.

"*Migo*!" Rafa said, jumping out of the car. "*Que pasa?*" He ran up the steps excitedly and jumped onto the porch.

Cheetah watched as Miguel came forward more slowly. Miguel, Cheetah thought, Warlord de Los Caballeros. "*Hola,*" Cheetah said quietly with respect. He cast his eyes downward.

"Hey Cheetah," Miguel said, smiling. "How are you?"

"Aren't you glad to see us migo?" Rafa asked. "What's the matter, eh?"

"Nothing," Cheetah said, quickly. He tried to shake it off. "Nothing, I'm fine. How es everything?"

"Good," Miguel told him. "They way you set Los Caballeros up, es perfect. We have no problems with anyone. But," he said softly, "everyone misses you."

Cheetah nodded.

"So eh…this es your new house now?" Rafa asked.

"No. It belongs to Stands Proud," Cheetah told him. "Es where I lived when I was a kid."

"How are things going, eh? You like it here?" Rafa inquired. He noticed the look on Cheetah's face, the way his eyes had darkened. Rafa glanced at Miguel. "Some thing bad happen Cheetah?"

"No," Cheetah said softly. "Nothing. Come in," he offered. He opened the door and walked into the living room.

Stands Proud saw Rafa and Miguel and he smiled, getting up from the chair. "Hey," he said, "I thought I heard someone out there." He extended a hand to both of the boys. He'd met them in the city. They were close friends of his son and Stands Proud

41

liked them. "Are you two hungry?" he asked.

"I'm starving," Rafa said.

Cheetah looked at him.

"Not for real, I'm just hungry," Rafa told him.

Cheetah walked into the kitchen and filled two plates with chicken and mashed potatoes. He put them on the table.

"Eat with us, come on," Miguel said, smiling.

"No," Cheetah said softly, "*no soy esta noche hambrienta*." He leaned back against the kitchen counter and watched them. How did they do this? He had been hundreds of miles away from them. Each and every time he had a plan to kill himself, they showed up.

"You better cook more than this," Rafa snickered. He glanced at Miguel.

"Eh...this isn't enough," Miguel announced.

Cheetah felt his anger simmer. Was Miguel stupid enough to come here and give him orders? "Not enough for you Warlord?" Cheetah asked coldly.

"No," Rafa said smiling, "not enough for the ones coming behind us."

They laughed.

Miguel looked up at Cheetah. "When we said we were coming to see you," he said, "a lot of people wanted to come, eh?" He smiled. "They stopped on the way but they'll be here soon."

Cheetah stared at him.

"Es ok? No?" Miguel asked. He didn't like the vacant expression he was seeing. Miguel stood up slowly and approached cautiously. "Cheetah...I thought you would be happy to see them. The rest of the Ten and a few others..." Miguel's eyes deepened with concern. "What es wrong Cheetah?" he asked.

"*No es nada, nada importante*," Cheetah replied.

"Ay then you are glad to see us," Miguel said, opening his arms wide. He wrapped them around Cheetah's shoulders. He was like stone, Miguel thought, a statue. Miguel moved back slightly. "Are you hurt?" he asked.

"No," Cheetah softly whispered.

Miguel noticed the way Cheetah was standing, with his hands in his pockets. He never stood that way. His arms were always at his sides. It was something he'd been trained to do. He was taught if he had his hands in his pockets, he was an easy target, not quick enough to react. Miguel knew Cheetah was hiding something in the pocket of the jacket. Ever so gently, Miguel took Cheetah's right wrist into his hand and pulled his hand out. Cheetah said nothing as Miguel reached into the pocket and pulled out the nine millimeter Beretta.

Rafa lifted his chin and lowered his brows. "Why are you carrying a gun, Cheetah?"

Cheetah looked across the room at Stands Proud.

"*Mi amigo*," Miguel said softly, "as long as I've known you…you've never carried a gun with you. Who es bothering you?"

"No one," Cheetah said.

"What es the gun for?" Rafa asked, standing up. "Cheetah, what es it for?" He looked over at Stands Proud and saw the big Indian's eyes were full of tears. "Oh no, not again. Tell me were not trying it again," Rafa said, slowly. "Five times?" he asked. "Cheetah!"

"Why?" Miguel asked. "Why Cheetah? I thought this es what you wanted. You said you had to come home. I thought it would make you happy. Es the only reason I took the mark, the only reason. I did it so you could go."

"I don't belong here," Cheetah said. He swallowed, hard. "I don't belong anywhere."

"You can have Los Caballeros back," Miguel said. "Es you they look for. You can go home with us."

"No," Cheetah said. "Don Antone has finally won, eh? There's no point to anything anymore, not for me."

"Don't say that! Don't you ever say that in front of me!" Rafa yelled at him. He stormed over to Cheetah, knocking a chair over as he went. "You will not do it! I will not let you! No one from Salcida will let you!"

Cheetah stared at him.

"Who do you think you are?" Rafa yelled angrily, tears coming to his eyes. "You think you can come in somebody's life, act like you care and then shit on them by leaving forever?" He grabbed Cheetah's shirt and twisted it in his fist. "You're not going to do it," Rafa said. "Do you hear me?"

"Rafa, don't," Miguel said. "Let him be."

"No, no I won't let him be!" Rafa yelled in Cheetah's face. "Es the problem! Everybody kiss his ass because he es Warlord, because these people think he es something special…no one tells him anything he does not want to hear."

Cheetah sneered at Rafa. "You're so full of shit Gonzalez."

Rafa yanked him away from the counter and shoved him backward. "Get outside!" he demanded. "I have a few things to tell you!"

"No Rafa," Miguel warned. "Don't do this now. Don't do it."

"I'm not fighting you Rafa." Cheetah's voice was slick, mean and deep. "*No quiero luchar un tonto estúpido corto que no sabe nada!"*

"Do you want to die?" Rafa yelled at him. "I'll kill you for that."

"*Máteme pero sería repugnado si usted era el uno terminar mi vida,*" Cheetah replied, glaring at him.

Rafa flew forward and knocked him down. They fell to the floor and Gonzalez was sitting on his chest.

Rafa's fist was back but he stopped. He glanced around. "How did this happen?" he asked. He looked down at Cheetah. It was a position he'd never been in before and one he'd never seen Cheetah accept. "*Madre de Dios*, for that you should kill yourself." He climbed off of Cheetah and stood up.

Cheetah sat up and leaned against the kitchen cabinets.

"Get up," Rafa said.

"Why?" Cheetah asked, looking up at him. He drew up one leg and casually rested his arm on his knee. "What difference does it make?"

"You really need to get back to the city," Miguel said. "This has been very bad for you. Where es you heart, Cheetah?"

"*No se,*" Cheetah murmured. "*No se*…haven't seen it in a long time." He looked up at Rafa. "What did you want to tell me?" he asked. "Go ahead, tell me, run your mouth."

"*Bueno,* I will do it," Rafa said, snapping at him. "I have waited a long time for this day."

"No Rafa stop," Miguel said. "Shut up."

"No, I won't shut up. He needs to hear this," Rafa said. He looked at Cheetah. "Everybody cares about you, eh? They look for you. All you ever think about es your own pain. I know what Tassiano did. I know what those men did to you…and for that I'm sorry. I know es never been easy for you. You had all of that and the weight of Los Caballeros on your shoulders…and

45

you keep saying you want to die. You keep trying to kill yourself. Do you know what es like when you disappear, eh?" Rafa demanded. "When you walk off and disappear for hours and we look for you? I can't do this anymore. I can't keep looking for you wondering if I'll find you dead. If you are going to try it while I'm here, I'm going home. Fuck you, I'm going home!" Rafa yelled. "You're not going to do that to me, eh? Every time I looked for you, all of this year, I was afraid of what I would find. Not because somebody else will kill you but because you would do this! *You* would do it…and not even care if I find you like that." Rafa stopped talking but his chest heaved up and down. "You wouldn't care if I found you dead. Es what I want to say to you! You're selfish Cheetah! You don't think about us. You think only about yourself."

Cheetah lowered his gaze and stared at the floor.

"You know what es like," Rafa said, in a raspy voice. "You found so many yourself. You found them dead, on the street, with no more chance for life. I'm not doing this," Rafa said. "I'm not doing it." He backed up, turned and stormed across the room, pushing the door open.

When it slammed shut, Cheetah closed his eyes.

"Get up Cheetah," Miguel said softly. "You don't want to stay down there. You don't *belong* down there."

Cheetah opened his eyes and looked up at Miguel.

"Stand up," Miguel said. He held his breath and waited. Slowly, Cheetah began to move. He got to his feet and arose to his full height. Miguel nodded. "Much better," he said. "*Ven conmigo*," Miguel said. "Es been a long time. I think you need to talk with me."

Stands Proud breathed out a sigh of relief. He walked over to the counter and picked up the gun, knowing how close he'd come to losing his youngest son. He looked at the clock. It was dark outside. Where was Wolf? He reached for his hat and put it on his head. The boys in the living room were sitting and talking. He heard Cheetah's voice broken and full of emotion. What Stands Proud had been trying to do for weeks, Miguel was able to do in a few minutes. Cheetah was talking, the words pouring out of him mixed with tears and sadness. Stands Proud was thankful that this son was all right, at least for now. He had to find Wolf and then he felt he could rest. As Stands Proud walked out of the house he decided that prison, for all its inconveniences, had been a very peaceful place.

Chapter Six

Stands Proud found Wolf on the basketball court, alone, bouncing the ball. He stood in one place and bounced it repeatedly, over and over again. Stands Proud sat down on the bleachers and waited. After a few moments of hesitation, Wolf came over to him.

"Where is he?" Wolf asked, still bouncing the ball.

"At home," Stands Proud said. "Are you all right?"

"Yeah," Wolf said, watching the ball bounce. "Shortwing is really mad. He's harassing everybody. He said if he catches Cheetah doing something that even looks wrong; he's going to nail him."

"He got out?" Stands Proud inquired, smirking.

Wolf grinned. "Yeah, Buddy went over with the Jaws of Life and had to cut him out. The whole paramedic crew and the rest of the cops were down there. It was pretty funny." Wolf stopped bouncing the ball and caught it. "He's definitely going after Cheetah though," he added. "Are you sure he's home?"

"Yeah," Stands Proud said. "Rafa and Miguel came in from New York. He's with them now."

Wolf's eyes lit up. "Rafa's here?"

"Yeah," Stands Proud said slowly, "and there are more coming. They missed your brother."

"You don't think he'll leave with them, do you?" Wolf asked.

"He might," Stands Proud said, honestly. "Before they got here, he told me he was leaving."

"Oh," Wolf said. He went back to bouncing the ball again, again and again. He stopped and looked at Stands Proud. "You know what I don't get?" he asked.

"What?"

"They treated him like he was special when he was a kid," Wolf said. "Why don't they do that anymore?"

"They didn't treat him like he was special Wolf. They treated him like he was different. Why do you think I did what I did? You were too young. Maybe you don't remember what it was like," he said. "Everywhere he went, to a Pow wow, the Broken Arrow with me, hell…even when I took him to the Trading Post, they whispered behind his back. It caused problems between the two of you; between your mother and me…she believed it and I didn't. Jake kept talking. He wouldn't shut up…" Stands Proud looked up at Wolf. "The day I killed Jake, I had your brother with me in the Broken Arrow. The place was full. Jake started telling everyone in there that I should be ashamed of myself because I brought the boy into the bar. He stood there and told me that when your brother was older he'd be whipped and raped…" Stands Proud's voice trailed off.

"He…told you that exactly?" Wolf asked.

"Yeah, that and more I didn't want to hear about my four year old son," Stands Proud said.

"So…it all came true?" Wolf asked, holding the ball under his arm. "All of it?"

Stands Proud nodded.

"Then he really is..?"

"Yes Wolf," Stands Proud replied. "That's why he's so different."

"He won't talk about it," Wolf said.

"He won't talk about it but everyone else still does. I thought it would stop after I killed Jake. It hasn't," Stands Proud said. He sighed heavily. "Come on, we better get home." He stood up.

"I've been thinking about going back to school," Wolf said. "I mean, this doesn't look like this is going to…"

"Go away?" Stands Proud asked. "Not unless he does."

"I don't want him to go," Wolf said, "but I don't think he believes me. I was hoping when summer gets here I could take him to a Pow Wow. You remember? Like when we were kids," Wolf said. "I guess that's stupid."

"No Wolf, that's not stupid," Stands Proud said, as they walked. "I was hoping for the same thing myself. I'd like to get him in a sweat lodge, a few ceremonies…" He shook his head. "He's a long, long way from all that right now." Stands Proud stopped and put a hand on Wolf's shoulder. "I have to tell you something."

Wolf knew whatever it was; he didn't want to hear it. He was learning his father's voice and knew what it meant when it broke and fell apart.

"He had a gun tonight," Stands Proud stated. "I don't know where he got it."

"A gun?"

"Yeah, Miguel took it away from him," Stands Proud said. "He was had every intention of killing himself. Your brother's in a real lonely place, son. He can't see his way out of it. I wanted to tell you…because if he…"

"I know dad," Wolf said quietly. "If he really wants to do it, no one will be able to stop him."

Stands Proud slung his arm around Wolf's shoulders. "I'm sorry I haven't been able to pay more attention to what you're doing."

"It's ok dad," Wolf said. "I understand it a lot better now than I did when we were kids. I used to want to be him. Not anymore."

They walked over the hill and looked down at the house. There were four vans parked in the yard and loud Latin music was blaring in the night air.

"How many kids do you think came in those vans?" Stands Proud asked.

"I don't know," Wolf said.

They walked down the hillside and over to the house.

Stands Proud opened the door and went inside. He was surprised to find the entire house was full but was relatively quiet. The Latin music had been turned down as soon as they saw him.

"Hey Papi!" Rafa called out. "Hey Wolfie!"

The rest of the kids yelled out a greeting.

Stands Proud laughed. He looked over in the candle lit corner of the living room and saw Cheetah talking in earnest to Miguel. Miguel was sitting on the coffee table and Cheetah was sitting on the couch, facing him, his face damp with fresh tears. They were undisturbed by the rest of the group and still talking back and forth.

"He'll be all right," Rafa said, coming up to Stands Proud. "Miguel's got him now, eh?"

Stands Proud nodded. "I'm glad," he said. "I couldn't reach him. I tried Rafa. He wouldn't talk to me at all."

"Cheetah has a lot of respect for Miguel. They're very close," Rafa explained. "The first time Tassiano whipped him… the rest of us…we didn't know. He walked around and said nothing. It got infected. He finally went to Miguel. They asked me for help because Cheetah was so angry. I was in the room with them and I saw how hard Miguel worked. He talked a lot and worked on Cheetah's back, trying everything to calm him down. For every injury he has ever had, Miguel has been there," Rafa told Stands Proud. "He trusts Miguel."

"Hey, you brought girls with you," Wolf said, noticing the group of Latina girls gathered together. They were all beautiful.

"Eh…yeah," Rafa said.

Stands Proud looked at the young ladies crowded in his kitchen. "Okay," he said rather slowly in a stern voice. But the truth was, he really didn't mind. They were all beautiful, as Juanita had been and it brought a fondness to his heart for them. They were young and full of life, laughing and talking, the way she was. He found himself smiling.

"We had to bring them, I'm sorry," Rafa said. "You see that one? Right there, her name is Angelina. She es very tight with your brother," he informed Wolf, "and she hates me. She said if I didn't bring her and some of our sister gang, she would do things to me I can't tell you about."

"She's gorgeous," Wolf breathed out. Angelina's raven hair flowed in waves over her slender shoulders. Her dark eyes flashed as she talked and her lips were full and cherry red.

"She es a snake," Rafa warned him, "A deadly viper. The others, Elisa, Rosa, Maria y Julia…they are all okay…but trust me, stay away from Angelina. Ah no…she has seen you, noticed you look like him. Good luck, eh?" Rafa slipped between the others and disappeared.

Wolf laughed at him but stopped as Angelina approached. She was wearing a tight red sweater and a short black skirt with heels. He'd never seen a woman walk the way she did. He smiled nervously.

"Ah so you are the twin brother," Angelina asked sweetly. She touched Wolf's chin with one finger and slowly studied his face.

Wolf's heart did a drum roll in his chest. He couldn't breathe.

"There es a difference," she said.

"Really?" Wolf asked.

"Si, your eyes are softer than his," Angelina purred. "I hope you weren't listening to that dog Rafa. He es so stupid."

"Uh no," Wolf stammered. "I mean…I never listen to Rafa."

Stands Proud chuckled at Wolf and looked away.

"You must be Stands Proud," Angelina said, slowly raising her eyes to his. "I see why they call you that. Es easy to see why Cheetah es so handsome, no?"

"Thank you," Stands Proud said, smiling at her. "It's nice to meet my son's friends."

"Cheetah and I are more than friends," Angelina told them. "He was Caballero Warlord and I rule the Latin Ladies. We are very close, Senor," she added. "Very close."

Wolf watched as she walked back over to the other side of the room.

"Take it easy," Stands Proud said, grinning, and patting his shoulder.

"She's amazing," Wolf breathed out.

Stands Proud laughed. "Yes she is, but I'll give you a small piece of advice…listen to Rafa."

"Why?" Wolf asked.

"First of all," Stands Proud said, "you don't want to end up fighting with your brother over any woman. And secondly, that young lady has a very dangerous quality."

"What's that?" Wolf asked.

"She'll devour you," Stands Proud said, "and there won't be anything left when she's done."

"Yeah, but it would feel so good," Wolf said.

Stands Proud laughed and went into the kitchen. They were sitting at the table, on the counter and on the floor. He couldn't even begin to count how many kids were in his house. He suddenly wondered what Juanita would say if she saw this. He smiled. She'd be laughing and pointing at him. Laughing with those beautiful expressive eyes of hers, he thought, like Angelina's. He turned and looked at the young lady and a pang went through his heart. He knew what it was like to be devoured, whole.

Chapter Seven

The next day when Stands Proud came home from work, he sat in the truck for a few moments before he shut the ignition off. Cheetah's friends were in the yard, on the porch and no doubt in the house. There seemed to be more kids than there were the night before. He hoped he still had a house left.

He turned the key, shut the truck off and got out. He walked by them as he went into the house and nodded when they said hello to him. Stands Proud was waiting to see the inside of his house before he decided whether or not to be friendly. Once again, the Latin music was turned down when he entered.

Cheetah was in the kitchen, cooking supper as usual but all the girls were gathered at the table and Angelina was leaning against the counter, talking to him. Wolf was on the couch talking to some of the boys.

"Hey Papa," Cheetah called out from the kitchen.

"Hey Papi!" all the kids yelled.

Stands Proud grinned and walked into the kitchen. "What are you cooking, son?" he asked. The aroma of spice and sauce enticingly filled the house, people were everywhere talking and laughing and a few were dancing.

"*Es pollo con arroz y frijoles*, a Latin dish," Cheetah said. "Everybody likes it so that's what I'm making." He stirred each of the four pots on the stove. "How was work, eh?"

"Good," Stands Proud said, glad Cheetah was talking more. He seemed a little happier.

"Grandfather called," Cheetah said. "He wanted to know what was going on over here so I told him. He seemed ok with it, eh?"

"It's all right, son," Stands Proud said.

"Ok es done," Cheetah said, turning around, "Ladies por favor," he said in a teasing quiet voice, "Eat before I set the pigs loose, eh?"

They giggled and lined up at the stove.

"Here es yours Papa," Cheetah said, handing him a bowl.

"Thanks," Stands Proud said, sitting down.

The girls gathered around the table, watching Stands Proud, giggling and eating.

He smiled when they spoke Spanish and thought that he didn't understand them. "Yes, Juanita was very lucky to have me," he agreed. He enjoyed it when they burst into a fit of roaring laughter.

"We forgot Senor," Rosa said emphatically, "of course you would know our language."

"We weren't trying to be rude," Elisa said. "You're very handsome and Juanita, she was sooo pretty."

All the girls agreed.

"I love the way she wore her hair, like this," Julia said, moving her hair to one side.

They saw Stands Proud's eyes flicker with sadness and they fell silent.

"What I loved about her most," he told them, trying to ease the sadness, "was her laughter. She was usually laughing at me, but I liked it."

Cheetah smiled a little. He leaned against the counter and folded his arms over his chest.

"She was funny," Rosa agreed. "*¡Ah Senor!* I have to tell you this story. One night we had a bad snow storm and we couldn't get home. Cheetah, he say, you can come to my apartment and stay there, no?"

The girls started laughing and nodding their heads.

"No, no," Cheetah said quickly, "don't tell this story!"

"Es funny, we have to," Julia said. "Ok, listen…so Cheetah, he cannot take the four of us through his Mama's apartment without her killing him so he sends us from the fire escape into his room."

"We were very quiet Senor," Elisa said. "We did not make one sound. Cheetah, he went to Calle de Azul to sleep, but he comes in the morning to get us out of his bedroom." She started laughing and couldn't stop.

Stands Proud smiled at them.

"I came in and sent them home," Cheetah said. "End of story."

"Ay no, es not what happened," Julia said smiling and correcting him, waving her finger. She smiled at Stands Proud. "We're all very lazy sleepers, eh? We'll sleep until noon if we can. So Cheetah, he tries to wake us and he can't. He decides to change his clothes…so he es half naked…"

"Juanita, she came into the room," Rosa said, "*¡Y ella se volvió loco!* Poor Cheetah, he keeps backing up saying, 'Mama! Mama! Por favor, es not how it looks!' He apologized to her over and over again. She yell at him. She call him a whore. We got up fast and ran for our lives."

Stands Proud's hearty laughter filled the kitchen.

"We got him in a lot of trouble that night," Rosa said, smiling.

The laughter slowed down a little and they ate. Cheetah called the boys in and they lined up in an orderly fashion and filled their bowls.

Stands Proud was impressed and relieved with their

behavior. He wasn't sure what to expect. He noticed that Angelina had stayed quiet during the whole story the girls told and she didn't laugh very much. He got the feeling she wasn't too happy about any other girl being in his son's room.

Miguel came into the kitchen and stood beside Stands Proud. "Senor…I have something to ask of you," he said.

Stands Proud lifted his head. "What?" he asked.

"We know how sad Cheetah is," Miguel said dramatically. He reached over and patted Cheetah's face. He laughed and slung his arm across Cheetah's shoulders when Cheetah gave him a stern look. "Anyway, in New York when he es like this, we like to cheer him up. We gather all of our music together and we go up onto the roof and dance. We have a little party…"

"A little party," Cheetah said dryly. "Es never *little,* Miguel."

"Ok, a very big party," Miguel said. "We dance; we sing…drink just a little…"

"A little?" Stands Proud asked.

"Si Senor," Miguel said, grinning. "We would like to do it here. If es ok?"

"Miguel…" Cheetah sighed and shook his head.

"You see? He needs to be happy," Miguel explained.

"You're on a reservation," Cheetah explained. "There es no roof top to dance on, eh?"

"We found some sheets of plywood," Miguel offered. "We can make a floor out there in the yard, eh?"

"You're asking me if you can have a party?" Stands Proud inquired.

"Si Senor," Miguel said. "There won't be any fighting. We will clean everything up and I promise it will be okay."

"Okay," Stands Proud said. He shrugged. "It's still a little cold out there but if you want to go ahead."

"Ay Senor," Angelina smiling at him, putting her hands on her hips, "when the Latin ladies dance, we will melt the snow."

All the girls agreed and laughed.

"As long as there are no fights, it's all right with me," Stands Proud told them.

They hurried to make preparations for the party. Cheetah watched as they carried the plywood to create a dance floor. Rafa parked three of the vans on the side of the house and one near the floor. He spent an hour hooking up lights and sound. Cheetah sat on the porch and watched them.

Stands Proud walked around, watching what they were doing and helping them to find places to plug electric cords in. He showed a few of the boys how to do things and found he liked being useful to them.

"What's going on?" Turtle asked, walking up behind him while he was hanging a wire.

"Oh the kids want to have a party," Stands Proud said.

"Need some help?"

Stands Proud turned around and looked at him. "You're asking to work? You'll have a heart attack." He laughed at the look on Turtles face. "Sure, help me with these wires."

Turtle held the wires so Stands Proud could fasten them on a pole. He looked over at Cheetah. "How's wild cat?"

"Not too good," Stands Proud said. "He's a little better since they arrived but I can't tell if it's real or not."

"The Council doesn't know what to do about that check."

"He didn't want it," Stands Proud said. He made sure the wires were fastened right. "You can't blame him."

"Five hundred million dollars," Turtle whispered hoarsely, leaning close to Stands Proud.

Stands Proud sighed. "I don't think he believes he'll be around to spend it," he said. He stopped to watch the kids carrying food and cases of beer into the house. He realized the vans were full of it. "How did they get all that stuff in there?" He shook his head.

"Wolf seems to be having fun," Turtle commented.

Stands Proud turned around to see all the Latin Ladies gathered around Wolf. He chuckled. His gaze went to Cheetah, still sitting on the porch. He was watching everything go on around him.

"He doesn't look so good," Turtle said quietly.

"No, he doesn't," Stands Proud said agreed. "I thought this might make him feel better but it doesn't seem to be working." Rafa came up to him. "Are the wires okay?" Stands Proud asked.

"Si Senor," Rafa told him. "It works. Don't worry too much. This happens with him sometimes. I think we can help."

"I hope so Rafa," Stands Proud said.

"I'm going to put our music on," Rafa told him. He went over to the van and began to organize the music for the night.

Miguel saw Cheetah sitting and staring the way he used to from his roof top in Calle de Azul. He walked slowly up the porch steps. "What do you see Cheetah?" he asked.

"The Tribal police have gone by seven times," Cheetah said. "Jack has been standing over there wanting to come over but he's worried about it."

Miguel looked over his shoulder and saw the Indian Cheetah was talking about.

"Up there on the hillside es Tommy and Luke Eagle

Chaser," Cheetah said. "My Grandfather es talking to my father, probably about me and Wolf es busy forgetting his own name."

Miguel laughed and glanced at Wolf. "He likes the Ladies." He walked over and sat down on a chair. He looked over at the van as Rafa got the sound on. The music started just as it was getting dark. "How are you doing, eh?"

"Eh…" Cheetah said. "I know you want me to be happy but sometimes I can't."

Miguel nodded. "I know it."

"Do you like it?" Cheetah asked quietly.

"Like what?" Miguel asked.

"Being Warlord."

"Si," Miguel said gently. "I can see you miss it."

Cheetah sighed. "I thought I was doing the right thing, coming here. Now, I'm not so sure."

"If you want to come back Cheetah," Miguel told him, "all you have to do es tell me and I will step down. That mark can be fixed."

"I don't know," Cheetah said, discouraged. "I'm not sure about anything, eh?"

Miguel looked around. "Eh these people coming around," he said, "will they have a problem with us?" He noticed more Indians gathering to see what they were doing.

"No," Cheetah told him. "Tribal Officer Shortwing might be a problem. The Eagle Chaser brothers also might try something. But eh…no I don't think anyone else will say anything. They will like it. There es not much happening here."

"You're bored," Miguel said.

"Si," Cheetah said. "I have nothing to do, no where to be." He shrugged. "I'm not used to it." He leaned forward and

61

listened to the music and smiled. "Rafa did a good job, eh?"

"Let's go a little closer," Miguel suggested.

Cheetah smiled and stood up. "I know what you're up to," he said. "I don't think it can work, eh?"

"The music has never failed us before," Miguel said. "Relax, eh?" he encouraged, "Have some fun Cheetah."

Chapter Eight

Cheetah watched Officer Shortwing stop in front of their house. Somehow Stands Proud and Turtle managed to deter him from coming into the yard. He saw Tommy and Luke Eagle Chaser coming and he sighed, shaking his head. "I knew it," he said hoarsely. "Tell Los Caballeros not to kill them, eh? They're trying very hard to be a gang here."

Miguel looked at the six boys. "Them?"

"*Si,*" Cheetah said, "they're more talk than anything. I've become their favorite target, no?"

"Eh they must not be too smart," Miguel said. "There are at least thirty five Caballeros here."

"They don't know that," Cheetah said. "You're not flying colors. They'll think you're just my friends. And eh…I haven't fought anyone. My leg was giving me some trouble."

"Ok," Miguel said, standing up. He went over to Rafa and told him what Cheetah had said.

Cheetah watched as they came closer but they didn't cross the road.

The lights came on. The girls rushed onto the floor and began to dance. They took the hands of the Caballeros and they danced, too. Cheetah smiled as their plan for a party had actually worked. He laughed at Wolf trying to move to a Latin beat. "He's clumsy," Cheetah said to Miguel.

"Ay si but very happy," Miguel said, grinning. He saw the Indian girls at the edge of the dance floor. "Hey Cheetah…who are they?"

"I only know that ones name," Cheetah said. "The girl wearing the blue jacket es Suzy. Those are her friends." He smiled when the Latin Ladies encouraged the girls from the rez to come out and try the steps. They seemed to get along and they were doing pretty good.

"She's pretty," Miguel said.

"Go dance with her," Cheetah told him. "She stays to herself. I've watched her. I don't know why she es so quiet. Maybe you can find out."

Miguel stood up and crossed the floor. He began to teach Suzy some of the dance steps and she smiled at him.

Cheetah grinned.

Stands Proud had walked through the house and the yard. There were people in the kitchen cooking and his sister's Leah, Martha and Jolene had come over to help. The women of the rez were more than happy to help out with the party. Once the food was cooked it was brought outside and served from the long tables. Stands Proud began to bump into people he hadn't seen in a while and they talked. Everything was going very well, he thought, except for Cheetah. His son was still sitting in the lawn chair, watching everyone else. He smiled every now and then but it would fade into the somber expression Stands Proud had gotten used to seeing. He was standing by the food table when Rafa grabbed his arm. "What's the matter?" he asked, expecting trouble.

"*Nada,*" Rafa said. "Come with me, eh? The party es going to start now."

Stands Proud gave him a strange look. The kids had been dancing for two hours.

"We are going to get him out of that chair," Rafa said urgently.

"Oh," Stands Proud said.

The dance floor cleared suddenly and the lights went out. Everyone gasped thinking it was a power failure. The lights came on and the Latin Ladies were wearing red satin dresses with

64

ruffles. They stood proudly, waiting for the music to start. When the Latin beat began, they danced in their heels, shaking their hips and swaying their bodies in a sultry way.

"If this doesn't get him on his feet, nothing will," Rafa said.

"What?" Stands Proud asked.

"To dance Senor," Rafa said.

"He dances?"

"Does he dance?" Rafa asked, with disbelief. "*Si*, he does. The girls will do everything they can to get him up. Es what they always do to him. If he doesn't get up, he will make them mad, no?"

The girls danced across the floor, turning around and shaking their hips in front of Cheetah. They smiled adoringly, daring him to get up and chase them onto the dance floor.

Cheetah laughed and sat up straight, but he stayed in the chair. He didn't feel like dancing. Rita beckoned him to come onto the floor but he shook his head.

"Ay, he's feeling bad," Rafa told Stands Proud. "He loves to dance. He sings too."

"He sings?" Stands Proud asked.

"Si, if he drinks enough Corona, you'll see," Rafa said.

"He's drinking?"

"A little," Rafa said. "The beer es ok. Es the whiskey we keep him away from." The song ended and Rafa shook his head.

Stands Proud laughed as the girls scowled at his son and told him off in Spanish. Cheetah leaned on one elbow on the chair and laughed at them.

"Ok, plan B," Rafa told Stands Proud. "The viper."

Stands Proud laughed. "You shouldn't call her that," he

said.

"Oh you watch this," Rafa said. "He will have to get up this time, eh? They used be together before Marisa. If he ignores Angelina, he'll pay for it."

Angelina walked to the center of the floor and lifted her chin. Whistles came from all directions.

"She es the best dancer of the Latin Ladies, eh?" Rafa said, "She and Cheetah entered a few contests together in clubs. He's her dance partner. She'll get him up."

The sultry beat began and Angelina moved perfectly, her feet stepping to the music. Her ruffled deep blue satin dress revealed most of one leg as she moved. She flounced the ruffles and drew closer to Cheetah a little at a time, tantalizing him with her movements.

The people gathered around the floor laughed and recognized what she was trying to do.

Cheetah smiled up at her and tilted his head to one side, letting her think he might be bored. He saw the flash in her eyes as the beat came harder and faster. When she was right in front of him, he yawned and patted his mouth. She glared at him and he laughed at her. She spun indignantly to turn away and he jumped up behind her, dancing and following her onto the floor. She glanced over her shoulder and saw him coming. She smiled at him.

Los Caballeros cheered as they danced to the center of the floor.

Stands Proud's jaw dropped. He laughed. Cheetah moved beside Angelina as if he were born to do it, taking her hand and spun her several times and pulled her close to him.

"Es it," Rafa said. "That es our dancing. They're good, no?" Rafa clapped his hands and called out to them.

Cheetah smiled as Angel wrapped herself inside his arm.

Their bodies pressed together and he began to tantalize her, leaning toward her but keeping barely an inch between their lips. He smiled and spun her around him. They'd danced together often and he felt the beat of the music in his heart. He'd forgotten where he was. He no longer had any worries.

"There," Rafa said. "He's all right now, eh?"

Cheetah danced with Angel and his Latin blood burned hot inside of him. They danced together often and easily. He'd missed doing it. When the dance ended, he smiled wide and tilted his head back. It was a relief. He could breathe again. She kissed his neck and he laughed. The music started and they picked up the beat. The floor filled with Caballeros and Ladies dancing together.

"You see?" Rafa said, nudging Stands Proud. "This es the party, eh?"

"He's happy," Stands Proud said quietly amazed.

"Very happy," Rafa said. "I told you he loves to dance. We've been doing this on the roof back home ever since I can remember. Es his Latin blood Senor," Rafa said, trying to make a point. When Stands Proud looked at him, Rafa knew the point had been made.

Stands Proud sat down in a chair and watched as Cheetah moved on the floor. His son was sweating profusely but smiling. He was quite a character too, Stands Proud noticed. Cheetah would pretend to be bored, ignoring the ladies, and then suddenly his face would light up with a smile. He danced up to them and took them into his arms. In the midst of his friends, dancing, Cheetah was full of life. He'd turned out so much like Juanita; it drew tears to Stands Proud's eyes. Because of the prophecy surrounding him, Stands Proud had forgotten Cheetah was Latino as well as Lakota. It pained him. How could he have forgotten?

Out on the floor, Miguel danced up to Cheetah. "We have trouble," he said, looking at the reservation gang. "Over there."

Cheetah saw Luke and Tommy Eagle Chaser and he sneered. "To hell with them, eh? What can they do?"

Miguel put a hand on his shoulder and they walked to the other side of the floor. "If you will go through the drills with us," he said. "I think they'll leave."

"I'm dancing, eh?"

"Cheetah, they haven't seen you fight. If you show them what you can do and let them realize there are ten others who can fight like you do, they'll go away," Miguel said.

"Si, ok. I can't feel my leg anymore so why not?" Cheetah conceded. He walked over and took a drink of his beer and set it down.

Once again, the dance floor cleared and the lights went out. The men whistled expecting to see the Latin Ladies. When the lights came on, Cheetah and *El Escogido Diez de Los Caballeros* were on the floor. Cheetah stood in the front of the group with Rafa on one side and Miguel on the other. Behind them were two rows of four Caballeros. Cheetah took a step forward and lowered into a perfect fighting stance. In unison, the Caballeros followed. "Begin!" he called out, in a clear voice. He started the first drill and they punched, blocked and kicked, moving together with precision. He moved faster and picked up the pace, spinning and kicking higher. They followed him exactly, without missing a step.

Suddenly, The Ten moved away from him and they lined both sides of the floor, giving him more room. Cheetah leapt high into the air and twisted his body, rolling in mid-air and landed softly on his feet. He punched and kicked, at a fast furious pace. He jumped into the air, kicked left, then right and landed right in front of Luke and Tommy Eagle Chaser. His chest arose and fell as he lowered into fighting stance and held it. Sweat streamed down the sides of his face. Cheetah looked into their eyes, with a daring gaze. They turned to walk away. He reached down, picked up his Grandfather's cane and tapped both boys on the shoulder, counting coup on them.

They stopped and glared at him, knowing the full impact of what he'd done. Long ago, a warrior counted coup on his enemy by getting close enough to tap them with a stick and get away with it, unharmed. Luke and Tommy stomped away from him, swearing.

His Grandfather laughed. Cheetah smiled and crouched down beside him. "How are you, eh?" he asked. "Are you having fun? I can get the Ladies to dance with you."

Jonathan Argent laughed until tears came to his eyes. He patted the boy's face gently. "I've missed you Grandson," he said. "Here's the boy I used to know. Where have you been hiding that smile?"

"I'm happy tonight," Cheetah said, smiling and standing up. "No worries, eh?"

Angelina came up and wrapped her arm around his. "Come sing with me Cheetah," she said.

"Go, go," Jonathan teased him. "I see you're busy."

Cheetah laughed and took the microphone from Angelina. Rafa had thought of everything, he realized. He drank more Corona and went out onto the floor with Angel. The slow pulsating music started and she sang to him in a sexy, sultry voice. Cheetah moved closer to her and his husky words flowed into a song.

Stands Proud gazed at them in awe. They were singing an old Latin love song that Juanita had often played. The girl sang to the boy of how much she loved him. The boy sang to her about the pain of love. Cheetah's face revealed the agony, the grief of losing love and he seemed to force himself away from Angelina. Angelina sang from the shadows calling him back to her. Cheetah closed his eyes and tears streamed over his face as he sang, lowering to his knees. Angelina's voice grew stronger, echoing in the night air. She called to him over and over but he sang that he

69

was lost and alone. Angelina came from the shadows and sang in a strong clear voice. She lifted Cheetah's chin with her slender fingers and brought him slowly to his feet. He arose beside her and they began to sing together that their love would bind them forever. Together, they would never be lost.

When the song ended the cheering from everyone erupted and hands clapped violently together. The Indian women trilled and the Latin Ladies cried.

Cheetah wrapped his arms around Angelina and pulled her close to him. The music began again and it was a faster beat. He smiled at her, took the microphones and set them down and they danced.

Chapter Nine

The party lasted all night and into the next day. Stands Proud thought they might get tired but they danced on the floor, on the porch and Rafa climbed to the roof of the van and danced up there. Cheetah spent more time talking to Miguel, dancing with Angelina and the girls and he seemed very happy. More food was cooked and it was brought into Stands Proud's kitchen. The people on the rez didn't mind at all and they stayed to eat and talk.

"I wanted to thank you Senor," Miguel said to Stands Proud.

Stands Proud faced him. "I've never seen him like this."

"He es happy sometimes, eh?" Miguel assured Stands Proud, "But it wasn't that often at home either. Cheetah…he es very serious, Senor, about life. He always had to stop dancing and go to Don Antone's or there was some business in the neighborhood to take care of. The music and dancing always makes him feel better, no?" Miguel paused, "If he hadn't gotten out of that chair last night, I'd be very worried about him."

Stands Proud saw Turtle and Danny Redboy bringing over a Pow Wow drum. He smiled. "You'll get to see our dancing now," he said, pointing to the drum.

Miguel nodded. "This es good. Everyone es having fun." He looked around the yard. "I haven't seen the ones who have been giving Cheetah trouble, have you?"

"No," Stands Proud said. "They're gone."

The Latin kids curiously watched as the Indians set up the drum and sat around it. When the beat began and the Indians sang out, their eyes widened with a pleasant surprise and they smiled.

Cheetah had been talking to Rafa on the porch. He heard the ancient beat and he moved so he could see where it was coming from. He watched the men drumming, their drum sticks coming down against the raw hide. The hollow sound matched the beat of his heart. He saw the people coming toward the house. Suzy Takes-The-Bear was wearing a fancy shawl outfit. The women walked together wearing long buckskin dresses, with intricate bead work. And the men, Cheetah saw, were wearing buckskin leggings, breech cloths, and shirts. He stared hard at the feathers, the paint and the war shirts.

"Somebody say Pow Wow?" Wolf's voice said, from behind Cheetah.

Cheetah turned around. Wolf was wearing a blue and silver fancy dance outfit. Cheetah smiled.

"I'll show you how to dance," Wolf informed him. He went down beside the drum and put his bustles on. He fastened one high on his shoulders and one to his waist. The feathers and ribbons glistened in the sun light.

Cheetah's smile grew as his friends from New York gathered closer to the floor. He knew they'd never seen this. They waited while Wolf prepared to dance. In silence, his brother walked to the middle of the floor. When the beat began, Cheetah moved slowly down the steps, watching Wolf step perfectly to the drum beat. The faster the drum beat, the faster Wolf's feet stepped to it. Wolf whirled and spun around. He jumped down into a split and bounced back up. When the drum stopped, Wolf struck an arrogant pose and turned his face toward Cheetah. Cheetah laughed and clapped his hands for his brother.

The drum called for an inter-tribal dance and the people came in droves. The area widened as they danced in a circle.

Tears came to Cheetah's eyes as he watched them. He remembered this from going to Pow Wow's when he was little, but the beat he recalled from a long, long time ago.

"Can you do that?" Rafa asked him.

Cheetah looked beside him and noticed Rafa had followed him from the porch. "What?" he asked quietly.

"Can you dance like them?" Rafa asked. "Do you know how to do it?"

"Yes," Cheetah said softly. He watched as the Latin Ladies joined Suzy and tried to imitate her fancy shawl dance steps. He laughed at the Caballeros attempting the traditional men's warrior step.

"I would like to see that, eh?" Rafa snickered.

"What?" Cheetah asked him, his attention on the dancers.

"You," Rafa said, laughing, "doing that." He pointed to Jack Dann. Jack moved to the ancient beat, warrior style, stepping to the drum.

Cheetah saw his aunts approaching. He saw what they were carrying in their hands. He grew nervous and stepped back a little. They stood in front of him proudly wearing their deer skin dresses. They presented him with finely beaded moccasins, leggings and breech cloth. "Thank you," he said quietly, taking the items into his hands.

"Your father is bringing the shirt," Jolene said, with a big smile. She winked at him.

Stands Proud carried the shirt carefully. It had been kept within the tribe for a hundred and fifty six years. It was old soft worn deer hide, dyed blue and yellow. He knew his son would recognize it. The Council had talked. It was time to return it.

Cheetah saw the shirt and his heart sped up inside his chest. It had belonged to him when he was a member of the Tokala Warrior society. How had they found it? He knew it was his because of the markings he'd placed on the shirt by his own hand. His gaze lifted to his father's eyes and his lips parted but he couldn't speak.

73

"You know this shirt?" Stands Proud asked.

Cheetah looked at it. He saw the side of it, torn from the wound at the Greasy Grass River fight. His gaze returned to his father's. Still, he didn't know what to say.

"The tribe believes it was yours," Stands Proud told him, "but they're not absolutely sure."

The drum had stopped. The wind blew. Cheetah looked around at the expectant faces of the people. His hand trembled as he touched the part of the shirt that had been torn with his fingertips. "Yes," he said quietly. "It's mine." He accepted the shirt from Stands Proud and the trilling of the women surrounded him. The men called out to him and someone hit the drum a few times.

"This isn't to force you into anything you don't want to do," Stands Proud told him. "They asked me to return the shirt. It's yours and the people want you to have it."

"*Pilamaya,*" Cheetah whispered, staring at it. Everything came back to him in a rush. He remembered his village, the move to the Bighorn Mountains and how his people, his mother, father and sisters they were slaughtered along the way. He had survived and went to a Sun Dance near the Greasy Grass River where the warriors fought the Seventh Calvary. Cheetah's breathing deepened and his chest a rose and fell. He remembered dancing near Wounded Knee creek…the Hochkiss guns rapid fire…people dying and falling into the snow. Cheetah remembered standing on a cliff, after watching them die, and wanting to leave this world. He remembered falling without caring that he was dying. He'd lost everything he loved, even then.

When Cheetah raised his gaze from the shirt, to look out over the people, Stands Proud saw the overwhelming sorrow and grief return to his eyes. The depth of his sadness was worse than before and Stands Proud instantly regretted returning the shirt. He started toward him but Cheetah turned away, ran up the steps and went into the house.

Miguel quickly followed him. The bedroom door slammed in his face but Miguel opened it and went inside. He found Cheetah sitting on the bed, holding the shirt in his hands. "Hey," he said gently, approaching him. Cheetah's hands were shaking. "I've never seen you like this. What does that shirt mean?"

"Es not a bad thing," he said, trying to explain. "It brings back a lot of memories, that's all."

Miguel looked at the shirt. It couldn't have been Cheetah's. He was four when he lived here. "Is it your father's?" he asked.

"No," Cheetah said quietly. "It's mine."

"But you were…"

"It's mine Miguel," Cheetah said clearly, looking up at him. "I told you about the prophecy. This was my shirt when I was Tokala."

Miguel didn't know what to say. He believed what Cheetah had told him. He'd seen the nightmares, heard the screaming and listened to a lot of drunken ramblings. "If it hurts you, don't keep it. Give it back to them."

"It wasn't all bad," Cheetah said. "I remember being… free. I know what it was like. These people, they don't know." He smoothed a hand over the shirt. "I was surprised to see it, es all. You know the scar on my side, eh?" Cheetah turned the shirt so Miguel could see where the buckskin was torn.

"What are you going to do?" Miguel asked. "You're not happy here. I know your not."

"It's a reservation," Cheetah told him. "The Lakota were forced to come here. They were kept here, given rotten meat and the soup. You never saw anything like that soup, eh? I swore…I would never…" His voice faltered. "It's not being with the people that upsets me. It's that I remember what it was like

75

before…how it is now…this es what is painful to me."

Miguel went to the window. The drum had started again and the people were dancing. "They seem happy today."

Cheetah stood up and went to the window. He watched the people dancing in the circle, the same as they had long ago. The pride shown in their eyes and they stepped to the beat. He saw the children dressed and dancing.

"Es a wonder you're all still here," Miguel commented, watching the people.

Cheetah looked at him. "You're right," he said. "They meant to kill us."

"And because of that special dance you told me about," Miguel said, "the Ghost Dance, that es how you've come back?"

"*Wanagi Wacipi*," Cheetah said. "It was said the old warriors would return to live again. I'm not sure."

"It must have worked migo," Miguel said to him.

"Maybe," Cheetah agreed, "but I don't know why…and I don't know why I'm the one who is back."

"Maybe there are other warriors somewhere," Miguel said.

"Do you think so?" Cheetah asked him. He'd never thought of it. What if there were? Where were his old friends?

Miguel shrugged. "Maybe," he said. "You're here. Why couldn't they come back too?"

"I don't know," Cheetah said.

"What are you going to do?" Miguel asked him.

Cheetah looked out the window. "Eh…I don't really have a choice and they know it. As Tokala warrior, my life es to be in service to the people, I come last. What they want always comes before my own wishes."

Miguel smiled and poked at him. "You *have* to dance with them."

"I know it," Cheetah said, defeated, "and Angelina will laugh at me."

"Probably," Miguel said, smiling, "but Rafa will tease you more, no?"

Cheetah rolled his eyes and sighed.

"I'll let you change," Miguel snickered. "Don't forget the feather for your hair, eh?"

"Get out Miguel," Cheetah said, smiling at him. The door closed and he began to get dressed.

Chapter Ten

When he stepped out onto the porch, the drum stopped. The voices of the people fell to a hush. The young man on the porch wore his hair loose, with two grey hawk feathers tied into it. There was a red painted line drawn from one side of his face to the other. Two black streaks were painted from the inner corners of his eyes. He wore a bone choker around his neck. The shirt hung from his broad shoulders and it fit him well. The rawhide on the sides of the leather leggings was fringed and he wore the soft elk hide moccasins on his feet. He left the porch and he walked to the circle. No one knew what to do. They did not expect him to do this. They were amazed to see him.

Cheetah watched as they moved away from him and his heart began to sink. They were staring at him again. He saw them whispering to each other. His eyes began to cloud with tears.

Jack Dann glanced at the young man and saw how the people were moving away, a little afraid, as if he were a spirit appearing before their eyes. He also saw the hurt on the young man's face. Jack walked into the circle and called over to the drum, "We want a sneak-up song!" he called out.

The drum started and Jack began to dance. He saw Cheetah watching him but the kid wasn't moving.

"Maybe he doesn't know how to do it," someone said. "He's been in the city a long time."

Cheetah looked over at Angelina. She wasn't laughing. Her dark eyes were curious. She gave him a short wave and nodded her head, telling him to dance.

"Why are you standing there?" Angelina called out, "I know you can move your skinny ass, eh?"

78

Cheetah laughed. He listened for the beat of the drum and his feet began to move. He stepped in time to the drum, a little nervous at first, but then, something happened and it became easy for him. He crouched down and danced inside the circle. When the drum beat at a very rapid pace he lowered to one knee and his head turned to the side. He acted as though he were searching for tracks, for prey or the enemy. The drum began to beat at its usual speed and he slowly bounced upright. He danced around the circle, weaving and bobbing his head, as he passed by the people.

"Stands Proud," Jonathan Argent said, nudging his son. "Watch his feet."

Stands Proud stared, hard. His son was dancing but he'd changed from the modern Pow Wow step to something unfamiliar and very, very old. He watched as Cheetah danced. Time seemed to go backward. The sage wafted through the breeze and the young man stepped to the beat of the drum. Something was happening. New time became old. Days were erased and days of long ago were brought back to them. The young man was no longer dancing on a make shift plywood floor. The reservation seemed to disappear. This became a day of celebration taking place in the old days, with the Lakota gathered together. Stands Proud found tears slipping from his eyes.

Jack stumbled, trying to dance beside the young man. He found he couldn't keep step. The ground seemed to move beneath him. He stopped and stared in amazement at the young man. He smiled. He laughed. "Here is the true warrior!" Jack called out to the people. "Silver Hawk!"

The women trilled loudly. The men raised their dance sticks and a few modern warriors raised their fists.

"*Ah Dios mio.* Do you feel that?" Angelina said with surprise, leaning toward Miguel. "What es happening? What es he doing?"

"*Ah si,*" Miguel said to her, "I feel it but I don't know what it is." It was Cheetah but it wasn't. Miguel felt a lot of power coming toward him, from the circle. The Latin dances gave off happiness, a fun energy and a lot of heat but this, Miguel realized this was something very new to him.

The song ended and Cheetah stopped on the final beat. Los Caballeros and the Latin Ladies cheered but the people of the reservation were quiet. Cheetah walked off the plywood floor and stood beside Angelina. He looked at the faces of the people in the crowd. They stared back at him.

"I…I thought you would laugh," Cheetah admitted to Angelina. "I'm glad you didn't."

"Why would I laugh, eh?"

"I don't know," Cheetah said thoughtfully, "es…different."

"But you are not like anyone else," Angelina told him. "Tell me, what were you doing?"

"Es called traditional dancing," Cheetah said.

"No, no I mean…why did that happen?"

"What?" Cheetah asked, not understanding her.

"Eh…I don't know how to explain it," Angelina said. "Everything moved."

He stared at her.

She gave him and impatient look. "Everything. The ground, the wind…it was like someone changed the channel on a TV. Everything moved. How did you do it? Was it eh…some kind of illusion? Magic?"

He shook his head. "I…I don't know Angel." Cheetah paused and looked around him again. The people were still staring. Some had begun to whisper behind their hands. He turned quickly and walked away from her and went up the steps. Cheetah went into the house and pulled the shirt off as he walked down the hall. He went into the bathroom and stared into the mirror, knowing he'd made a terrible mistake. Some how, time had gone backward. They wouldn't forget this. They would talk about it for months and even he could not explain how it happened. Quickly, he washed the paint from his face.

Once inside his room, he folded the shirt and put it away in the closet. He put the rest of the outfit in there, too. He changed back into his black pants and pulled the muscle T-shirt over his head. Cheetah picked up the trench coat and put it on. The people had reacted in the same way they always did. He'd done what they'd wanted and he'd gotten an even worse result. It was bad enough they thought he was different, he thought, now they would also be afraid of him. Cheetah went outside and walked over to Angelina. "Enough of this, eh?" he said, taking her hand. "Let's go for a ride."

"You're done dancing?" Angelina asked surprised. She walked with him over to Miguel's car.

"*Si*," Cheetah said shortly, "I'm done."

"What are you angry about?" she asked him.

"It's nothing," he said. "Let's get out of here." Cheetah got in behind the wheel and turned the key in the ignition. He put his sun glasses on and turned the car around, driving down the reservation road. He muttered and slowed down seeing the Tribal police car with Shortwing inside of it. "Eh…he's always waiting somewhere for me," Cheetah complained. "That guy hates me."

"Why?" Angelina asked. She looked over at him. He said he wasn't angry but she knew better.

"He tried to lock me up," Cheetah said. "I shoved him into the cell and took the keys."

Angelina laughed. "Cheetah," she said slowly, "you didn't."

"*Si,* I did."

"I don't know how you are living out here," she said,

81

looking out the window. Miles of emptiness stretched before them.

"I don't know either," Cheetah told her. "I'm getting sick of it fast. They wanted me to come but now that I'm here es like I'm some kind of freak."

"Why? Es it because you're from the city?"

"No, es always been like this," Cheetah told her. "I can't go anywhere that someone isn't staring at me."

"So?" she asked. "What of it? Eh? They do it at home too."

He glanced at her.

"When you're on the street," Angelina said. He gave a small growl and rested his hand on the steering wheel. "What? Tell me you did not know this."

"Es different, the look they give me es different," Cheetah explained. He drove for a while and his anger subsided. Angelina hadn't been talking. She knew his moods. "How have you been, eh?" he asked, more gently.

"The same," she said. "Nothing different at home. Es all the same only you are not there."

"I'm sorry I didn't come by to see you before I left," Cheetah said.

"Are you?" she asked, smiling at him.

"Of course," he said.

"Eh well, I was going to come to Calle de Azul but you said to stay away," Angelina reminded him.

"There was too much going on before I left," Cheetah told her. "I didn't want to have you mixed up in it."

"I know. I listened, didn't I?"

Cheetah smiled. "For the first time since I've known

you," he said, glancing her way.

Angelina smiled at him. "I do what I want to," she said, "but I'm not stupid."

Cheetah laughed. "I know that," he admitted.

She sighed. "Where are we going?"

"I have no idea," he said.

"There es nothing ahead of us," Angelina stated, "and nothing behind us. What kind of a place es this?"

Cheetah sighed and turned the car around. He started back to the reservation.

"We're going back?" she asked him. "God that was exciting!"

"Sorry, eh? I just wanted to get out of there for a while," Cheetah said, grinning at her. "The next town es a hundred fifty miles away."

"I'm sorry but I like New York, eh?"

Cheetah smiled. "Es different here. I haven't figured out what to do yet," he said. "That's part of the problem."

"What es the other part?" Angelina asked him.

He shrugged.

"Were you really going to do it, eh? Miguel said you had a gun."

Cheetah sighed heavily.

"You must miss your mother and Marisa very much," Angelina said softly.

"Don't do this Angel," he said. "I don't want to talk about it. Miguel took the gun and Rafa has already chewed on my ass, eh?"

"Eh well," she said flippantly, "you want to kill yourself?

Go ahead. I won't miss you."

"If you didn't miss me," Cheetah stated, "you wouldn't be here."

"I came for the scenery," she replied.

Cheetah smirked. "Es that right?"

"Si…I love eh…that one tree over there…and hey, that barn es nice," Angelina told him, "for a barn."

Cheetah laughed. He turned onto the road that led back to the reservation. As they got closer, he could see they were still drumming and singing. He parked the car in the field across the road from the house. He got out and went over to Angel's side to open the door. When she started to walk away, he slipped an arm around her waist and gently pulled her back to him. "Let's stay over here, eh?" he suggested. Cheetah lowered his face to hers and kissed her soft lips.

Angelina backed up and looked into his eyes. "You could show me your room," she said.

He grinned at her. "You've seen my room."

"I think I want to see it again."

"Ah, do you?" He laughed and took her hand in his. They walked across the road, past the people and the Pow wow drum. He led her up the porch steps, into the living room and down the hall. Cheetah opened the door to the bedroom and closed it behind them. Inside the room, he gently laid her down on his bed. "Es this more exciting for you Angel?" he asked in a husky voice, lying down beside her.

"Es a start," she said, smiling at him.

"Better than the scenery?"

"Ah si," Angelina said.

"I can make everything in this room move for you too," Cheetah told her, smiling.

84

She smiled at him. "You've already done that."

"I'm going to do it again," Cheetah promised and he leaned over, kissing her lips.

Chapter Eleven

Stands Proud sat in the lawn chair and tried not to look at his house. He shifted uneasily. Every now and then, Jolene raised an eyebrow and looked over at him. He'd seen Cheetah take the young woman into the house and they hadn't come out. The sun set behind it. Everyone ate supper. The drum began again and someone built a fire and still, Cheetah and Angelina did not appear. The women talked, glanced at the house and shook their heads. The men shared secret grins and nodded to one another.

"I guess you're ready to be a grandfather," Jolene said to Stands Proud.

He opened his mouth, started to speak and made a funny sound.

"You should stop this," she said.

"I…uh…" Stands Proud glanced at the house. A soft warm glow flickered from Cheetah's bedroom window, candle light, Stands Proud supposed. He cleared his throat and shifted in the chair. "He's eighteen," he offered, growling.

"They're talking about him."

"Jolene…" Stands Proud began. His son came out of the house with the young woman and Stands Proud breathed a great sigh of relief.

Jolene turned and followed Stands Proud's gaze. "He should know to act better when everyone is around," she said, "or at least…" she added, "be a little less arrogant about it." She walked away.

When Stands Proud saw what was happening on his porch, he wished they would have stayed in the house. Cheetah had the young lady backed up against the post and he was kissing her neck. They were one being with two heads, Stands Proud decided. He sighed heavily and lumbered across the yard and over to the porch steps. He rested his hand on the railing and looked up at his son. Cheetah hadn't bothered to put his shirt on; his hair was loose and disheveled.

Cheetah noticed Stands Proud staring at him. "Do you want something Papa?" he asked.

"Uh…oh boy," Stands Proud said, glancing away from them.

Cheetah laughed. "What?" he asked.

Stands Proud sighed again and went up the steps and on to the porch. He stood next to his son. "Stop," he said.

"Stop what?" Cheetah asked.

"Your aunts have been pecking at me," Stands Proud told him. He glanced at Angelina and then looked at his son. "You paraded this young lady past everyone and you've kept her in the house for hours. I understand you haven't been living here but you should know this isn't what they expect from you."

Cheetah's dark eyes flashed. "I don't care what they expect of me," he said.

"You could be a little quieter about…"

Cheetah scowled at him, released Angelina and walked away in a huff. Angelina smiled at Stands Proud, flipped her hair over her shoulder and left the porch.

Stands Proud emitted a low growl from his throat. He knew the boy wouldn't understand. "That went well," he muttered sarcastically.

Cheetah walked over to the van. Rafa had moved the stereo equipment and was sitting inside the van, watching the Lakota dance. Cheetah sat down next to him and reached behind him and into the cooler. He took out a can of beer, opened it and drank from it.

"Ehhh…I guess you would be thirsty," Rafa grinned, teasing him.

Cheetah didn't answer him. He watched the people moving in the circle.

"Where es the viper?"

"Don't call her that," Cheetah snapped.

"You know what she calls me," Rafa reminded him. "I have to get even some how, no?" He noticed the anger coming off of Cheetah. "What es wrong? Did you fight with her?"

"No," Cheetah said.

"I would think eh…you'd be in a good mood," Rafa said to him.

"Let it go," Cheetah warned, lifting the can to his lips. He drank more of the beer. "Es nada."

Rafa nodded and fell quiet.

Cheetah saw his grandfather watching him. The look in the old man's eyes had changed. "Ah shit," Cheetah muttered. He drank the rest of the beer and tossed the empty can into the van.

"What?" Rafa asked.

"Stands Proud said I'm not doing what they expect of me," Cheetah informed him.

"Eh…what are you supposed to be doing?"

Cheetah reached for another can of beer. "I don't know Rafa," he said. He opened it and saw his grandfather stand up. He lowered his brows as the old man approached him. His grandfather stopped in front of him and took the can of beer out of his hand.

"You can't do this here," Jonathan said to him.

"What?" Cheetah asked.

"Listen boy, you're too close to the circle and the drum," Jonathan told him. "If you want to sit here and watch the dancing, that's ok but if you want to get drunk, you should go away from here."

Cheetah stared at him. Slowly, he stood upright. "We were drinking here last night," he said.

"That was different," Jonathan said.

"I'm not the only one drinking Grandfather," Cheetah stated. He'd smelled the alcohol as he walked through the crowd. He'd seen a few others stumbling.

"I know," Jonathan said. He walked over to the garbage threw the can away.

"What was that about, eh?" Rafa asked Cheetah, watching the old man. "Why did he do that?"

"My behavior es unacceptable to the people," Cheetah said scowling and crossing his arms over his chest. He glanced over at Angelina who was talking with the Latin Ladies and swore softly under his breath. A boy wearing regalia came over to him and Cheetah had to look twice before he realized it was Luke Eagle Chaser. "What do you want, eh?" Cheetah demanded.

Luke stared at him.

Cheetah stood up and menacingly glared into his eyes.

"You better get out of here Indio," Rafa warned Luke.

Luke glanced at Rafa and his intense gaze returned to Cheetah. "I think you should go back to New York, fag," he said, shoving into Cheetah's chest.

Cheetah drew back his fist and plowed it into Luke's face. The boy flew backward and fell. Cheetah jumped on him. He swung again and again. Blood covered his fist and sprayed over his chest.

Rafa grabbed him; pulling him backward and Cheetah spun, punched and kicked. Rafa ducked to avoid the punch but Cheetah's fast high side sweep had always been unstoppable. His boot slammed into Rafa's arm. There was a loud crack and immense pain spread through his entire arm. He crashed to the ground, lying on his side. "Damn it Cheetah!" Rafa yelled at him, clutching his arm and moaning. "Ah damn you.".

Cheetah stopped cold and stared hard.

"You broke it!" Rafa yelled at him, cradling his arm against his chest. "You broke my arm, eh? I know you're mad, eh? But you didn't have to do this."

"I…" Cheetah said, stunned. "I didn't know it was you,"

"You could've looked," Rafa retorted, scowling at him.

Cheetah noticed everyone staring at him. He looked over at Luke Eagle Chaser lying on the ground. The boy's face was beaten beyond recognition. The people gathered around him. His chest heaved with left over rage. "You know better than to…" Cheetah held back the rest of what he was going to say. The people were listening. He fell silent and lowered his chin.

Miguel walked over to him. "Cheetah," he said.

Cheetah looked at Miguel and his eyes moistened to tears. "I didn't see him Miguel. I didn't," he said in a throaty voice.

"I know," Miguel said, gently. "I know you didn't. Come with me. We'll have to take him to a hospital now, eh?"

Cheetah swallowed, hard. He nodded. He left the circle with Miguel and Rafa, walking into the darkness. He felt the warm tears leave his eyes and slip over his cheeks. "I'm sorry Rafa," he said, in a muffled voice.

"You're always sorry," Rafa muttered.

Chapter Twelve

When they went back to the house, Cheetah opened the door and went inside. He knew everyone was looking at him and at the cast on Rafa's arm. He knew Stands Proud expected him to say something, to explain what had happened but Cheetah knew his father wouldn't understand. But there was one person Cheetah knew who had always understood him. He walked into the kitchen and picked up the phone. He dialed the number and waited, praying for an answer.

Stands Proud watched his son in the kitchen but asked Rafa, "Are you all right?"

"Eh…" Rafa said, sitting down, "it will heal."

"Who's he calling?" Stands Proud asked.

Miguel shrugged.

Cheetah paced back and forth with the phone to his ear. "Khan," he said, suddenly. "Khan es that you?" He paused. "Es Cheetah." His vision blurred again as Khan asked how he was doing. "I'm…eh…" He couldn't speak. He drew in a deep breath and shuddered as he exhaled. He tried to steady his voice. "Can…Can I come to Okinawa? I need…I need to talk with you." Tears began to fall from his eyes and he blinked. Cheetah turned his back to everyone in the living room and leaned against the wall. "I know we're talking now Khan…I can't…" He paused as Khan asked him what was wrong. "I need your help Khan. Please, can I come?" He paused. "No, I'm not in New York anymore. I'm home but…" The tears fell harder and faster. "Pine Ride Indian Reservation, South Dakota but I…" Cheetah stopped speaking and listened as Khan told him to be still and that he would arrive the next day. Khan asked if he were in danger. Cheetah swallowed, hard. "No Khan," he said in a hoarse voice, "but…the way I've been acting lately everyone else is." His voice broke and he couldn't say anything else. He hung up the phone and turned around.

"Isn't Khan the one who trained you to do these things to people?" Stands Proud demanded, motioning to Rafa's arm.

"No, Khan didn't teach me to do that," Cheetah said. "I did that, eh? And I said I was sorry. I didn't mean to break his arm."

"Why did you?" Stands Proud asked.

"I don't know what happened," Cheetah said.

"You attacked Luke," Wolf said, putting his feet up on the coffee table. "Rafa tried to stop you and you kicked him."

"I know that," Cheetah said. "What I don't know...es why I can't..." His voice faltered and looked at Stands Proud. "I can't remember it."

"What do you mean you can't remember it?" Stands Proud growled at him. "It was just a few hours ago."

"I heard what Luke said to me," Cheetah told him. "After that, I..." He didn't want to say anything else. Everyone already believed he was crazy. "I don't know."

"What do you mean, you don't know?" Stands Proud asked angrily, standing up. "You broke his arm!"

"I know what I did!" Cheetah yelled back. "I don't know how it happened!"

"Did you black out?" Miguel asked, quietly.

"No," Cheetah said.

"If you didn't see Rafa," Miguel said, "and you didn't black out, what did you see? Anything?"

"Khan es going to help me," Cheetah said. "He's the only one who can."

"Khan is the one responsible for this!" Stands Proud

yelled at him. "If that man hadn't taught you these things, you wouldn't know how to do them…and you wouldn't be hurting anyone."

"Es not true!" Cheetah yelled back. "Khan didn't teach me to hurt people"

"Then why are you doing it?" Stands Proud demanded. "This isn't the first time it happened. You broke Jack's nose the other night. Do you think I don't know about that?"

"This es not Khan's fault," Cheetah told him.

"The hell it isn't," Stands Proud said evenly. "I talked to Frank. I know what they were training you for."

"You don't know anything!" Cheetah yelled at him.

"I know that you don't have any control over what you're doing!" Stands Proud roared, charging toward him. "You don't eat! You don't sleep! You act as if you're still living in that god damn place!"

Cheetah backed up, moving away from him. "Be quiet," he said.

"You broke Jack's nose! You broke Rafa's arm! And you crushed Luke's cheekbone! What the hell are you doing Hawk?" Stands Proud yelled at him. "Are you mad at me? Are you going to attack me?" He moved forward until his son's back hit the wall of the living room. "Come on! Come after me! I'm right here!"

"Stop it," Cheetah pleaded with him. "Don't do this."

"Why? Are you going to hurt me? Would you attack your own father?" Stands Proud roared. "How crazy are you?"

"Stop it!" Cheetah screamed. The agony twisted his face. Angry tears came to his eyes. "Back up…" he said, begging Stands Proud. "Please…back up."

"What if I don't?" Stands Proud asked, towering over him.

"Back up," Cheetah warned.

"No," Stands Proud said in a deep voice.

Cheetah glanced at the door. He moved to one side, attempting to run. Stands Proud's hand slammed against the wall, trapping him. He went to the other side and Stands Proud slammed his other hand down. Cheetah flinched, expecting to be hit. He raised his arm and began to shake.

Stands Proud's heart ached. "Why aren't you attacking me?"

"Because…" Cheetah said, in a throaty voice.

"Because why?" Stands Proud asked. "I made you angry. I yelled at you but you're not fighting me. You're shaking. You're afraid and you want to run. What are you afraid of?"

Cheetah lowered his arm and looked into his father's eyes. His chest heaved slowly and his throat ached. "If you touch me…" he said, tears sliding over his face, "I will hurt you." His entire body shook. "Don't…touch me."

"Angelina touched you," Stands Proud said. "You didn't beat her up."

"No *Senor*," Angelina said quietly. "I never touch him. He holds me but I…I can't touch him. I used to be able to but not anymore."

Stands Proud gave her a surprised glance and looked back at his son.

Cheetah closed his eyes and turned his head aside. His shoulders began to quake and choked sobs erupted from his chest. He slid down the wall and crouched down on the floor, burying his face in his hand.

Stands Proud backed up.

"Es not Khan's fault," Cheetah sobbed. "Es not." Angrily, he wiped his face with his arm.

94

"Is it because of what those men did to you?" Stands Proud asked, crouching down beside him.

Cheetah looked at him, tears running down his face. "Es not all that happened," he said. "There are things you don't know. Things that no one knows. Ah God… please…just go away and leave me alone."

"I can't leave you alone. I won't do it," Stands Proud said tenderly. "Tell me. What things? What are you seeing that scares you?"

"I didn't see Rafa and I didn't see Jack…I didn't even see Luke…" He closed his eyes and struggled to regain his composure.

"What do you see?"

"I see...I see Don Antone putting a black hood over my head…and I hear…his voice," Cheetah said, "saying to me…no mercy…show no mercy…and I feel something hot…burning my hands." Cheetah opened his eyes and looked directly at his father. "Show no mercy," he said. He lifted his shaking hands up where Stands Proud could see them.

Stands Proud looked at his son's scarred hands.

"They took me...to a room," Cheetah said, "and they brought a man into this room. Don Antone told me to kill the man very slowly. I was to use a high front kick to crush the ribs in his chest. Next, I was to use a lower side sweep to break both of his legs so that he couldn't stand up. I refused to do it. I told him I would never kill anyone for him. No mercy, he would say, show no mercy." Cheetah stopped speaking and his jaw quivered with suppressed rage. "He poured something hot over my hands, burning me. He said one day…my hands would kill for him. But I never did it. I never did it for him."

"You told us you burnt your hands at the chemical plant," Miguel said.

95

"I wasn't working anywhere," Cheetah said in agony. "I was with Don Antone, always with Don Antone."

Miguel's eyes saddened. "Cheetah…"

"He told me…this would happen. He told me one day I wouldn't think anymore, I'd just react and then…I'd be able to do it. I'd be able to kill for him."

"He's not here son," Stands Proud said quietly. "Don Antone is dead."

"I can hear him," Cheetah said. "He planned this, don't you understand? I have to find a way to get his voice out of my head. The only one who can help me es Khan. Khan will know what to do."

Chapter Thirteen

The next morning Los Caballeros and the Latin Ladies packed up their things. Cheetah watched and wished he was able to go back with them but he figured he wasn't good for anything, anymore.

"Well Cheetah," Miguel said to him, "We've got a long drive back to New York, eh?" He finished loading the trunk of the car. "I hope that Khan can help you."

"I hope so too," Cheetah said. "I'm sorry for the way things happened while you were here."

"You've been through too much," Miguel said. "Don't blame yourself. I always told you that. What Don Antone did to you wasn't your fault."

"I know it," Cheetah said. He watched as the rest of the Caballeros and Ladies packed their vans and said good bye to everyone. He glanced over his shoulder at Rafa, who was sitting on the porch. "I feel bad about Rafa. He hasn't talked to me at all," Cheetah said quietly.

"He's a baby that's why," Miguel snickered.

Cheetah smirked. "How long do you think he will be mad?"

"Until he gets home," Miguel said, "then he will say how Los Caballeros es not the same without you, how no one can run Los Caballeros like Cheetah could and he will talk about *all* the good old days."

Cheetah laughed. "You get a lot of that, eh?"

Miguel smiled and shook his head. "You don't know," he said. "I hear it from Patty down at the Diner, from the people on Salcida...even homeless people come around mumbling about how everything was better when Cheetah was Warlord," Miguel sneered.

"Keep trying," Cheetah told him. "It will get better for you."

"I doubt it," Miguel said. "Hey! Rafa! *Vamanos!*"

"I'm not getting in that car with you," Rafa called back.

"*Ah Dios*," Miguel uttered. "*Por que no?*"

"Because I'm not going."

Cheetah turned and looked at him.

"I said," Rafa repeated, walking over to the car, "I'm not going. I like it here."

Miguel and Cheetah exchanged a glance.

"What?" Miguel asked.

"I said, I like it here," Rafa said. "I'm staying. I already talked to Stands Proud. He said es okay if I get a job. Besides, if I go…who es going to make sure this one doesn't do anything stupid like killing himself?"

Cheetah looked at Rafa. "Do you really want to stay here?"

"No," Rafa said smartly, "I'm just saying it because when you kicked me last night I fell on my head and I can't think straight no more."

Cheetah smiled at him.

"All of New York will celebrate now, eh?" Miguel teased Rafa.

"I wouldn't be surprised," Rafa admitted. "So…if you want to gather Los Caballeros together and jump me out, let's get it over with."

Miguel called out in Spanish to Los Caballeros. He told

them Rafa was leaving the gang and would they come to jump him out?

Cheetah laughed as the Caballeros climbed into their vans, waving him off and ignoring the whole idea. They drove past and waved, calling out to Cheetah. The Ladies claimed their hearts would be broken forever, but not because of Rafa. Cheetah waved back.

"Es time for me to go, eh?" Miguel said, watching the vans pull on to the main road. "Ehhh…maybe I'll come out here one day, no?"

"I'd like that," Cheetah said.

Miguel nodded and got into the car. "*Honro y orgullo* Cheetah!" he called out, driving away.

"Ay," Rafa said. "Finally…some peace and quiet."

Cheetah laughed. "I can't believe you decided to stay," he said.

"Are you kidding?" Rafa said. "I've been waiting for years to dump them some where."

"Looks like they were waiting to dump you," Cheetah teased.

"Eh…not the first time," Rafa said. "You're the only brother I got. I can't let you walk alone out here."

"But they were all your brothers," Cheetah told him.

"You're not the Warlord," Rafa reminded him. "You don't have to talk that kind of crap no more. You know they didn't like me."

Cheetah laughed. "Es because you harass everyone," he said.

"They asked for it," Rafa said.

They went into the house, laughing.

Stands Proud gave them a strange look. "I thought you'd be upset when they left," he said to them.

"Hell no," Rafa replied, "I have a head ache. That whole gang will fall apart now, eh? Cheetah and I, we were the true Caballeros, not those clowns."

Cheetah smiled at Stands Proud. "Thanks for the new brother," he said.

"After having a house with forty two kids," Stands Proud said. "How bad can you three be?"

Wolf looked at him from behind the magazine he was reading. "Dad?"

"Yeah?"

"You shouldn't have asked that question," Wolf said. He looked at Rafa. "Do you shoot hoops?"

"Do I?" Rafa asked, tapping his chest. "I am the best on Salcida Avenue unless," he said, looking over at Cheetah, "someone breaks my arm."

Cheetah sighed. "That's why you stayed here, isn't it? If I do live to be an old man, I'll still be hearing it."

"You owe me," Rafa said, going into the kitchen.

"I told you I was sorry," Cheetah said, following him.

"You still owe me."

` The phone rang and Cheetah picked it up. "*Bueno?*..Eh hello?" He nodded. "Okay, I'll come to pick you up." He hung up the phone. "Khan es at the airport. I'm going to get him."

Stands Proud didn't say anything.

"Papa," Cheetah said. "I swear nothing terrible I've done es because of Khan."

"That man taught you to fight," Stands Proud said, looking up at him from the chair. "He's your friend and I'll respect that but the way I see it is different. He knew what was going on in that place and he didn't do anything to stop it. He only taught you more fighting moves so Don Antone could continue to use you."

"He couldn't stop it from happening Papa," Cheetah said. "No one could."

Again, Stands Proud fell silent.

Cheetah sighed heavily. "I asked Grandfather to come over to meet him," he said. "Es that all right? I'll make supper."

"That's fine," Stands Proud said.

"Good," Rafa said, sitting down and putting his feet up. "You go get him. I'm waiting to meet this Khan because I'm going to tell him you broke my arm."

Cheetah scowled and went out the door.

"Rafa," Stands Proud said, folding up the newspaper.

"Si Papi?"

Stands Proud smiled. "I'm glad you decided to stay," he said.

"Someone has to keep him in line, eh?"

Cheetah scowled the whole way to the airport over what Rafa had said. He would do that too. If Kahn stayed every day he would hear Cheetah broke my arm. The only way out was if Khan could take him to Okinawa. There, Cheetah thought, he could have peace. He arrived at the airport and began to search for Khan. When he saw the Japanese man waiting for him, his eyes filled with tears. The old man was wearing a dark blue kimono with a gold sash around his waist. "Khan, I'm so glad to see you," he said, embracing him.

"Very good to see beloved son," Khan said. "How much trouble you in this time?"

Cheetah lowered his gaze.

"Hmm, must be bad," Khan said. "Come. Take me to your house. We will wok on your troubles."

"I hope you can," Cheetah said, walking beside him.

Khan nodded. "You not like being home Cheetah-san?"

"I like it," Cheetah said, "but if I don't do something soon, I'll have to leave."

"What happen?"

"I've lost control fighting. I broke a man's nose, someone's arm…which, you will hear all about…and I crushed a boy's cheekbone," Cheetah said. He opened the car door so Khan could get in. He went around to the other side and got in. He turned the key and the engine roared.

"You broke many bones fighting in the arena," Khan said. "I never approved of force Tassiano made you use."

"I know," Cheetah said.

"Why this different?"

"Because one man is a friend, it was Rafa's arm and Luke…eh…he had it coming but not as badly as I beat him," Cheetah said quietly.

"Why you do this?" Khan asked.

"There's something wrong with me," Cheetah admitted, glancing at Khan. "I hear Tassiano's voice telling me to…" He gripped the steering wheel and stared hard at the road. "I think I'm going crazy, Khan. You know some of the things he did to me but not all of them. When you would go home to Okinawa… he…" Cheetah paused. "He was training me to kill."

"Khan not understand," he said. "Any one can kill."

"He tried to make me do it," Cheetah told Khan, "but I wouldn't. I remembered things you told me and no matter what he did, I got through it but now…I have nightmares and it feels like these things are happening to me all over again. I wake up

102

screaming. I can't eat. I can't sleep. Es so bad now…when anyone touches me, I fight. I can't control it. I see him. I hear him. No one can touch me anymore…at all…not even a woman. I can't stand it."

Khan said nothing.

Cheetah looked over at him. He knew when Khan was angry. "I'm sorry if I said something wrong," he apologized.

"I not mad at you," the old man said. He blinked his eyes. His voice was strained. "So sorry this happen. Not your fault."

"I'm finished with living like this," Cheetah said. He drew in a deep breath and tried to find courage, but it wouldn't come to him.

"What you mean finished?"

"The other day," Cheetah said hesitantly, "I had a gun. I was going to go up in the hills to kill myself. I thought…it would be better that way. I don't trust myself anymore. I don't want to hurt anyone." He swallowed, hard. "Es not the first time," he said, looking over at Khan. He wished he hadn't. There were tears flowing over the old man's eyes. "I'm sorry Khan," he whispered. "I'm sorry."

"Truly believe world is better without Cheetah?" Khan asked.

"Yes."

"You right. This very bad."

"Everyone I love, I lose," Cheetah said softly. "Es always been that way."

"Khan still here," he reminded him.

"I'm glad," Cheetah said, "very glad."

"Find reason to live," Khan said.

"I don't have any."

"Where is boy who told Don Antone 'I am Oglala, Lakota. I was born with honor in my blood'?" Khan asked.

Cheetah's eyes flooded with tears. He blinked. "I don't know Khan."

"You in a big mess now," Khan said, looking out the window.

Cheetah wiped his cheek with his hand and stared hard at the road. He turned onto the reservation road. He drew in another breath of air, wiped his face and went around the car to let Khan out. The old man was waited for him at the porch steps.

"This reservation?"

Cheetah nodded.

"Happy here?" Khan asked.

"Not really," Cheetah said, looking at him, "but it's where I was born."

"Second time?" Khan asked, going up the steps.

"Yes."

"Hawks flew above this house?"

"Es what they tell me," Cheetah said. He opened the front door so Khan could walk inside. His grandfather, father, brother and Rafa were in the living room. "Khan, this es Jonathan Argent, my grandfather and my father, John Stands Proud. This es my twin brother, Seth Lone Wolf and my friend but also my brother, Rafael Gonzalez."

"He broke my arm," Rafa said, pointing at Cheetah.

"Khan will try to help."

"Someone should," Stands Proud said.

"Nice to meet you Khan," Jonathan said, shaking his

hand. "How was your trip?"

"Good flight," Khan said, "but land in very bad news."

"Well, here's some more for you," Stands Proud said, looking at Cheetah. "They can't wake up Luke. He's in a coma."

Cheetah sucked in a breath and turned his face away. "*Madre de Dios*, what have I done?" he asked.

"Go. Make tea," Khan said to Cheetah.

Stands Proud sat up straighter and gave the Japanese man a strange look. "How's tea going to help anything?" he asked.

"Tea is for Khan," he said, "and for Cheetah. Long journey ahead."

Cheetah nodded and took Khan into the kitchen. "You can sit here Khan," he said. "I'll make it."

"You remember how?"

"*Si,* I remember." Cheetah opened the cupboard and reached for the cup. It slipped out of his hand and crashed, shattering into the sink. He looked at his shaking hands and turned around, showing them to Khan.

"Come. Sit down," Khan said. "Take off coat."

Cheetah took off his coat and sat down.

"Khan will make the tea," he said. "Why you shaking?"

"I don't know. It happens a lot though," Cheetah told him.

"Take drugs?"

"No Khan, I drank a little but I haven't done any drugs in a while," Cheetah told him. He watched as everyone else hesitated and slowly came into the kitchen. He was mad it took them so long. He could tell they didn't like Khan at all.

"Any one else?" Khan asked. "Tea?"

105

They shook their heads.

"I'll make coffee," Stands Proud offered. He walked over next to Khan, towering over him. The man's head barely reached his chest. "Khan, can I ask you a question?" Stands Proud inquired.

"Certainly."

"You were there when that man was abusing and torturing my son," Stands Proud said. "Why didn't you do anything to stop him?"

"Tassiano never abuse boy in front of Khan."

"But you knew it was happening," Stands Proud accused.

"Leave Khan alone," Cheetah warned, standing up.

"Sit," Khan said to Cheetah. He put the water in the kettle over the flame on the stove. "Khan knew," he admitted. "Plan many ways to rescue boy. Take boy to Okinawa. No one *ever* see boy again. Tassiano very smart. Never leave Khan alone with boy."

Stands Proud glanced at his son. "You were going to take him to Japan?" he asked.

"Cheetah most beloved son of Khan. He not deserve life he forced to live," Khan said.

Stands Proud fell silent.

"Eh...my arm hurts," Rafa complained.

Cheetah glared at him and rose up in a fury, knocking over the chair he was sitting in. "I said I was sorry!" he yelled.

"Sit," Kahn said calmly.

"He keeps giving me a hard time about his arm," Cheetah told Khan, "I told him a hundred times I was sorry!"

"Cheetah want Khan's help?"

"*Si,* of course I do but…"

"Sit."

Cheetah scowled at Rafa and up righted the chair. He sat down. Rafa kicked his leg underneath the table and Cheetah stood up and started around the table.

Khan moved in front of him.

"I'm sorry Khan."

"What boy sorry for now?" Khan asked. "All the way home. Sorry it raining Kahn. Sorry Cheetah late. Don't be sorry. Drink tea." Khan put the cup on the table. "You sit here, beside Khan."

"Thank you," Cheetah said quietly.

"So you're the one who taught him to fight?" Wolf asked. "He's really good."

"Cheetah is best quality fighter," Khan agreed. "Very good student. Some time he not listen but he learn fast."

"*Madre de dios*…this pain," Rafa uttered.

Stands Proud chuckled.

"Ok," Khan said. "Rafa tell Khan whole story of broken arm."

Cheetah leaned an elbow on the table and put his face in his hand.

"Es like this, eh?" Rafa said, sitting upright, "Luke came over and shoved Cheetah. He says you better go back to New York and he called him a fa..." Cheetah glared at him and Rafa faltered, "Yeah, anyway, so Cheetah jumped him and started to pound his face in so I go and grab Cheetah. He swung at me, then he kicked me. I heard this loud crack and...."

Cheetah bolted out of the chair and ran for the bathroom.

Everyone fell silent in the kitchen.

107

Stands Proud sighed. "He's throwing up again."

"This worse than I thought," Khan said.

Cheetah came back to the kitchen. He leaned against the door frame.

"How many days sick?" Khan asked, looking up at him.

"I don't know," Cheetah said tiredly. Hesitantly, he glanced at his father and grandfather. He didn't want to talk in front of them.

"I know he's been sick since he got here," Stands Proud informed Khan.

"How many days sick?" Khan repeated.

Cheetah walked over to the table and sat down. "I was sick in New York," he confessed quietly. "It's getting worse. I was hoping you could train me again."

"First time Khan train, no good?"

"Ah no Khan," Cheetah said. "What you taught me was the best but what Tassiano trained me to do…I think es what's making me sick. I thought if I can train all over again, go back and start over…maybe I can get things right."

"You want to go back to start over?" he asked. "I was young man of seventy years when started your training."

"I need your help."

"Remember first day of training?" Khan asked him.

Cheetah thought back. "*Si,* you had me fight the entire group of men to find my place to stand. I was first."

"What else?"

"That was all we did," Cheetah said.

"Think hard. You remember meditation exercise? Past life memories?" Khan asked him. "Boy tells Khan this not

Khan's business. Boy tells Khan to leave him alone. That was first day. You want to go back to first day?"

"Yeah," Cheetah said quietly.

"You ready?"

"Yes," Cheetah said. He glanced at his father and grandfather and settled his gaze on Khan.

"Khan is not."

Cheetah gave him a hurt look. "You won't help me? The only time I ever felt good was when you were training me."

"You not listen first time," Khan said. "You cut Tassiano's plants in half with sword. You chase kitchen help with staff. You play mind tricks, move here to there. You difficult student."

Cheetah smirked. "You said I was a good student."

"Khan was being nice."

Everyone laughed.

"Khan…I promise I'll listen to you," Cheetah said.

"You not student," Khan said, "You master now."

"I'm not a master of anything," Cheetah replied softly.

"Master of yourself," Khan told him. "You miss big part of training because you tell Khan past life not Khan's business. Leave part of yourself behind you. Other part runs ahead. Khan warned you one day it would make boy only half of what he could be." He paused. "If both parts together you complete, whole man. Left half of you empty for Tassiano to fill. You half ruined now."

"Es my fault?" Cheetah asked.

"Yes," Khan said. "Khan not accept just anyone as student. Leave homeland and spend life searching for warrior of days past, special warrior. You tell Khan his life mission was not his business. Khan was to leave you…but when Khan saw boy,

Khan's heart was full again. I could not leave you."

"You knew?" Stands Proud asked, "About him?"

"Knew long time," Khan said. He reached down into his sack and brought out a box. He looked at Cheetah. "Look familiar?"

"*Si,*" Cheetah whispered nervously.

Kahn took the lid off the box, revealing a silver, pearl handed knife. "This knife from seventeen generations of Khan family warriors. Knife made long time ago and carried by Samurai. Khan family knew one day this knife would travel to America and be given to a warrior who was not Khan's blood, but very close to Khan's heart. This knife tells story of warrior who comes from long time ago, who would be lost to his people. This knife belong to special warrior named Silver Hawk. Boy called *Igmu.*"

Cheetah sadly lowered his gaze and stared at the table top.

"Sixty years Khan search for warrior," he said. "Try to give knife to boy long time ago. Tell boy when he accept knife he must accept his right place, his true name." Khan took the knife out of the box. "Great silver bird etched in the blade of the knife. Very good, very powerful knife," he said. "Boy refused knife three times." Khan put the knife back into the box and closed it. "We go back to first day," Khan said.

Cheetah's eyes filled with tears as he looked Kahn. "I don't know if I can do this," he whispered.

"What is your name?" Khan asked.

Cheetah sat back and the chair and turned his face away from everyone. He regretted inviting his grandfather to the house. He could feel Stands Proud watching him but if he didn't answer, he knew Khan would take the knife away and leave.

"What is your name?" Khan repeated.

"*Cetan Maza,* Silver Hawk," he said, in a throaty voice. He looked at Khan as an overwhelming sorrow returned to him that he'd tried hard to forget.

"Who are your people?"

"The Teton Oglala, Lakota." .

"Where is homeland?" Khan asked.

Cheetah stood up and moved away from the table. He walked over to the window and gazed at the prairie and the Black Hills. Tears slid over his cheeks. "I was born to Dark Moon's village," he said, "a few miles away from here. I was called Igmu."

"How many in village?" Khan asked. "You remember?"

"Three hundred."

Stands Proud sat back in the chair. He exchanged glances with his father and stared as his son stood at the window.

"Tell Khan about family."

Cheetah turned and looked at him with tears streaming over his face. "I can't...I..." He saw Khan put his hand on the box that held the knife. "They were killed," Cheetah said. "I had a mother, a father and two little sisters...we were on our way to the Bighorn Mountains. We thought we'd be safe there but...the soldiers came..." He walked back over to the table and rested his hand on the back of the chair. "Everyone I knew my entire life was killed on that day," he said. "I was the only one left alive."

"How old when this happen?"

"Thirteen winters," he said. "I traveled alone to the Bighorn Mountains and joined with *Tashunka Witko's* band. He called me *wabluska,* a bug, because he said I was a pest. But then, he named me Silver Hawk and I became a warrior, a hunter...but there was nothing to hunt. The people were starving and we were told to go to the reservations. I spent one day at Fort

Robinson. They killed *Tashunka Witko* and I ran off. After that, I was no longer a warrior."

"This life time, you throw away honorable name."

"Yes," he whispered.

"Who is Cheetah?" Khan asked, looking up at him.

"It's a good name, a gift from friends," he said, "but it's not who I am."

"Again, what is your true name?"

"Silver Hawk of the Oglala, Lakota."

Kahn slid the box across the table. "Be ready Silver Hawk," he said. "We start tomorrow."

Rafa raised one eyebrow. "Es true then?" he asked.

"Yes," Silver Hawk replied. "It's true."

"Holy shit," Rafa uttered. "You're from the past, for real?"

Hawk nodded.

"But how…how does this happen?" Rafa asked him.

"Some think it happened because of the *Wanagi Wacipi,*" Stands Proud said, "the Ghost Dance. It was told to our people that one day, the warriors would return."

"I was there," Hawk told them. "I was with Chief Bigfoot. He was sick and in a wagon. We were ghost dancing in the snow. We heard the soldiers were coming to take us to the reservation. We headed back but the Calvary came. They surrounded us. In the middle of the night, I snuck away…because I was afraid of confinement. I knew if they caught me, I was going to the guard house." He paused. "I got away but then I heard a shot fired and….many, many were killed. It was near Wounded Knee Creek. I couldn't stand this anymore. It was the second band of people I traveled with and most of them were

112

dead. Again, I survived but I had no heart left. I went into the hills, found a cliff and was about to jump when I heard a voice saying to me, 'you'll be back.' A silver hawk flew out of the mist and wrapped around me. I didn't care," he said. "I jumped anyway."

"You killed yourself?" Rafa asked him flatly, "Even way back then?"

"But something is not right," Hawk told them. "My spirit never left the Black Hills. It's trapped here."

"Why do you say that?" Jonathan asked, listening to him with intention.

"Because," Hawk told him, "in this life time…I can't die."

Stands Proud stared, hard. "That part of the prophecy is true?"

"Yes, I've tried," Hawk told him. "I've tried to go." He shook his head. "It does me no good. Somehow…my spirit, my soul has been trapped and unable to leave here." He looked at Wolf. "Now you really think I'm weird, don't you?"

Wolf stared at him.

There was a knock at the kitchen door. Wolf got up and opened it. "Officer Shortwing," he said.

"I came by to tell you that Luke is awake," Officer Shortwing said. He looked directly at Hawk. "You're damn lucky. His family isn't pressing charges against you but I want you to know, I'll be watching you."

"You won't have any trouble from me," Hawk promised.

"I'd better not," Shortwing said. "I don't want you anywhere near my jail." He stomped out of the house and down the steps.

Stands Proud laughed and the others joined in.

Wolf smiled and closed the door.

"Khan missed joke," he said.

"I locked him inside of his own jail," Hawk admitted, looking over at Khan.

"You not student," Khan said slyly. "You master."

Chapter Fourteen

Stands Proud sat in the kitchen the next morning and watched the little Japanese man preparing a meal. He discreetly took a look at the stuff but didn't recognize it. He pretended to read the paper while Khan placed all of it at one setting. Stands Proud realized it was either for the man himself or for Hawk. Either way, it was a relief that the entire table wasn't set.

Hawk came into the kitchen. "Good morning Papa," he said. "Good morning Khan."

"Good morning. Sit down," Khan said. "Eat."

"Thank you," Hawk said.

Stands Proud winced as his son ate. He raised the paper to hide the expression on face.

"Stands Proud hungry?" Khan asked.

"Oh no," Stands Proud said. "I already ate, thank you."

Wolf came in and looked at Hawk's meal. "Eeeeww," he said. "What is that?"

"Wolf," Stands Proud reprimanded, smirking.

Khan smiled. "Good food for a strong fighters," he said. "You like some?"

"Nah," Wolf said. He put the box of chocolate cereal on the table and reached for a bowl. "You could give some to Rafa. He's a fighter."

"He won't wake up until noon," Hawk said. He sat up and looked at Khan. "There's too much here. I can't eat all of it."

"Eat as much as you can," Khan said.

Hawk only ate a little more of it. "That's all," he said.

Khan nodded. "How long is road to this house?"

"About five miles," Stands Proud said.

"Good. Hawk, go outside. Run road away from house and back ten times."

"It's…raining," Hawk said, looking out the window.

"You want Khan's help?"

Hawk sighed and stood up.

Wolf laughed at him.

Hawk scowled and went outside. The rain poured over him as he ran down the steps and started down the road. His boots sloshed in the mud, making it harder to run.

"You should not laugh at brother," Kahn said. "He very sick."

"I know," Wolf said. He put the bowl in the sink. "I was just teasing him. Is it all right if I run with him? I used to play basketball. I'm still in pretty good shape."

"Yes," Khan said, "but no talking. Run quietly. Silence very important to strengthen mind."

Wolf nodded and went out the door.

"We've been waiting a very long time for him to talk about the prophecy," Stands Proud said. "It meant a lot to my father also."

"Hawk not talk about prophecy. Hawk spoke about his life."

"Yeah, I guess I forget that sometimes," Stands Proud said, "that he lived it."

"Both life times full of pain," Khan said. "This life time very old soul in young man's body but body is worn out. Tassiano too hard on him. He fight with many wounds and he never complain before. He never tell Khan he is sick."

116

"Never?" Stands Proud asked.

"No, never. Hawk asked Khan to go to Okinawa," he said. "Khan say no. Silver Hawk must use the spiritual medicine of his people to get well. You know person who knows this medicine?"

"Yeah, I do but Hawk doesn't want anything to do with it."

"He fighting to get well now," Khan said. "You offer. He will accept. He very, very sick."

"I'll try," Stands Proud said.

Rafa stumbled into the kitchen and sat down at the table.

"How is arm today?" Khan asked.

"Es all right," Rafa said. "It does not hurt that much *Senor* but I complain to nag at him. If I don't…he forgets how strong he is and how easy he can hurt someone."

"You good friend to Hawk," Khan told him.

"We used to live next to each other," Rafa told him, "until my family moved away. After that, I hung out in Cheetah's apartment and at Calle de Azul."

"Family move without you?"

"Es right," Rafa said. "Eh…I don't care. Mi Papi y Mami…both crack heads. Who needs that?" He studied the food across the table.

"You hungry? Eat."

"*Gracias,*" Rafa said. He accepted the Japanese food without hesitation. He caught the look on Stands Proud's face. "Listen, once you live eating out of dumpsters, you'll eat anything, eh?"

"Good food," Khan told him. "Good food for fighters."

"I'm a fighter," Rafa said. "Cheetah taught me."

117

"Oh," Khan said. "Hawk good teacher?"

"Si, very good," Rafa said. "He's eh…very picky but very good."

The door opened and Wolf came in, soaking wet.

"Where brother?" Khan asked.

"He's coming," Wolf breathed out.

Hawk came in and leaned against the wall, gasping for air.

"You race back?" Khan inquired.

"No," Wolf said, sitting down. He flung his long wet hair over his shoulders. "He stopped to help Jack get a car out of the mud."

"You run ten times and push car?"

Hawk nodded unable to talk.

"Sit," Khan said. "Relax. You in sad shape."

Hawk nodded, gasped for air and tried to catch his breath. He rubbed his thigh to ease the ache inside of it. "I messed up this tendon," he told Khan.

"We will fix," Khan said. "Hawk better now?"

"Yes," he said.

"You talk?"

Hawk nodded. "I can." He looked over at Rafa, eating the food Khan had prepared. He grinned. He hated that stuff.

Khan arose to his feet. "Come here."

Hawk walked over and faced Khan.

"Turn around."

Hawk looked at him suspiciously. His mouth grew dry. "Why?" he whispered.

"You trust Khan?"

"Yes."

"Turn," Khan said.

Hawk turned with his back to Khan. His heart beat rapidly in his chest. He hated having anyone stand behind him. He was breathing so hard his shoulders were moving. He waited. Sweat streamed over his face. Suddenly, a hand pushed into his back and he spun, throwing a punch. Kahn caught his wrist before the blow could strike him.

Khan let the wrist go. "Turn," he said.

Hawk turned around and lowered his chin. He waited through the agonizing minutes.

"Find center," Khan told him. "You know this is Khan. Relax."

"I'm trying," Hawk said. He drew in a deep breath and exhaled. The shove came to his shoulder. He spun, throwing the punch and again, Khan had to catch his wrist. His eyes burned with tears. He lowered his arms. "Do you see…what he's done?"

"Again," Khan said.

"No," Hawk said. "I don't want to do it anymore."

"Hawk is in control," Khan told him, "not Don Antone. Turn."

Hawk turned around and closed his eyes. He breathed deeply trying to center himself and find the control he'd lost.

Khan motioned silently for Wolf to come and stand where he had been standing. Wolf shook his head, refusing. Khan urged him forward. He placed Wolf directly behind Hawk. Khan nodded. Wolf shoved hard into Hawk's shoulder blades.

Hawk spun and threw the punch. Khan blocked it again. Hawk gasped and looked into his brother's eyes. "I'm sorry," he whispered.

"Not see brother?" Khan asked.

"No," Hawk admitted.

"What scar from?"

"What? A knife," Hawk said, questioning him with his eyes.

"Where?"

"Eh…Ninth Street."

"Why?"

"Fighting. Eh…Carlos Martinez. *El Caudillo de Los Serpientes.*"

"This one?" Khan asked, pointing to another. "Answer questions. What from? Where? And why?"

"A whip. The training room," Hawk said in a throaty voice, "I don't know."

"Why?"

"Because I was drunk."

Khan walked around him. "Right shoulder."

"A bullet, the alley behind Louie's grill and I was running from the police."

"Why?"

"They wanted to arrest me."

"Your hands and your wrists."

"A whip. And…"

Khan stopped in front of him. "What else?"

"I don't know. Why am I doing this?" Hawk asked, backing up.

"Answer question."

"I don't know what it was," Hawk repeated. "I couldn't see. They covered my eyes."

Khan took a dish towel from the counter. "Tie over eyes."

"Ah Khan I don't want to do this," Hawk said.

"Khan leave today for Okinawa."

"All right," Hawk conceded roughly. He tied the towel in place, covering his eyes.

"You not see?"

"No."

"What this?" Khan asked, waving a spice under his nose.

"Cinnamon."

"This?"

"Lemon."

Khan walked a few steps very quietly. "Where is Khan?"

"To my right," Hawk said.

"Think of hands. What you smell?"

Hawk's breathing increased from fear. "Aftershave. Antonio es there. Garlic…sauce…."

"What you hear?"

"Don Antone. No mercy…" he said, in a raspy voice, "no mercy."

Stands Proud looked away. He couldn't stand watching it happen. He knew what Khan was trying to do but it didn't help him to accept it.

"What else you hear?"

"Shoes…walking…Don Antone is laughing…" Hawk shook his head. "The stove…they're cooking, boxes opening…"

"Your hands. What you smell?"

Hawk's head wrenched back and his entire body shook. "No mercy...show no mercy..." He started to scream. Hawk scrambled backward and his shoulder hit the wall.

Khan pulled the towel from his eyes. "Look here. Look here!" The young man was shaking, scared to death and believed he was being hurt. "Look here!" Khan yelled.

Terrified and hurt, Hawk looked at him.

"Who you see?"

"Khan," he said, breathing heavily. "I see Khan."

"Ok. You not hurt. Sit down," Khan said gently.

"The kitchen, Tassiano Estates and because I refused to kill a man," Hawk said, violently shaking. "Hot oil...he poured hot oil all over my hands."

"What you say?" Khan asked him.

"Where, why and what," Hawk scowled bitterly. He glared at Khan.

"Control anger."

"Why did you do that to me?" he yelled, still shaking.

"Father told Khan what you see when lose control fighting," Khan said.

Hawk reluctantly sat down and cast an angry look at his father. Who knew they were all in on it? What would they to him next? He tried to stop shaking. "I'm cold," he said, suddenly.

"Get blanket for brother," Khan told Wolf.

Wolf went into the living room and brought back a blanket. He gave it to Hawk.

"What about scars from past life time?" Khan asked.

"Only one," Hawk said. He wrapped himself in the warm blanket.

"What? Where and why?"

"From a Springfield Carbine, Greasy Grass River fight and because I…" He smiled, suddenly. He started to chuckle and then he laughed. "Because I was a warrior."

Khan nodded.

Stands Proud smiled.

"It wasn't a bad wound," Hawk said, "and we had won that day. We fought all afternoon. There was so much dust, you couldn't see the sun. It was a good fight." He stood up. "I…I still have it," he said. He moved the blanket and showed Khan his side.

Stands Proud leaned over to look at it. "Does that happen?" he asked. "Can someone carry a scar from a previous life time?"

"They can," Khan said.

Hawk sat down. He felt better and calmer.

"Your first life easier?" Khan asked him. "One scar."

"No," Hawk said. "It was harder because I couldn't see a reason for it happening. We were free and happy. Then…" His voice faltered. He paused, thinking about it. "There was so much death around me. People dying from not having food, from being sick…with diseases we had no medicine for. There was no reason for it to happen. This time, with Don Antone…he gave me a lot of scars…but I knew what was happening… and I knew why."

"Ok," Khan said. "Enough for today. You rest. Real work begins tomorrow."

Chapter Fifteen

"Things are getting weirder around here," Steve Battisse said, bouncing the basketball on the asphalt and watching Wolf's brother. He was standing at the end of reservation road. "What's he doing?" Steve asked.

Wolf laughed. He glanced at Hawk. He'd been standing in the same place for over an hour. "It's probably something Khan told him to do," Wolf said.

"He's not doing anything. He's just standing there, staring at everything," Steve said.

"Yeah, I know," Wolf said, catching the ball and bouncing it. He bounced the ball again and again.

"Who's Khan?" Steve asked.

"The Japanese guy staying at our house," Wolf said. "He's from Okinawa. He's the one that taught my brother to fight."

"I saw him," Steve said emphatically. "He's really weird."

Wolf laughed. "He's just different."

Steve tucked the ball under his arm and stared down the road at Hawk. "How does that teach you how to fight?" he asked. "I mean, I saw all those fancy jumps and kicks he can do the other night but when he jumped on Luke, he just bashed his face in."

"Yeah, well…" Wolf said, slowly. "I think that's why he's standing down there." Wolf caught the ball in his hands. "Khan said he has to master self discipline so he doesn't have to fight anymore."

"That doesn't make any sense," Steve said.

Wolf shrugged. "It does to Khan," he said. "Our people said the same thing. The greatest battle is the one not fought, or something like that."

"Huh?" Steve asked. "I think you're all weird."

Wolf laughed. "If you think we're weird out here," he told Steve, "you should see what goes on inside my house. Stands Proud has been working with Danny Redboy, learning all the old ways stuff about sweats and ceremony. Khan does this thing called Tai-chi every morning and he eats raw fish. Hawk talks to Danny Redboy about old ceremony stuff, cooks Latin food or does some weird martial arts thing. And Rafa sings Latin love songs at the top of his lungs, walks around eating chocolate cake and watches Spongebob Squarepants on TV," Wolf explained, "Oh, and Grandfather and all his friends have started hanging around playing poker."

Steve Battise stared at him. "That is weird," he said.

Wolf laughed. "I have to go," he said. "I promised Khan I'd help him with Hawk after he's done standing down there."

"Yeah?" Steve asked, grinning. "What's he going to do next?" He pointed in the other direction. "Stand over there and stare at stuff?"

Wolf shrugged. "I don't know. Khan never tells anyone what he's thinking about doing, he just does it." He started off the court and Steve ran up to him.

"Hey," Steve said.

"What?"

"Can I come with you?" Steve asked Wolf. "There's nobody at my house. Luke's still not coming out and the rest of the crew is at school."

"Sure," Wolf said, grinning. "Why not?"

They walked down the hillside and into the house. Rafa was lying on the floor, eating and watching cartoons. He started laughing and rolling around.

"You lazy," Khan told Rafa. "Good fighter never lazy."

"My arm's broke, eh?" Rafa said, sitting up. He held the cast close to his chest and pouted.

"You use arm in all fighting?"

"No…" Rafa said slowly, looking up at Khan suspiciously. "Eh…you're going to make me do something, no?"

"Go outside. Hawk coming," Khan said.

Rafa moaned getting up off the floor and turned off the TV. He went out the door.

"Hey Khan," Wolf said. "This is Steve Battise. He's a friend of Luke's."

Khan nodded. "Hello friend of Luke."

"Yeah hey," Steve said, watching the old man bow. He was wearing some kind of weird dress and he was probably the shortest guy Steve had ever seen, except for some guy he met at a pow wow the year before and he was a Hopi.

"How is Luke?" Khan asked.

"He's okay," Steve said. "He's got a scar right here," he said, pointing below his eye, "and he gets head aches sometimes but he's all right." He didn't want to tell the man that Luke and Tommy were still pissed off about what Hawk did and they were planning on getting even with him.

"You tell Luke, Hawk very sorry lose temper," Khan advised, "Not happen again."

"Yeah, okay," Steve said.

"Come outside," Kahn said.

Steve dropped the basketball onto the couch and followed

126

Khan and Wolf out the door.

Hawk saw Steve on the porch and wondered why he was there. He quietly waited while Khan walked on the old plywood platform, studying the floor.

"What this for?" Khan asked Hawk.

"We were dancing on it," Hawk said.

"You dance?" Khan asked.

Hawk smiled. "Sometimes," he admitted.

"Come here," Khan said. "I'll show you a dance."

Hawk laughed and stepped onto the platform. He noticed Khan looking at his old steel toe street boots. They were covered with mud.

"Why you wear those?" Khan asked him.

Hawk shrugged. "Tassiano gave them to me. He wanted me to wear them when I fight. I guess I just got used to them."

"Boots broke friend's arm," Khan said. "You take off. Throw away."

"I don't have any other shoes Khan," Hawk said. He liked the boots. He'd worn them for a long time, running on the streets and jumping roof tops in his old neighborhood. They were a special brand that was light weight but still had the steel-toes. He felt defenseless without them.

"You not need shoes," Khan said. "Take off. Throw away."

Hawk sighed and lowered to untie the laces. He pulled them off and tossed them aside.

"Throw away," Khan repeated.

Hawk bent down, picked them up and walked over to the garbage can. He took off the lid and dropped them in. The cold wet mud squished between his toes and stuck to his feet. He scowled.

Rafa laughed at him.

"What you wear on feet?" Khan asked.

Rafa lifted his foot to show Khan a cloth tennis shoe that was ripped; half missing and a few toes were sticking out.

"That not shoe," Khan said. "That sandal."

Rafa shrugged.

"Those ok," Khan told him. He looked at Wolf. "Tennis shoe. Very good." He looked at Steve. "You help us?"

Hawk glanced at Khan, then at Steve. He wondered if Khan knew who Steve was? He was the one who always started shit, ran his mouth and caused trouble.

"I don't know how to do this stuff," Steve said.

"Khan show you. Not hard."

"Ok," Steve said. "I'll try it."

"What you wear?"

Everyone looked at Steve's cowboy boots with the pointed toe and the hard soles.

"You leave boots on," Khan said.

Hawk gave Khan a curious look. The old man was holding a piece of thin rope in his hand and staring at everyone.

"Rafa stand here," Khan said.

Rafa moved over to where Khan was. "Eh, what are we doing?" he asked.

Khan didn't answer him. He motioned for Hawk to come forward. "Hawk come here," he said.

Hawk approached him.

"Turn," he said.

Hawk turned and swung. He felt a hand on his wrist. He spun around and delivered a low side sweep. His leg slammed into Kahn's but the old man didn't move. He looked into Khan's eyes, and then lowered his chin.

"Again," Khan said. "Turn."

Hawk huffed out a breath and turned. He'd never be able to do it. He didn't know why Khan did this all the time. It was obvious he wasn't getting used to it and he couldn't stop himself from reacting. Again Khan's hand went to his wrist. Darkness came before his eyes. He turned and threw a powerful punch. Khan caught his wrist but the old man didn't release it. Hawk's heart sped up. "Let go Khan," he warned.

"Why does he keep doing that?" Steve asked, whispering to Wolf.

"He can't help it," Wolf explained. "If someone touches him, he fights."

"That's weird," Steve whispered.

"Kahn…" Hawk said, his mouth growing dry. "Please… let go."

Kahn tightened his fingers around Hawk's wrist, using a hold he knew Hawk could not get out of. His gaze leveled with the boy's dark frightened eyes. He watched the sweat forming on his forehead and drip down the sides of his face. Hawk's shoulder's moved slightly and Khan knew the punch from the free arm was coming. He blocked it and caught the other wrist.

Hawk yanked backward, trying desperately to pull away but couldn't free himself. He tried to kick but Khan blocked him.

"Focus," Khan said. "You angry. Too afraid."

"Let go of me!" Hawk yelled angrily. He pulled and struggled.

"You forget teachings of Khan," the old man said. "You

master. You think, not act!"

"How old is that guy?" Steve whispered, behind his hand to Wolf.

"Eighty three," Wolf whispered back.

"Shut up!" Hawk yelled at Wolf. "Stop saying shit about me!" He'd seen them standing on the side of the platform whispering back and forth. He moved toward them but Khan had his wrists in an iron-like grasp. Khan turned his hands and a sharp excruciating pain went up into his arms. It took him to his knees. He stopped. Shame swelled up inside of him and he lowered his head. Khan dropped his wrists.

"Hawk get up," Khan said.

Slowly, he arose to his feet, glaring at Steve and Wolf.

"Hold arms up, wrists together."

Hawk looked at him and at the piece of rope in Khan's hands. He sighed and raised his arms and watched while Khan tied his wrists together without his fingers touching Hawk's skin.

"You fight Rafa now," Khan said. "Rafa use one arm. Two legs."

Rafa grinned. "You're in trouble now, eh Cheetah? Es my turn to look good."

"I don't want to fight him," Hawk told Khan. "Tie my legs together too. Let him kick my ass. I don't care."

Khan studied him. "You teach Rafa to fight?"

"Yes," Hawk said quietly.

"You have no faith in teachings?"

"He's good but I'm afraid I'll hurt him again," Hawk told Khan. Khan walked over to the side of the platform and stood between Wolf and Steve. Hawk sighed and faced Rafa.

Rafa grinned and bounced around a little. "Ok Cheee-tah,

130

open wide here comes my shoe." Rafa ran forward, jumped spun and slammed his foot into the side of Hawk's upper arm. Hawk stumbled to one side from the force of it and did nothing to block him. Rafa glanced at Kahn. Khan nodded for him to continue. "You're not going to fight back, eh?" Rafa asked Cheetah. "I know you're angry…" Rafa sang out, stalking around him. He swung his leg into Hawk's, knocking him to his knees.

Hawk stared straight ahead. He remained on his knees and didn't get up. His anger whirled inside of him like a hurricane wind but he fought hard to shut it down, to stop the wind and make it calm.

Rafa looked over at Khan and shrugged. Khan nodded again. Rafa knew he was supposed to make Hawk fight him. He didn't know why Khan wanted them to do this, but Rafa understood his mission. He walked around Hawk, reached down and gently stroked the side of Hawk's neck with his hand.

A complete blackness came before his eyes and Hawk shot upright.

"Oh shit!" Rafa yelped and he scrambled backward fast attempting to block the kicks. Hawk delivered a high front kick and a low side sweep. Rafa jumped and ran to get out of the way.
.

Hawk felt a hard kick to his chest, another came to his legs. His legs started to buckle and another powerful front kick slammed into his chest. He landed flat on his back. The jolt to the hard ground startled him and he stared up at Khan, standing over him in a fighting stance.

"Eighty three?" Steve whispered to Wolf.

"Yes. Khan eighty three," Khan said, looking over at Steve. "You come here."

Steve trembled a little. The short Japanese guy was a lot weirder than he thought. At eighty three, he should be sitting in a chair on a porch somewhere. Steve looked at Hawk who was still

131

on the ground. "Me?" Steve asked, putting a finger to his chest.

"Yes. Come here," Khan said.

Steve walked casually out onto the platform. He shoved his hands in the front pockets of his jeans and waited.

"Hawk turn over. Lie on stomach."

Hawk's chest arose and fell quickly. His rage boiled under his skin. "No," he said coldly.

"Khan leave for Okinawa."

Hawk glared at him. "Fine," he said. "Go!"

Khan turned and walked toward the house.

"Damn it!" Hawk roared. He jumped to his feet, running after the man. "Khan I'm sorry. Listen, I can't do it. I can't. I don't know why you want me to do that but..."

Khan kept walking. His foot rested on the first step and he stopped. "You not want to do what Khan tells you."

"No, I don't," Hawk admitted. "I don't want to."

"Khan cannot help Hawk."

"Please," Hawk said, "I'll do anything else."

"No bargains," Khan said. "Store closed. Time to go home."

Hawk visibly shook. "All right," he whispered. "All right...I'll do it. Don't leave."

"Go to platform," Kahn said.

Hawk walked back to the plywood. He glanced at Rafa and Wolf. He lowered to his knees. He watched as Khan cut the rope between his wrists, freeing his hands. He laid down on the platform, with his cheek against the scratchy wood and felt tears coming to his eyes. He closed them and his chest began to ache.

Khan looked at Steve and pointed to Hawk's back. "You

stand here."

"What?" Steve asked.

"You friend of Hawk's enemy. You take revenge for friend," Khan said. "You stand on Hawk's back."

Steve swallowed, hard. He looked down at Hawk, forced to lie on the ground. He could see the agony on Hawk's face and he knew why. Hawk hadn't liked what those men did to him at all. He'd been raped and humiliated. It had to be killing him to lie there. Steve glanced at the old man but quickly looked away.

"You friend of Luke?"

"Yeah," Steve whispered hoarsely.

"Eagle Chaser brothers planning revenge?"

Steve looked at Khan. "Yeah," he said, in a raspy voice.

"This end here," Khan said. "You take revenge for friend now. Stand on back of man who hurt your friend."

Steve raised his cowboy boot and gently placed it on Hawk's scarred back.

"You not like your friend much?" Khan asked him.

Steve put his right boot down and stepped up onto Hawk's back.

"Good. You stay here," Khan said. "Hawk knock boy down. Khan on first plane to Okinawa." He walked away and went into the house.

Rafa blinked and tried to get the tears out of his eyes. He sniffed. "Oh damnnn," he moaned. He glanced at Steve standing on Hawk's back, then at Wolf. "I can't watch this migo," he said and he went into the house.

Wolf sighed. He didn't want to stay there either but he found he couldn't make his feet move. If he left, he'd be leaving his brother lying face down with somebody Hawk hated, standing on top of him. Wolf stood there and watched them. Every now and then someone would drive past and slow down to look. The school bus came and the kids got off of it, pointing and laughing but a few simply stared at them.

Suzy Takes-The-Bear got off the bus and slowly walked across the field. Her eyes were drawn to Steve Battise standing on Hawk's back. The spring breeze chilled her. She stared at them and walked forward, clutching her library books to her chest. One book was about Crazy Horse and the other was the story of Mary Crow Dog. The high grass brushed against the legs of her jeans as she walked, swish, swish, swish. When she stopped, she stood right next to them and raised her eyes to meet Steve's. "Do you feel better now?" she asked him.

Steve glared because she'd made tears come to his eyes but he refused to look at her. He stared straight ahead. He didn't talk. He didn't move. He stared hard at what was ahead of him and discovered the hills he'd been living next to all his life, the Paha Sapa.

"He's a warrior Steve," Suzy Takes-The-Bear said. "He's not a fag. Even if he is a two spirit you had no right to say those things to him."

Steve wanted to get off Hawk's back and run for those hills. He wished he had a horse to ride and he'd go with the wind....away, away, away.

Suzy crouched down, with the books against her chest. Slowly, she reached toward Hawk's cheek.

"Don't do that," Steve yelped out. He trembled. "He doesn't like it."

Suzy's tears fell from her eyes. Her hand lowered slowly and she softly touched his cheek. He closed his eyes and didn't make a sound. "Silver Hawk," Suzy Takes-The-Bear whispered to him, "you never talked to me but I've been crying for you." She stood upright, her back straight and her chin lifted in a proud,

134

defiant way.

Steve wondered why she wasn't going anywhere. Was she going to stand there and stare at them? He knew she might. She was weirder than most people. He glanced at her but quickly looked away when her gaze tried to capture his.

"Idiots," she said. "You're both Lakota." She turned and walked away.

Hawk opened his eyes and saw Suzy walking through the prairie grass, going home, alone. He'd never heard her voice before, it was sweet and melodic. She was another silent one... but today, she had something to say.

Chapter Sixteen

The sun began to set beyond the hills. The evening breeze blew Steve's long hair over his shoulders and he waited for the Japanese man to come out of the house. He wondered why he was still standing there. After Suzy came and went, there no longer seemed to be a point to make. She'd made it for them. Steve stood there because he knew if he got down, it might upset Khan and Khan would leave and he thought Hawk had earned the right to have his friend stay. Steve realized when he first placed his boot on Hawk's back; the whole problem between them seemed stupid. It was a battle over name calling, not for life or death. After a while, Steve began to think about the prophecy. If it were true, if the man beneath him rode beside Crazy Horse, what kind of man did that make him? What kind of warrior was he? He felt stupid and ashamed for being so ignorant. When Luke and Tommy came walking down the hillside, Steve looked once again toward the hills.

They laughed.

Steve had gotten used to the slow rhythmic rise and fall of Hawk's breathing. He noticed it did not change. Hawk did not seem to care if they were laughing or he no longer had the energy to get angry.

"What the hell are you doing?" Tommy asked, smiling.

"Kahn told me to stand here," Steve said.

Tommy came closer to study them. "Who the fuck is Khan?"

"He's the Japanese man living with Wolf," Steve said. "He told me to stand here and take revenge for Luke."

Luke looked at Hawk lying on the ground, huffed a breath and turned his head to one side.

"And you bought that?" Tommy snickered. "Do you think standing on his back is going to even up what he did to Luke?" His voice changed and turned cold. "He almost killed my brother." He bent forward and spit into Hawk's face.

"Leave him alone Tommy!" Steve yelled.

Tommy Eagle Chaser looked at him. "Are you defending him?"

"You didn't have to do that," Steve said, angrily. "We're all Lakota. If this were the old days, we'd be riding next to each other."

"I wouldn't be riding with him. He's half spic," Tommy muttered, "and he's a fag."

Steve heard the screen door open and Khan stepped out under the porch light. Tommy and Luke took off running up the hillside.

"You afraid of eighty three year old man?" Kahn called out to them. He walked over to the platform and looked at Steve. "They afraid of eighty three year old man."

Steve nodded. "Yes Sir."

"You get down now," Kahn said.

Steve watched as Hawk slowly began to move. He offered a hand to help him up but Kahn gently moved Steve backward.

"You go now," Khan said.

"But I...I wanted to tell him I'm sorry," Steve said. "I mean I..."

"You go now," Khan said. "Come back tomorrow."

Steve nodded and started home. It was dark. Night had arrived. He glanced over his shoulder and saw Khan wrapping the blanket around Hawk's shoulders. He heard a sad moan, followed by deep throaty sobbing. Khan held Hawk close to him

137

and patted his shoulder. Steve's vision blurred as he put his head down, and walked the rest of the way home.

"There now," Khan said. "You all right." He sat beneath the stars and moon, listening to the young man cry. Khan, at his age, knew life and death. He knew many things in between. He knew enough to know he could not make every thing all right again. That was a myth people told. A man lived. A man hurt and healed but it was never all right again. A man died. So simple, Khan thought, but so very complicated. Finally all tears for that day fell out of the young man's eyes. He sat up somberly and drew in a deep breath. "You all right now," Khan said quietly.

"It'll never be all right Khan," Hawk said.

"You learning," Khan told him.

"I killed Antonio."

Khan nodded. "That what make you cry?"

"No," Hawk said, "I don't have any feelings about that. It's what he did that makes me cry. I don't care that I killed him. I just thought I should tell you."

"You not less of a man because Antonio less of a human being," Khan told him.

"That's easy to say," Hawk said. He pulled the blanket closer around his shoulder.

"Khan understands," he said. "Very hard when such things happen. Act of rape used between warring male tribes long ago in all parts of world. Not first warrior this happen to."

"I didn't know that," Hawk said quietly.

Khan nodded. "Wife of Khan raped by enemy of Khan long ago."

Hawk looked at him.

"Long ago, Khan had beautiful wife name Suki. She gave

Khan strong first born son to carry on Khan family name. We very happy. Live in village and have many good days. One day, Khan hear enemy coming to village. Khan hurry to find man, hurry to kill man. Khan was young. Always hurry." The old man looked up at the night sky. "Khan did not know there plenty time. Enemy knew Khan would hurry. Enemy waited and went to house of Khan…kill first born son. Enemy rape and kill wife."

Hawk didn't know what to say. He raised a hand and placed it on Kahn's shoulder. He saw tears glistening in the old man's eyes.

"Khan discover secret too late," he said sadly, "spend eighty three years here. No need to hurry."

Hawk wrapped his arms around the old man's small shoulders. He knew there was nothing he could do to ease Khan's pain so he did as he'd been taught. "There now," he said, with a little smirk. "You all right."

Khan laughed. His shoulders shook. He sat upright and patted Hawk's face. "You fine young man," he said.

"Thanks Khan." He smiled mischievously. "You fine old man."

They laughed.

"Go in house," Khan said. "Cold out here."

Hawk walked beside him. "You smart old man, too," he added. He hadn't liked what Khan had done, at all. When anyone touched his back, it made him want to scream. When Steve stood on his back, he wanted to fight. Bad memories flooded through his mind of being face down on the floor. Fear came and went. Anger subsided. Finally, all Hawk heard was his own heart beat and he realized Steve was not that heavy. He thought about the earth beneath them, how it supportive it was, and he heard a distinct heart beat coming from below the ground. When Suzy touched his face, a soft gentle caress, he welcomed the warmth of her hand. He hadn't liked being spit on but with one life time gone and traveling through this one; he was wise enough to know some people never change. But Steve had changed, Hawk realized, and he went from standing on him and conquering to defending him. He opened and held the door for Khan to go into the house, admiring the man's patience and his wisdom as he walked by.

Wolf came out of the darkness and up onto the porch.

"Where were you?" Hawk asked him.

"I was sitting in the field," Wolf said, quietly.

"Why?" Hawk asked, following him into the house.

"Don't be stupid Hawk," Wolf said. He glanced at his brother and saw that he seemed to be all right. He almost thought he'd have to get up when Luke and Tommy came around but Khan took care of that. When Hawk started crying, Wolf remained hidden. He'd thought of a lot in that field. Seeing Steve stand on Hawk's back reminded Wolf of what he'd done to Hawk when they were kids. He always tried to stay on top of Hawk, to be better than him and now he saw how stupid that was. He thought of how he laughed at Hawk, the first time he saw him in handcuffs and shackles. Wolf knew the prophecy was true and if he'd laughed at his brother, a brother who'd fought at Little Bighorn? What kind of warrior did that make him?

Hawk went over to the couch and sat down. Stands Proud was reading a newspaper but he seemed to be doing that a lot lately. "Hey, any good news?" Hawk asked him. He saw the paper tremble. "I'm all right Papa," he said, seeing the anger in his father's eyes.

Stands Proud folded up the paper. He watched as Khan went into the kitchen, out of hearing distance. He leaned forward and a stern look came to his face. "What did that prove?" he demanded in a hoarse whisper.

"Actually, I learned a lot."

140

"Like what?" Stands Proud asked.

"That carrying the weight of another man es not that hard," Hawk said. "Es not necessary to be on top all the time, eh? In fact, the man under the first is kind of important too. He is the support. If he moves the wrong way, the man on top will fall."

Stands Proud sat back in the chair.

"That's like me and you, huh?" Wolf said, coming over to the couch, "only I never gave you anything to stand on."

Hawk tilted his head to the side and looked up at him.

"You've always been first, even though I was born first," Wolf explained. "Everybody always talked about you because of the prophecy. That's why I did all those mean things to you when we were kids."

"You threw rocks at me because I was part of a prophecy?" Hawk asked him.

"No," Wolf said, "boy, some times you are dumb." He sat down on the other end of the couch. "Everyone notices you. Everyone pays attention to you."

"Es funny," Hawk said. "I thought the man on top was you."

"What?" Wolf asked.

"You stayed here with the people," Hawk said. "You went to school, played ball and you don't mess with drugs or alcohol. The only reason people notice me is because they don't understand me. They think I'm…eh….wierd."

Wolf smiled at him. "You are weird," he said.

Hawk laughed and got up from the couch. "Hey," he said looking down at Wolf, "remember, we *are* identical twins." He looked around the room. "Where's Rafa?" he asked, "speaking of weird."

"He's in your room," Stands Proud said. "He's been back there since this whole thing started. I don't think he was too happy about it."

Hawk sighed. When Rafa went into seclusion it was never good. He lived to annoy other people which made him a very social being. Hawk went past the kitchen, where Khan was making tea, and opened the door to his room. Rafa was lying on the bed listening to some loud music and he was glaring at the ceiling.

"You know? Sometimes, I don't like that old man," Rafa said, sitting upright on the bed. "He had no right to do that to you."

"Es ok Rafa."

"No, es not okay," Rafa said, standing up, shaking and pointing a finger to where Khan might be on the other side of the wall. "That old man had no right to humiliate you like that. Es not okay to do that to somebody!" Angry tears came to his eyes. "You don't stand on someone! You don't treat them like dirt… like they're nobody!"

Hawk walked over to him. "Es all right Rafa."

"No it isn't," Rafa said. He sniffed. "Es not all right."

Hawk sighed heavily and wrapped an arm around Rafa's shoulders. If anyone knew about being treated like dirt people walked on, it was Rafa. "There now," Hawk said. "You're all right."

"Stop hugging me you fag," Rafa said, pushing him away.

Hawk stepped back surprised and then he gave a hearty laugh. "You're going to die for that, eh?" Hawk said, starting after him. Rafa jumped up on the bed, ran across it, and headed for the door. Hawk ran after him down the hall. He went into the kitchen where he found Rafa hiding behind Khan. Hawk sneered at him. "Come out here coward."

"Sit down. Drink tea," Khan said to Hawk.

"*Si migo,*" Rafa taunted him. "*Sientate. Tenga más té.*"

The kitchen door opened and Danny Redboy came in with Jack. About six more men were behind them. They smelled like smoke, tobacco and leather. They stood quietly, watching the Japanese man pour tea.

"Hey," Hawk said, greeting them. "Are you looking for Stands Proud, eh?"

"Yeah," Danny said. He glanced at the little Japanese man. "Are you okay Hawk?" he asked. He'd seen the kid outside, on the ground. He saw Steve a little while ago too, crying his heart out over by the Trading Post.

"I'm okay," Hawk said. "I'm good, eh?" He noticed their curiosity about Khan and realized he was being impolite. "Sorry, I wasn't thinking," he said. "Khan this es Danny, Jack and some of Stands Proud's friends. I'm sorry; I don't know your names. But this es Khan. He es the finest master of martial arts in the world and he es my friend."

"Not finest," Khan said. "One man beat Khan in 1963."

Hawk smiled at him.

Stands Proud came into the kitchen. "Hey," he said.

"The lodge is ready," Danny told him.

Stands Proud nodded. "Okay," he said, taking his jacket from the hook.

"Are you having eh…sweat lodge?" Hawk asked.

"Yeah," Jack said. "Do you want to come?"

"Are you kidding?" Hawk asked. "I've needed a good sweat for the last hundred and forty years, eh?" He took his jacket from the hook. The men stared at him. Someone in the back whispered something. "Unless, eh…you don't want me to go with you?"

"I think it's a good idea," Stands Proud said bravely.

The men nodded.

"You have tea when you return."

"I will," Hawk said. "Thank you Khan. I'm glad you're staying. I'm sorry I was rude to you earlier."

"Khan cannot leave."

Hawk looked at him. "You can't?"

"No," Khan said. "Khan sees boy. Khan's heart is full again." He turned and smiled at Hawk. "You go. Men are trying to leave without Hawk. You tell Khan about Lakota medicine?"

"I will," Hawk promised. He nodded and went out the door, running to catch up with the men.

Chapter Seventeen

After the grueling day of training he had combined with being in the sweat lodge, Hawk fell into an exhausted sleep. Pleasant dreams floated in his mind. *He saw the shining mist and the silver hawk slipping around the pine trees in the Black hills. He rode upon Midnight's back across the open prairie, feeling the wind and sun upon his face.* But good dreams ended and nightmares returned. *The decision was made to ride to Fort Robinson. Tashunka Witko was killed. He was wet and frozen from the snow, sick, hungry and cold.* He began to moan in his sleep and chatter angrily at the soldiers keeping him under control at the Fort. Time spun and weaved through his nightmares *He was alone in the vault at Tassiano's. He was cold and hungry. Comfort is not necessary, Don Antone's said. Mistakes will not be tolerated. You will not lose! Don Antone gave the order for Antonio to whip him and the long leather braided whip slashed across his back. Hawk could smell the disinfectant before it reached him. They poured it over him.*

Hawk screamed.

Stands Proud jolted up right. The screaming echoed between the walls of the house. His eyes widened as he had to orient himself to time and place. The first few times this happened, he'd jumped out of bed, crashed into a few walls, stumbling in the dark and ran to his son's room. Now, he sighed heavily. His heart sank a little lower and he rubbed his eyes. Khan had been working with him for over a week and still, every night, Hawk screamed. Stands Proud stumbled out of the bed in his boxers and lumbered down the hall.

Rafa was coming the other way, from Hawk's room. He'd already been there and was going back. "He'll be ok," Rafa told Stands Proud. "Same as always. You can't do anything when he's like that anyway."

145

"Is he ever going to stop doing that?" Wolf called out irritably from his room.

Khan was standing in the door way of Hawk's room. The young man was sitting upright, with his back to the wall, wide awake but staring straight ahead. Every night Khan came to the room when he screamed. Khan flipped on the light and he would stop screaming but he became frozen and unreachable.

Stands Proud sighed again and looked into the room. "I hate it when he's like this," he said. "I don't know what to do. Is it better to leave him like that or should we try to snap him out of it?"

"Khan find out," he said, starting into the room.

"Okay," Stands Proud said, yawning sleepily. "You go first."

"Hawk," Khan called out. "Hawk. You wake up now."

Stands Proud shook his head. His son remained perfectly still and hadn't acknowledged Khan's presence.

Khan poked at him. The young man did not move. "This very curious," Khan said. He waved a hand in front of Hawk's face and got no response. Khan looked over at Stands Proud. "Turn out light."

"I don't think that's a good idea," Stands Proud said.

"Turn out light," Khan repeated.

The room filled with darkness. Khan heard him move. "Hawk? You all right?"

"Don't...please don't..." Hawk said, *moving away from the shadow in the dark.*

"This Khan," he said. "You not be afraid."

"I'm sorry Antonio," Hawk said. *"Please...let me go... don't do this..."*

146

Stands Proud jaw set tight and he turned his face away from the room.

"No…no…let go of me…I won't do this anymore…" Hawk began to cry. *"…kill me…kill me…"*

"Hawk," Khan said in a louder voice. "This Khan! You hear Khan!"

There was silence. Breathing and more silence.

"Are you done Antonio?" Hawk asked.

Stands Proud's hand went to the light switch with a slam. Light flooded the room. Hawk backed up against the wall, staring. "I can't listen to that," Stands Proud said.

Khan reached down and put his hands on Hawk's shoulders. He shook gently at first, then harder. "He not here," Khan said.

"What?" Stands Proud asked.

"Hawk not here," Khan said, looking across the room at the tall Indian. "You not wake him up from this. He not here."

Stands Proud walked into the room.

"His spirit travel elsewhere," Khan said. "This empty shell."

"Do you think so?" Stands Proud asked.

"Yes," Khan nodded. "Khan have no answer for this. Khan will write friend in Okinawa."

"We know spirits can travel," Stands Proud said.

"His is gone," Khan said.

Stands Proud sighed.

"You turn out light," Khan said, "Hawk return to nightmare. You turn on light. Hawk travel elsewhere." He walked over to a chair in the corner of the room and sat down.

"You turn out light. Khan sees how boy wakes up."

"You're going to sit in here all night?" Stands Proud asked.

"Must see how Hawk wakes up," Khan insisted. "Tell Rafa come here."

Stands Proud nodded and went down the hall. He looked in the living room. Rafa was sound asleep and snoring. Stands Proud walked over. "Hey Rafa, Khan wants to talk to you." He tapped the boy's shoulder. Rafa exploded upright, jumping to his feet and into a fighting stance. Stands Proud stumbled backward, his heart slammed inside of his chest. He clenched his teeth together. "Damn you kids," he said. "Rafa wake up!" Stands Proud yelled.

Rafa lowered his hands to his sides. "What are you yelling at me for?" he asked.

"Khan would like to see you," Stands Proud said, glaring in the dark. He was being very polite because the short little bastard had just scared the hell out of him.

"Khan, Khan, Khan," Rafa mumbled going down the hall. He leaned on the frame of Hawk's door and stuck his head in the room. He heard Hawk moaning again. "What you want, eh?" he asked, seeing Khan's silhouette sitting in the chair. The moonlight shone behind him.

"You come here," Khan said.

"Where? I can't see nothing." Rafa walked into the room and slammed his toe off of something excruciatingly hard. A stream of profanity left his lips. "Man," he said, "if you're thinking of training something, anything, forget me. Ok?"

"No training," Khan said.

"*Dios gracias.*"

"What you say?"

148

"I said," Rafa repeated very plainly, "thank-God!"

"Oh," Khan said. "You see Hawk like this many time?"

"Yeah."

"Always?"

Rafa sat down on the floor and leaned against the wall. He scratched his arm. Since the cast come off, it was very itchy. "No," he said, "not always." He knew he wasn't getting away. Besides, he was the one who used to sit in Hawk's room at Calle de Azul, he reasoned, so what was the difference?

"When screaming start?" Khan asked.

"After they whipped him," Rafa said. "Most times he eh...just moans about Antonio."

"You turn on light?"

"Eh...not a good idea," Rafa said.

"What happen?"

"I thought the light would wake him up, eh? But it doesn't. I don't know what happens to him. One time, I left the light on, the sun light came in the window and he sat like that all day," Rafa said. "Es too creepy for me. I leave it out."

"You wake him up?"

"When he's screaming?" Rafa asked. "Yeah, all the time."

"How you do this?"

"Next time he screams, I'll show you," Rafa said.

Khan nodded. "How he wake up in morning?"

"Pissed off," Rafa said, "but like anybody else. He's always mad though. He doesn't sleep enough." Hawk's moaning grew louder. "Eh, he'll be at it again soon." Rafa leaned over and lit a candle. "Don't turn the light on, ok? I hate that."

"Light from candle okay?"

"Yeah," Rafa said. He watched Hawk toss and turn. Rafa stood up and waited. When Hawk started screaming, he jumped on top of him. Hawk stood straight up. They fought and crashed into a wall.

Khan stood up and moved back.

Rafa grabbed Hawk and slammed him against the wall. "Shut the fuck up!" he yelled in his face. "Your screaming es making me crazy! SHUT UP!" Hawk threw one punch after another. In the small space he attempted to kick. A lamp crashed to the floor and they fought across the room. "You fucking bastard!" Rafa yelled. "SHUT UP!"

Stands Proud and Wolf heard things crashing, breaking and shattering. They ran down the hall as Rafa's angry voice roared inside of Hawk's room.

Rafa had his hands around Hawk's throat. "SHUT THE HELL UP!" he yelled.

Hawk's eyes widened, his nostrils flared and he glared at Rafa. "Get off of me," he said in a slow evil tone.

"He's awake," Rafa said, letting go of Hawk. He turned to walk away.

Hawk grabbed him and threw him to the floor. "You..." he said. "I told you not to do that."

"Eh well," Rafa muttered. He sat up on the floor. "I think everyone's heard enough of that screaming shit, eh?"

Hawk looked at Khan standing in the corner and saw Wolf and Stands Proud in the door way. He grabbed his jeans and stormed out of the room.

"Hawk!" Stands Proud yelled, going down the hall. He expected to hear the door slam. Instead, he found his son in the kitchen making coffee. He looked at the clock. It was three in the morning.

Hawk glared at Rafa and slammed the coffee can on the table. "You never listen to me," he said angrily.

"I can only take so much, eh?" Rafa replied.

"You know what happens and you do it anyway!" Hawk yelled. He winced from the pain inside his head. "Ah you bastard," he whispered.

"I wish I was," Rafa sneered back, "it would be better than a crack head father, eh?"

"What's the matter Hawk?" Stands Proud asked him. His son was holding a hand to his head and fixing the coffee maker with his other hand.

"Every time he does that I get a pain in my head like some one es stabbing through my skull."

"Eh…es from screaming so much," Rafa muttered.

Hawk turned and glared at him. "I hate you," he said slowly.

"Es that right?" Rafa said, looking up at him. "If it wasn't for me staying in your room at Calle De Azul, your crazy ass would be splattered on the street, eh?"

"What you mean?" Khan asked.

Hawk looked over and scowled. He hadn't even noticed Khan was there. "Nothing," he said quietly. "Es nothing."

"He walks around sometimes," Rafa said. "Lots of nights he almost fell off the building, out windows, off the roof…I don't know how you did it in your apartment."

"Es not your business," Hawk replied. Holding his head, he sat down in the chair.

"How you not fall out window?" Khan asked, walking over to the table.

"I locked the window," Hawk said sneering at Rafa.

"Even in summer?"

"Yes," Hawk said.

Khan sat down beside him. He placed his elbows on the table. "Put head in Khan's hands. Khan fix for you."

"Thanks Khan," Hawk said quietly. He closed his eyes and lowered his head. It was the only touch he never minded the entire time he spent at Tassiano Estates. Khan's hands held medicine. The warmth seeped into his head and the pain faded until it was gone. Slowly, he sat up and opened his eyes.

"Better?" Khan asked.

"Yes," Hawk said. "Thank you."

"How did you do that, eh?" Rafa asked, watching him.

Khan ignored Rafa. He looked at Hawk. "What make you scream?"

"I have nightmares about the men pouring that disinfectant on my back," Hawk said, "after they whipped me. It burns like hell. Anything that burns does it." he said. "That's what makes me scream."

"Antonio?"

Hawk scowled. "No," he said. "I never screamed. I didn't fight. I was afraid of the dark." He got up and poured a cup of coffee.

"Khan try to wake you up. Hawk not hear Khan."

Hawk shook his head. "I hear Don Antone's voice and Antonio's. That's all I hear." He picked up the cup and returned to the chair.

"Khan turn light on. What happen?"

"Gone," Hawk muttered fiercely.

"Gone where?"

"Anywhere," Hawk said, staring at the coffee.

"You know you leave body?" Khan asked him.

"Yes."

"Why you leave when light come on?"

"Because," Hawk said, "as long as the lights are out, you can't see anything. When the lights come on…you see everything."

"You can choose to stay?" Khan asked him.

"Why would I?"

"You in safe place. No one here to hurt Hawk," Khan said.

"I…I don't know that," Hawk said, quietly.

"What do you mean you don't know that?" Stands Proud asked, leaning on the table.

Hawk gave a frustrated sigh. "The dreams are very real to me, eh? Es like everything is happening the way I see it in the dream. I think Don Antone or Antonio are here."

Stands Proud sighed and stood upright. "They're dead," he stated.

"In my head they are alive," Hawk said fiercely, glaring at his father.

The kitchen grew quiet and Stands Proud threw his hands up in the air, turned and reached for a cup. He was at a complete loss. There wasn't anything he could do and he hated being in that position. Silently, he poured a cup of coffee.

"If you not fight in dark," Khan said, "why you fight Rafa?"

"It wasn't dark," Hawk muttered. He glared at Rafa. "He lights candles. For some reason, it works."

"I told you," Rafa said, "I can only take so much screaming, eh?"

"Candle light keep spirits close by," Khan informed them.

"Ah…" Hawk said, seething, "so he keeps my spirit here and then he attacks me. Rafael Gonzalez you are very mean, eh?"

"I think I hurt my arm doing that," Rafa told him. He rubbed his arm. "It hurts a little."

Hawk scowled at him.

"Maybe in time," Khan said, "nightmares leave you."

"No," Hawk said, "I have bad dreams about going to the Fort and about seeing the people slaughtered also."

"Khan very sorry," he said sadly. "Khan cannot fix."

"Es all right," Hawk said. "Es all right. Es something I live with."

"Unless he shoots heroin," Rafa added to the conversation, "then he doesn't scream."

"That," Stands Proud stated coldly, "is not an option!"

"Did I say it was?" Hawk asked angrily. His gaze fixed on Rafa. "You can shut up now, eh?"

"He's only trying to help," Stands Proud offered. "We don't know what to do with you."

"You don't?" Hawk asked, standing up. "Eh well, that *can be fixed.*" He started for the kitchen door.

"Don't you walk out that door," Stands Proud growled sternly.

Hawk opened the door.

Stands Proud bolted, throwing his body against the door and slammed it shut. He stood in front of it, enraged. His chest heaved and he glared at his son.

"It's three thirty in the morning," Wolf moaned. He plopped his body into the chair, folded his arms on the table and put his head down.

"Every time you run off," Stands Proud said, glaring at Hawk, "everyone worries about you."

"What am I supposed to do?" Hawk demanded of him. He glanced at Wolf and Rafa. They were exhausted. Even Khan seemed tired. "Do you think I like having the nightmares? Do you think I enjoy this?"

"I didn't say that," Stands Proud told him. Hawk's hair was tousled, his shoulders caved forward slightly and his entire body seemed limp. He shuffled when he walked. "I know you're tired of it," Stands Proud said softly.

An easier quiet grew between them.

"You slept so well when you were small," Stands Proud said softly.

"I hardly slept at all," Hawk confessed. "At night, when you and Mama were sleeping, I would go out the window and go over to Uncle Pete's to watch the horses run in the field. Watching the horses made me feel better." He turned and shuffled across the room, away from Stands Proud. He stood in the door way, which led to the hall. He didn't want to fight with Stands Proud. "I had nightmares then too," he admitted, "but I didn't scream."

"You were always in your bed in the morning," Stands Proud said, watching him.

"I came back, " Hawk told him.

"He didn't start screaming until…" Rafa began. He saw the fire flash in Hawk's dark eyes. He faltered. "He eh…used to sleep ok. Not a lot but okay."

"There es nothing I can do about it," Hawk said coldly. "I'm sorry for waking everyone up." He turned and walked down the hall. Stands Proud followed him. "You can go back to sleep. I'll stay awake, eh?"

"That's not good either," Stands Proud said.

Hawk went into his room and sat on the bed. He watched as his father came into his room and went over to the window. Hawk sighed heavily and turned his face away.

Stands Proud saw that Hawk had nailed the window shut. A deep ragged sigh left him. "When did you do this?" he asked.

"When I got here," Hawk said. "The people think I'm weird enough as it is, eh? I didn't want to be seen walking around the rez at three in the morning." He paused. "I was going to put a lock on the door too but then you wouldn't be able to get in."

"You can't...confine yourself," Stands Proud said uneasily.

Hawk looked up at him. "Isn't that what you do with a freak?"

"No," Stands Proud said, folding his arms over his chest, "usually they're given away to a circus. I could get a good deal if I send Rafa with you, two for one."

Hawk smirked.

"Try to get some rest," Stands Proud said. He left the room and closed the door.

Hawk sighed and leaned back against the head board. He picked up the book about Crazy Horse and began to read it. Some one had left it on the front porch. He saw the black and white photo and rolled his eyes. They were claiming it was Tashunka Witko. Hawk knew it wasn't. Tashunka Witko never allowed his photograph to be taken. It was believed if someone took your image, they could steal your soul. Hawk sighed and started to read. He sat upright, staring hard at the words. The story was wrong. There was no truth to what he saw written in the book. It angered him. After everything they'd gone through, history was recorded but it wasn't right. He sat and stared straight ahead, looking at the wall but seeing a vast open prairie, an endless place where he used to ride.

Chapter Eighteen

A few hours later, Stands Proud left for work. Rafa and Wolf began to discuss basketball. As soon as it was light they headed off to the court. Hawk watched them leave as he stood on the plywood platform, training with Khan. Khan had him go through all sixteen drills. It was late morning when Hawk noticed Steve sitting on the hillside watching him. Khan tossed a staff to him and he nearly missed it.

"Focus," Khan reprimanded.

Hawk nodded. He began to spin the staff easily, waiting for Khan to toss him another one. Khan armed himself with a staff and came forward, in a vicious attack. Hawk deflected the blows, one after another. No matter how Khan swung, Hawk moved the staffs smoothly with an acquired proficiency, blocking the multiple strikes that came at him.

Khan observed the young man's bare feet. Hawk stood firm and had not moved one inch in any direction. Khan stopped swinging the staff and tucked it under his arm. "Hawk bored with training?"

"Ay no Khan," Hawk said, quickly. He learned long ago to never tell Khan he was bored but the old man was smart. He worried a little as Khan walked around him, thinking. "I'm not bored at all, eh?" he said. "This es very exciting. I like it."

"Good," Khan said. He turned and looked at the roof of the Argent house. "You go up there."

Hawk looked at the roof. It wasn't flat like the roof tops on the city buildings. Both sides of the roof came down at an angle. He grinned. "The house es old Khan," he said, trying to get out of the task, "What if the roof doesn't hold me?"

"Find out," Khan said.

Hawk sighed with a smile. "Ok," he said, yielding to the old man's wishes, "but if I fall through Stands Proud will wonder why rain's falling on his head."

Khan smiled. "Rain cool down hot temper," he said.

Hawk laughed. He walked over to the house and climbed up onto the railing of the porch. He went up the post and swung a leg onto the porch roof.

"Take staff," Khan said.

Hawk turned and caught the staff. He walked on the porch roof, studying the roof of the house. There was no place to stand up there. The very top was a sharp angle. "Here?" Hawk asked, standing on the porch roof.

Khan shook his head back and forth. He pointed to the top of the roof. "You not have far to fall," he said.

"Great," Hawk muttered. "You got mad at me once for almost falling off a roof," he reminded Khan.

"This building not twenty five stories high."

Hawk muttered under his breath and tucked the staff under his arm. At an angle, he scaled the roof to the top where it made a point. "There es no place to walk, eh?"

"Man walk on rope," Khan said. "Hawk walk on father's roof. Try not make hole."

"Yeah…" Hawk said slowly as he stood upright. He placed his feet, one in front of the other, and balanced himself with the staff.

"Drill number fourteen," Khan said.

Hawk laughed. He slipped and nearly fell. "Fourteen, eh?"

"Number fourteen. Khan waiting," he said. "Focus."

"Can you drive a car?" Hawk asked.

"Why?"

"I'll need a ride to the hospital when I break my leg," Hawk told him, smiling.

"Focus!" Khan said. "This not play. No more talk."

On the hillside, Steve Battise stood up. He glanced over at the guys on the basketball court. "Hey! Come here! Look at this," he said.

Wolf, Rafa and a group of boys walked over to where Steve was standing. They looked at the Argent house and saw Hawk on the roof. His long hair was tied back in a tight pony tail. He was standing on the roof top, wearing his fighting pants and holding a long stick. Behind him, the mist swirled around the Black hills.

"He's going to break his neck," Wolf said, slowly.

"The old man es crazy, loco," Rafa said. "That es not a roof to walk on." He scowled. "Es all we need…if he falls he'll be screaming in the day time too."

"That's not funny Rafa," Wolf said.

"Es not a flat roof," Rafa said, with a shrug. "Everybody knows you don't stand on a roof like that, eh?"

Hawk walked the length of the roof and back like a tightrope walker trying to find balance. There wasn't much, he realized. He sighed.

"Make staff sing," Khan told him.

Hawk knew Khan wanted him to spin the staff but instead he turned it on end and began to sing into it like a microphone.

"You play. You fall," Khan reprimanded.

Hawk forced the grin from his face. He crouched down slightly, held his breath and took the staff in both hands, horizontally in front of him. "Number fourteen," he said quietly. He began to spin the staff in front of him. He focused all of his attention on the staff. There was a breeze, he noticed, coming from the west. Hawk swung the staff to his side, spun it and jumped, extending his leg outward. He wavered and fell to the roof. Hawk hung onto the roof top with his fingers and tried to keep the staff from rolling away.

"Again," Khan said from below.

Hawk sneered and whispered. "Again, eh? Easy. No problem." He crawled on his belly to the roof and reached the top. He sighed heavily and got back up.

"Number fourteen," Khan said.

"It can't be done," Hawk said, looking down at the old man. Khan disappeared for a moment. When Khan's head popped up above the porch roof, Hawk's lips parted. He stared as Khan climbed up onto the roof.

"Old man show you."

Hawk stared him. Khan easily scaled the roof and stood at the top, balanced. Khan spun the staff and it sang through the air. The old man swung the staff to his side, leapt into a front kick, crouched down, spun the staff around him and advanced forward until he reached where Hawk was sitting. Hawk looked up at him, speechless.

"Hawk have question?"

"You are amazing," Hawk breathed out, watching him descend the roof top.

"Not amazing," Khan said, going down to the roof of the porch. "Many roof top like this in Japan. Hawk thinks too much," he said. "You named for bird. You fall maybe you fly."

Hawk smiled at the old man as Khan disappeared from the roof.

"Number fourteen," Khan said, "eighteen year old man."

"I'm a hundred and fifty six," Hawk replied smartly. He

smiled. Khan had no answer for that. Satisfied, he rose upward to his feet and closed his eyes. He felt the breeze on his face. He focused and began to spin the staff, opening his eyes. He stared straight ahead and swung the staff to his side. Hawk leapt into the front kick, turned, spinning the staff and it began to sing.

Rafa held his breath and winced as Hawk spun his body in mid-air, spinning the staff beside him, and landed on his feet. "Holy shit!" Rafa exclaimed. "Es number fourteen!"

"What's number fourteen?" Wolf asked, smiling and watching his brother.

"A staff drill," Rafa told him. "Es the hardest one."

"He has a black belt, doesn't he?" Steve asked them.

"He has more than that, eh?" Rafa told him.

"What level?"

Rafa looked at Steve. "He's a master."

"Whoa look," Wolf said. He smiled when he saw the hawk in the air, circling the house. "It's a hawk! A silver hawk!" The beautiful bird's wings seemed to flash in the sunlight.

Hawk felt the wings slap into his shoulder and he stumbled. His entire body wavered when he realized what had happened. He watched as the hawk flew back up into the air and turned. The hawk screamed with its wings spread out wide and swooped straight at him. Hawk's eyes widened and he ducked to one side. The huge bird slapped a wing at his shoulder and he dropped the staff. It fell to the roof top and rolled, falling over the edge. He stared, hard, as the bird circled again and came at him. "What do you want?" he screamed at the bird. He held his breath. The bird was coming back. He crouched down on the roof top. The hawk slammed into him again. He lost his balance and fell flat to the roof. He clawed into the shingles, holding on, and tried to upright himself.

The hawk screamed above him. It flew down from the air

and landed on the chimney.

Breathing heavily, Hawk stared at the bird and got to his feet. Slowly, he rose upward. "What do you want from me?" he asked the bird.

The hawk screamed, opened its wings and flapped them, but it remained on the chimney.

"What do you want?" Hawk asked again. The bird opened its wings and flew at him, talons out. Hawk raised his arms to protect his face and he fell backward. His body slammed onto the roof and he slid, outstretching his hands, trying to stop the fall. He screamed as he fell over the side. He hit the ground with a thud and angrily, he scrambled to upright himself.

"You not fly." Khan said.

Hawk glanced up at him but returned his gaze to the bird. It was flying low and coming back. "Shit!" he yelled. "GO AWAY!" he screamed at it. It swooped past him.

"Maybe you in his territory," Khan said, smirking.

"Ah no Khan," Hawk said, glaring at the bird. "That… that thing… and I go way back," he said, backing up. The bird started to dive again and Hawk scrambled backward. The bird came at him, screaming and flapping its wings. "Leave me alone!" he screamed back. The hawk drove him to retreat until his back slammed against his Uncle Pete's fence. Hawk hung onto the fence and glared as the huge bird came at him once again. He felt the talons rip his flesh of his chest and blood dribbled to his stomach. "You…" he said in a low wicked tone, glaring at the hawk as it flew away. Hawk furiously climbed over the fence and jumped on to a horse's back. He yelled and charged, jumping the fence and racing out into the field, chasing after the bird.

Wolf stared, his mouth hung open and he could not speak. He watched as his brother rode hard toward the Black hills, chasing after the silver hawk.

"What the hell was that thing?" Rafa asked.

"A hawk," someone said.

"That wasn't a hawk," Steve said quietly. "That was a spirit."

Rafa looked at them. He wasn't sure what was going on. "No se, no se," he said quickly, "I don't know what it was. I didn't know he could even ride a damn horse. And where the hell es he going? Chasing a bird? I don't know anything but I do know…one thing," he said. "All of you Indian people are weird, eh?" Rafa ran down the hillside and into the house.

Khan stared as the young man disappeared into the pine trees at the foothills of the mountains.

Chapter Nineteen

Hawk scowled and followed the bird. It would fly a small distance and land in the pine trees ahead of him. He wasn't worried about getting lost. He knew exactly where he was. He'd been thinking of coming up into the hills since he arrived home but he hadn't been able to. When he realized where the hawk was taking him, his chest began to tighten. His throat ached. Beyond the trees was the cliff where he'd jumped, taking his life, long ago. "Damn bird," Hawk said roughly. He urged the horse forward.

Hawk rode beyond the trees and stared at the scene in front of him. His heart ached and shattered. "No," he whispered. "Ah no." He got down from the horse. The cliff was gone. Huge pieces of heavy road equipment sat along the hillside. Bulldozers had scraped the earth, reshaping it and moving it. He froze in his tracks and realized, his bones, from long ago, were somewhere beneath these bulldozers. "This can't be right," he whispered, but he knew it was. He'd thought maybe he could come here, to this place, and apologize for taking his own life. He wanted to do it right and in a good way...but now there was nothing to come back to. Tears filled his eyes. The people who had driven him to this place the last time were the same ones who were destroying it now. Now there was nothing, nothing left and he could not come back. It was gone. His soul would be trapped here forever. The tears slid over his face as he stumbled through the mud, staring at the destruction.

Stands Proud knew something was wrong as he approached his house. There were people gathered in the yard, standing and waiting for something. His heart filled with dread as he stopped the truck. He didn't want to get out. He didn't want to know but the eyes of the people had always told the story. All he had to do was look and he knew it had something to do with

165

Hawk. He saw his father on the porch, waiting for him. Stands Proud gripped the door handle and swung the truck door open. Solemnly, he walked toward the house and up the steps. "Where is he?" Stands Proud asked.

"We don't know," Jonathan said gently.

"What happened?"

"Khan had him up on the roof today, practicing," Jonathan explained. "Some people say it was a hawk that circled the house four times. It dove at him and knocked him off the roof. It chased him into the field. He started screaming at it, telling it to leave him alone. He told Khan that he and this 'thing' go way back. The bird clawed his chest with its talons. He got mad, took one of Pete's horses and chased the bird into the hills. The horse came back but he's been gone since just before noon."

Stands Proud trembled. "You said some people say it was a hawk. What are the others saying?"

"Danny Redboy saw it," Jonathan said. "Danny said the bird wasn't real. People are saying it was a spirit." Jonathan sighed. "We were told it was a spirit of a silver hawk that tried to keep him from jumping off that cliff…the last time. I think it came back."

"Is anyone out looking for him?" Stands Proud asked gravely.

"We were up there all afternoon and we came back because it's getting dark," Jonathan said. "If he doesn't show up, we'll go back out in the morning."

Stands Proud nodded and went into the house. Wolf was sitting on the couch, stunned. It was easy to tell he'd seen what happened. His mouth was drawn into a thin line and he was staring straight ahead. "Wolf," Stands Proud called out, "are you all right?"

Wolf turned to look at him. "I…I can't explain it dad."

"Your Grandfather just did," Stands Proud said. His house was full of people who were full of questions and Stands Proud didn't have any answers. He turned and went back outside. There was no where to sit so he lowered down onto the front porch step and waited. The people slowly wandered away as time passed. He could feel Wolf or Khan coming to the screen door every now and then, but they would turn around and stay inside the house. It was chilly, early morning, just before the sun rose up into the sky. There was a light mist of fog and the grass was wet with dew.

Stands Proud realized, he was sitting on that same step Hawk had sat on when he was a boy. Hawk sat here thirteen years ago and waited for Stands Proud to come back home but Stands Proud was on the Interstate, headed for anywhere, trying to out run two State police cruisers. Stands Proud's vision blurred as he did his time on the step. How long had the boy waited for him? Had Hawk understood that he wasn't able to come home? He heard the screen door open and he wiped his face with the sleeve of his shirt.

Khan handed him the cup of tea and sat down beside him.

"What was he doing on the roof?" Stands Proud asked, in a muffled voice.

"Drill number fourteen."

"What's that?"

Khan smiled. "Very difficult. Only best can do it. Hawk not believe he best quality." Khan nodded. "He best quality."

Stands Proud nodded. He shuddered and sighed. "Did you see the bird?" he asked.

"Not bird," Khan said. "Old spirit. Old spirit take Hawk away into those hills."

They sat for a while in silence. Finally, Stands Proud began to speak in a throaty voice. "This is what I was afraid of," he said. "This is why I killed Jake Many Horses. I told people I didn't believe the old man. I said he was some kind of nut. I didn't want it to be true, not for my own son. I wanted Hawk to be like Wolf, a regular kid, but all along I knew he wasn't."

"How did you know?" Khan asked him.

Stands Proud huffed a breath. "I could see it. Everyone did and that was the problem. I thought if I killed Jake, it would all stop…because of some kind of bad taboo or something, but it kept going. Now look at him," Stands Proud said. "All he does is suffer."

"You see suffering," Khan said, "but there is more. He kind to all people. He smiles and they like him. Hawk tries very hard find the good in life."

"I know Khan," Stands Proud said, desperately, "but will he ever find it? Or is his entire life going to be this huge battle to find happiness?"

"You happy today?"

Stands Proud sighed. "No," he said softly.

"No guarantee for happiness each day," Khan said. "It happen today, maybe not tomorrow. Hawk battles for some thing but not for happiness. He battles to make peace in his heart."

Stands Proud saw Suzy-Takes-The-Bear coming through the morning fog. Her long hair was down and it wisped against her face as she walked. She was clutching a book to her chest and walking toward the house.

"I came for my book," Suzy said.

"Your book?" Stands Proud asked.

"I left it on the porch for Hawk."

"Oh," Stands Proud said, remembering. "The one about Crazy Horse." He paused and sighed again. "He's not here Suzy."

"Crazy Horse?" she asked with a little smile. "I hope not. You have enough trouble Stands Proud."

Khan and Stands Proud laughed a little.

"I know Hawk is gone. Can I have the book?" she asked.

"Sure," Stands Proud said. "I'll get it. I saw it in his room." Stands Proud slowly arose to his full height. He felt an ache in his back. He opened the screen door and it slammed behind him.

"Okinawa is beautiful," Suzy said to Khan.

"You go there?" Khan asked.

"No," Suzy said softly. "I've seen it in a book."

"Okinawa very beautiful," Khan agreed, "but must some day see with own beautiful eyes."

Suzy smiled at him and shyly looked downward.

Stands Proud's chest ached as he walked out onto the porch with the book in his hand. He didn't want to tell her it was ruined, but he had no choice. Hawk had taken a black felt pen to it and crossed out whole paragraphs. He'd written the word 'Lie!' in several places and had slashed the pen across the photograph. On the inside of the cover, he'd written, 'Maybe if someone hadn't been a coward…this story would have been told correctly,' and he signed his name.

"What's wrong Stands Proud?" Suzy asked, seeing pain on the man's face.

"I'm sorry Suzy," Stands Proud said, handing it to her. "He ruined it."

Suzy took the book into her hands and flipped through the pages. "It's not ruined," she said, studying it.

"He wrote all through it with a pen," Stands Proud said.

"Listen," Suzy said, in a sweet melodic voice, "My name

is Silver Hawk. I tell you these words are wrong. We were not stoic braves, painted up and riding fiercely on wild ponies. Tashunka Witko was tired and so was I. We hadn't eaten meat for days. We were far from stoic and tried to make jokes about stupid things to keep ourselves sane. We wore no paint. We had no time to prepare it, no time to put it on and we had a long way to ride." Suzy lowered the book. "Hawk wrote that in the margin. He fixed the book Stands Proud." She handed it back to him. "Maybe you should keep it a little longer and read it but save it for me. I'm going to type everything he wrote and tell the story the right way."

Stands Proud accepted the book from her. "Thank you," he said.

She stood there for awhile. She raised her gaze to meet Stands Proud's. "I have to tell you something."

Stands Proud went to the step and sat down, watching her. "What's that Suzy?" he asked gently.

"My sister lived with a monster," Suzy said. "The monster used to beat her and he raped her. She never left her house. She was embarrassed to go outside. I saw her the other day and she was smiling," Suzy said. "I asked her what she had to smile about. She told me the monster beat her so badly she decided to kill him. She pulled a knife out of the kitchen drawer and ran it through his heart but that wasn't why she was smiling. She said for some reason it made her very, very sad to kill the beast. After the way he beat her, she was surprised she had the strength. It took all of her strength to walk to the clinic the next morning. The people stared at her. She was bruised, bloody and beaten again. They'd seen her like that a million times so she went over to the window to watch the birds flying in the sky. That's when she said she met a warrior." Suzy paused. "I wondered if she was crazy from being hit in the head so many times. She told me a tall handsome warrior came over to her. He stood beside her. She could feel strength coming from him. He

170

had taken a bandana and wet it under the fountain. He offered it to her to wipe her face. She was so grateful she cried and he held her close to him. The Tribal Police came in and grabbed him, seeing him with her; they thought he'd killed the monster. She told them she was the one who had done it, not him." Suzy reached into her pocket and took out the crumpled piece of cloth. She put it in Stands Proud's calloused hand. "But he did kill the monster that was living inside my sister. She hated herself. She doesn't anymore."

Stands Proud watched as Suzy walked away. He opened his hand and looked at the red and black bandana. The Spanish words written across it read, Los Caballeros. His eyes overflowed with tears and they ran down his face. He stared hard at the mist on reservation road, waiting for the warrior to come home.

Chapter Twenty

The next morning before sunrise, Khan took his walking stick and set off for the hills. He knew something was wrong but he did not wish to alarm the boy's father. Hawk ran off many times during and after training but he always came back to Khan. This time, Hawk did not come back. Khan knew the old spirit; the hawk that harassed and chased the boy was a guide. The guide had taken him for a reason and that was all right but Khan wanted him back.

Khan enjoyed the walk into the Black Hills. He knew the other men had come looking for the boy but Khan had a slight advantage over them. Khan was gifted with extraordinary sight and he saw many things most people did not see. Khan also appealed to the hawk spirit, appeasing it, offering it bits of food and asked to be taken to the boy. Khan heard the distant screeching near the east side of the hills and so, he traveled there. The branches of a great pine rustled. He looked above him and saw the silver hawk.

"Ah, there you are old boy," Khan said gently. He dropped the offering. "You take me to young man."

The hawk screamed and swooped down, stealing the offering and flew a little farther.

Khan followed. At first, he saw nothing. It would have been easy to miss but Khan stayed in the spot a little longer, knowing there was more to see. He saw the ancient cabin, built into the hillside. It was covered with leaves and pine branches. The branches had turned brown; the cabin was the same color of the hillside. In front of the cabin, sitting on a wooden bench, was the young man. Hawk's head was bent forward, his long hair cascading down the sides of his face. His shoulders were at a slouch. He stared at his dusty bare feet. Khan quietly walked closer and saw a bottle in the boy's hand. "Good morning," he called out. "Beautiful day!"

Hawk lifted his head and stared in disbelief. How had the old man found the place? It hadn't had a single visitor for nearly two hundred years.

"Good morning," Khan said again, walking over to him. "You ready for training?"

Hawk scowled and raised the bottle to his lips.

"You not ready," Khan said. He sat down beside him. "Khan will wait."

Hawk sighed and rolled his eyes. He turned his face away from the old man. What was the point, he wondered. It didn't matter what he did, he would never find peace. He knew he was doomed to walk the earth in torment.

"You not train today?" Khan asked.

"I don't feel like it," Hawk said, glancing at him.

"Ok," Khan agreed. He looked at the bottle. "You share?"

Hawk gave him a strange look and handed the bottle to the old man. He'd never seen Khan drink any alcohol. "Be careful," he warned, "it's very old, eh?"

Khan took a sip and coughed. "Whooooo!" he said. "Khan like old dragon now. Breathe fire."

Hawk smiled a little. Khan gave it back and didn't say anything when he took another drink.

"This very old house," Khan said, looking at the cabin.

"It was mine," Hawk told him, "a long, long time ago. I came up here to hide like a coward when everyone else was put on the reservation. I spent thirteen winters here."

"Mmmm," Khan said. "Long time but maybe you not

coward. You escape enemy." He reached over and took the bottle from the boy's hand. "Khan taste whiskey like this long time ago." He took another drink.

"Eh…I escaped," Hawk said, "but only by abandoning my own people."

"This house keep you here?" Khan asked.

"No," Hawk said, lowering his gaze to the ground. "Come with me," he said quietly. "I'll show you."

Together they stumbled and drank their way to where the cliff had been. Hawk showed Khan the bulldozers and explained the way it had been before.

"My old bones are under there," Hawk said, pointing beneath a huge earth moving machine.

"Ooooo," Khan winced. "That not good."

"Tell me about it, eh?" Hawk lifted the bottle and turned starting back into the forest of pines. "My bones are either crushed or broken or they're in a museum some damn place."

"Not good," Khan said, walking beside him. "Not good."

"No," Hawk said, "es not good at all. There es nothing I can do…es destroyed. I can't go back and apologize for taking my own life; I can't fix what I've done. I'm doomed to wander the earth forever."

"Forever long time," Khan said.

They walked to the cabin and Hawk took him inside. He drank the rest of the whiskey and found another bottle while the old man looked around.

"Who this picture?" Khan asked, squinting at the WANTED poster.

"That's me," Hawk said, grinning. "I escaped by telling them I was Jose Argento and told them I was a Mexican. I never lied before but I learned do it."

174

"You wanted dead or alive?"

"I was," Hawk told him, "for shooting every white man I saw. That's when I decided to come up here."

"Nice guns," Khan said, "Khan see in old cowboy movie."

Hawk walked across the room and handed Khan the whiskey. "Pearl handled Colt revolvers," he said. "They worked very well."

"Hmmm, guess so," Khan said, tapping the poster. He surveyed the room. "You have many things here. What this?" he asked, picking up the stick with long pieces of hair attached to it.

"Scalps," Hawk said, smirking.

Khan quickly and politely put it back. He walked around the cabin, slowly. "You happy here?"

"I was," Hawk said, "for a while. No one found me. After three or four winters, I relaxed and lived the old way. I hunted game, fished…swam in the river below…" He paused. "It was the last time I had peace."

"What happen you not stay?" Khan asked.

"The people sent someone to find me," Hawk explained. He sat down on the hearth of the stone fireplace. "Ghost dancing started. The people believed everything would turn around. The game would come back, the old ones would return…" He sighed heavily, "But instead, I ended up at Wounded Knee. Shortly after that, eh well. Es when I jumped."

Khan listened to his story and walked along, looking at the bits and pieces of the boy's first life time. There were raw hide beaded shirts, beautifully bead pouches and many weapons. He walked over to the fireplace and stared hard, at an old tintype photograph which had been placed on the mantle.

"That's Sally," Hawk said, grinning. He drank more whiskey. "She was a saloon girl at the Broken Arrow. She was

175

very, very pretty."

"You look," Khan said gravely.

"I know, I've seen it," Hawk said, smiling. "I liked her a lot, eh?"

"You look," Khan said, more fiercely.

Hawk narrowed his brows. Khan seemed angry. Slowly, Hawk arose to his feet. "I knew a few saloon girls Khan; the other ones didn't want anything to do with an Indian."

"Look at picture."

Hawk looked at the picture and saw Sally wearing the low cut satin dress. It was a jade green with intricate lace. She had gorgeous red hair and green eyes, the same color of the dress. In the photo, everything was brown and white but he remembered the colors. He remembered a lot of other things too, he thought and he smiled. In the photo, he stood beside Sally, dressed in his warrior shirt, leggings and moccasins. "I made the photographer come to the room," he said, "and made him promise not to tell anyone I was Indian, eh? I threatened to kill him if he said a word." He paused. "She wanted something to remember me by."

"Look at picture," Khan insisted.

"I am," Hawk told him, thinking Khan had too much to drink. "She's beautiful."

"Name of photographer," Khan said, pointing to the bottom of the picture.

Hawk moved closer and read the words, 'Tassiano Artistic Photographs.' "Ah no…" he moaned, stepping back.

"What you do?" Khan asked him.

"Ah no…" Hawk said, moving away from it. He glanced at the photo again. It was there, one hundred and fifty six years later, for anyone to see.

"Ah yes," Khan stated. "What you do to photographer?"

"I eh..." Hawk stammered, "I threatened his life. He was a squirrel of a man, no? Tassiano..." he said. "Ah shit."

"What else you do?"

Hawk sank back down to the stone hearth. "This es much worse than you think Khan," he said. "That's the answer."

"What answer?" Khan asked.

"My people believe when someone takes your photo, they take your image," Hawk said in a hoarse whisper, "and they steal your soul."

"What you do?" Khan reprimanded him.

"I eh...damned him to hell," Hawk admitted, "and eh..."

"And ehhhhhh?" Khan said impatiently.

"I told him to take my soul with him," Hawk said gravely. He leaned back against the stone fireplace and stared, straight ahead.

"You do this?"

"Yes."

"Why you do this?" Khan demanded. "You not smart man in first life?"

"I was showing off," Hawk said, with agony. "Sally was there and the photographer was this little skinny white man...I was full of hatred...I..."

"You big fool," Khan huffed.

"Very big fool," Hawk agreed quietly, "and now Tassiano es dead."

"Guess where he is," Khan retorted.

"Ah no," Hawk said drunkenly. He lowered his face into one hand.

Khan took the whiskey bottle and drank a healthy gulp of

it. His eyes were glassy. "You do this," he said. "You do this."

"I know, I know," Hawk moaned.

"You not need to stand on cliff, apologize. You stand here, say sorry. Not good bones lost. Body fall, spirit rise. That you fix," Khan said, drunkenly. "This…" he said, pointing to the picture, "This very bad." He took another drink and moved closer to the photo, looking at the woman. "She very beautiful," he said.

"Yes," Hawk agreed, in agony, "she was."

"She…." Khan's voice slurred, "dance like in cowboy movie? Lift skirt show legs?"

Hawk looked up at him and smiled. "Yeah," he said. Khan was wavering on his feet, gazing at Sally.

Khan snickered and laughed. "You lucky short time," he said.

Hawk laughed.

"We better take with us," Khan said. He picked up the photo and put it in his pocket.

"Take it where?" Hawk asked, the smile sliding from his face.

"Back to reservation."

"I don't want to go there." Hawk stood up and stumbled.

"This not first life," Khan said, hobbling to the door of the cabin. "Hawk come with Khan. Father worried."

"Ehhh…" Hawk said, lifting the bottle.

"Father miss many days work," Khan said. "He look for you. Parole Officer calling. Stands Proud lose job he have much trouble."

Hawk sighed. "I don't want him to get fired," he said.

They staggered from the cabin, taking another bottle of

whiskey along, and wandered down the hillside.

Stands Proud was sitting on the porch when he heard the singing coming from behind the house. When his son and Khan stumbled into view, Stands Proud smirked. Except for their highly intoxicated state, they were okay. Hawk's arm was draped over Khan's shoulder and they were singing, in Japanese and at the top of their lungs while Hawk waved a bottle. Stands Proud, amused, tilted his head to one side as they staggered onto the platform.

"What the…" Rafa uttered coming out onto the porch.

Wolf arrived shortly after him, laughing.

"Turn," Khan told Hawk.

"Eh no…" Hawk said, smiling at the old man. "Not while I'm drunk."

"Why?" Khan asked.

"You know why," Hawk said. He lifted the bottle and drank from it.

"Bah…old man kick your ass," Khan informed him. "Turn!"

Hawk stumbled and turned.

"Oh shit," Wolf said, grinning. He sat down beside his dad on the step. "I can't believe their doing this."

"I can't believe they're standing up," Stands Proud said.

Hawk stood waiting and smiling. When Khan shoved into his back, he opened his arms as wide as he could. He turned and bear hugged the old man. "Ahhhhh," he said. "How was that?"

"Better," Khan said. He looked up at Hawk. "You have three things to learn."

"I know everything," Hawk bragged, smiling at him.

"Ah, you not know," Khan said, waving a finger at him.

179

"Three things and you only one in whole world with ancient Khan family wisdom."

Hawk stared at him, wavering. "Huh?"

"Only one in whole world."

"Why?" Hawk asked. He gave Khan the bottle of whiskey.

Khan took a drink. "You best quality."

Hawk laughed.

"You best quality," Khan repeated. He nodded. "Maybe some day I hear boy say this?" he asked, looking up at him.

Hawk smiled at the old man. "I'm best quality." He saw Suzy Takes-The-Bear walking across the field. He jogged over to her. He stepped in front of her, smiling. "*Hola chica bonita*," he said. "I'm best quality."

Suzy's cheeks flushed and she lowered her gaze.

Hawk laughed. "You said I never speak to you. I'm speaking to you."

"Hi," she said, quietly. She smiled and looked at the ground.

"You're very pretty," Hawk told her. He grinned when she backed up a little. "Ah don't let me scare you," he said. "I'm harmless today. I wanted to tell you something, eh?"

"What?" she whispered, looking up at him.

Hawk looked into her eyes and couldn't think. He'd never looked into her eyes before and now that he had, he found they were the most beautiful eyes he'd ever seen.

"So what did you want to tell me?" she asked, bravely. She gave a satisfied smile.

"Eyes like yours should never cry for someone like me," Hawk said with amazement, lifting a gentle hand to touch her cheek. "They should never cry at all."

Suzy smiled and took a few steps backward, and then she ran off into the field. Hawk smiled and watched her go. He went back toward the house where Khan, Wolf and Rafa had been watching him. "She says I'm best quality," he told them.

They laughed at him.

"Are you okay?" Stands Proud asked him, smiling. "Those scratches look a little deep."

Hawk looked down at his chest where the bird's talons had cut him. "This?" he asked, stumbling toward his father.

"Yeah."

"This es nothing," Hawk said. He saw Khan coming and tried to help him to the porch.

"Well, I'm glad you're all right," Stands Proud said.

Hawk laughed, hard. "*No, no esta bien,* eh? I am so far from all right...I'll never find it again if I look for three lifetimes."

"He best quality," Khan said drunkenly, "but he very much screwed."

"What?" Stands Proud asked, smiling at the old man. "What do you mean he's screwed?" He laughed.

Khan reached into his pocket. He looked up at Hawk. "Okay to show picture?"

Hawk shrugged.

Stands Proud's brows raised and he looked at the woman. "Wow," he said. The woman was strikingly beautiful. He studied the man next to her. It didn't look like his son, he thought, but the body would be different. "Is this...?"

"Es me," Hawk said. "First time."

"Let me see," Wolf said, looking over Stands Proud's

181

shoulder. "Was she one of those saloon girls?"

"Lift skirt show leg," Khan said.

They laughed.

Khan pointed to the name of the photographer, tapping his finger on the tintype.

The laughter stopped.

"Shit," Rafa muttered, staring at it. "That can't be right."

"Ah es right," Hawk said. Slowly. He extended a hand to Stands Proud. "Allow me to introduce myself, eh? I am Silver Hawk, Oglala, Lakota of the Kit Fox Tokala and Strong Heart Warrior societies but when it came to women, the entire west knew me as that arrogant asshole, eh?"

"Very big fool," Khan added.

"Very big," Hawk agreed. "Bigger than Paha Sapa."

"That big?" Wolf asked, snickering.

"Huge," Hawk stated. "I was showing off for her and I told the skinny white man photographer named Tassiano…eh damn you to hell and eh…take my soul with you."

"I don't get it," Rafa said.

"We believe someone takes your picture," Hawk said, "They capture your soul."

"It was an old ways belief," Stands Proud said.

"Old ways, eh? Like es not true?" Hawk asked him.

"I've had my picture taken a million times for basketball," Wolf said.

"I didn't say it's not true," Stands Proud said, slowly. "It's just…old ways."

"This man's name es Tassiano," Rafa said matter-of-factly.

"Old ways," Hawk said to Stands Proud, "as in don't believe that, no use for it, eh? What?" He crossed his arms over his chest. "And if you don't believe old ways things anymore, what am I?"

"The camera was new then," Stands Proud said.

"No kidding?" Hawk said, mocking him. "Es that true? I bet the iron horse came after that, no? Or was it before? Teach me, oh great wise one."

"All I'm saying," Stands Proud said, a little louder, "is that I don't believe the man took your soul. The name is a coincidence."

"Ahh," Hawk said, protesting.

"You have a soul," Stands Proud told him. "If you didn't, you wouldn't do the things you do like getting Ricky off the water tower or handing Suzy's sister a bandana to wipe her face at the clinic..."

"That was her sister?" Hawk asked.

"Yeah, she came by the other day and told me about it," Stands Proud informed him. "Some of the women on this rez have decided you did a nice thing for her and they're glad she isn't angry with herself anymore."

"What's her name?" Hawk asked.

"I don't know. She's in jail. She stabbed her husband because he was beating her and..." Stands Proud's voice faltered. "The point is you have a soul."

"Maybe Don Antone took some of it," Hawk said quietly. He drunkenly thought it over.

"Tassiano did not steal your soul," Stands Proud stated. He paused. "Where did this tintype come from?"

"Hawk's cabin," Khan said. "He have many interesting thing in cabin. Scalps. Many scalps."

Wolf smiled. "Where is it?"

"Es disgusting," Rafa said. "You did that?"

Hawk smiled and leaned against the railing, next to the steps.

"Where is it?" Wolf asked. "I never found a cabin up there."

"You wouldn't want to see it," he said, sneering at Stands Proud, "es old ways cabin."

"You're being a smart ass," Stands Proud informed him.

Hawk smiled at him. "Es that right, eh?" He smirked. "Eh well rodeo man you know how to ride old ways?"

"What?" Stands Proud asked, pointedly.

"Ride-a-horse-old-ways."

"Without a saddle?" Stands Proud asked. "Sure I can."

"I want to see you do this," Hawk said, challenging him. "I don't believe you."

"You don't believe…" Stands Proud began.

"Don't listen to him when he's drunk," Rafa advised. "Ignore him, eh?"

"Be quiet crack baby." Hawk laughed when Rafa flipped him the finger. "Come on, eh?" He nudged Stands Proud's shoulder. "I want to see you on a horse."

"This isn't a rodeo arena," Stands Proud said flatly.

"Ok, I'll show you *old ways* and you tell me if you can do it," Hawk said.

"Leave Pete's horses alone," Stands Proud reprimanded. He watched as Hawk walked over to the corral and opened the gate. All the horses ran for the field but the black one followed him. "Pete's going to kick your ass if you keep letting those horses out."

"They hate the fence," Hawk stated. He patted the horse. "Ok, he's right here. Are you going to show me something?" he asked Stands Proud.

"You shouldn't ride that horse," Stands Proud said. "You're drunk."

"Hurt less when fall off," Khan said.

"Es my way of thinking Khan," Hawk said. He jumped from the ground to the horses back in one swift movement.

"Are you running away again?" Stands Proud asked, taunting him.

"No, I'm going to show you how to ride a horse."

Stands Proud smiled and stretched out his long legs, crossing them. He leaned back on one hand and nodded. "Why don't you do that then?" he said. He smirked as his son rode off. "He's going to fall and break his ass," he said.

Wolf laughed as Hawk charged into the field at full speed. Suddenly, his brother was gone from his view, but Hawk hadn't fallen off. Wolf stood up. "Dad...?"

Stands Proud watched, amazed, as Hawk slid to the side of the horse and rode hanging onto the horses back. Hawk appeared again, on his belly on the horse and gave a shrill whistle. One of the other horses came riding at him. Hawk brought his feet beneath him, crouching down. When the other horse came by, Hawk jumped from one to the other and took off in the opposite direction.

"Dad?" Wolf asked.

"I see him," Stands Proud said nervously.

Khan nudged Stands Proud. "Your lost warrior home now," he said.

Stands Proud nodded. "Is that picture what kept him in

the hills?"

"No," Khan said. "Bird took him to place where he jump off cliff in first life time. Gone now. Bones under big machines. Earth all chop up. He say bones crushed, broken or in museum some damn place. Hawk say he doomed forever."

Stands Proud watched his son ride as though he were possessed. He raced through the field as if he were trying desperately to bring his old ways back. "They started construction up there last month," he said. "Some of the boys were trying to stop it but the construction crew won. I had no idea that's where he…" Stands Proud sighed. "No wonder he didn't come back."

"Does that mean he's stuck here?" Wolf asked.

"I don't know Wolf," Stands Proud said. "There are questions about your brother that I can't answer."

Hawk rode the horse thundering toward the house and turned sideways. The horse reared up on its hind legs, kicking the front ones high in the air. He hung on and waited for the horse to settle down. Hawk let the horse pace back and forth. He looked at Stands Proud. "This is how a Lakota warrior rides," Hawk stated. "Can you do it?"

Stands Proud smiled up at him. "Get off and I'll show you."

Hawk narrowed his eyes on the man.

"All right, so I'm lying," Stands Proud said, with a shrug of his shoulders.

Hawk let out a fierce war cry and charged back into the field.

Stands Proud cringed when he saw his brother Pete come out of his house.

Chapter Twenty One

"You!" Pete yelled at Hawk. "Come here you!" Pete walked out into the yard, motioning for Hawk to come to him.

Hawk brought the horse to a complete stop in the field and smirked.

"Come here!" Pete yelled again.

The neighbors began to gather.

"I tried to warn him," Stands Proud said, grinning. His brother Pete wasn't quite as tall as he was. He was stocky and muscle bound from years of hard work. He was the only one on the rez who owned that many horses and it was very personal to him, especially since Hawk 'stole' them every chance he got.

Hawk nudged into the horses sides. At a slow pace, he walked the horse toward Pete but stopped about twenty feet away. Every time Pete tried to approach him, Hawk moved the horse.

Everyone laughed.

"You go get the rest of those horses," Pete said, pointing to the back field where they were grazing, "and put them all back."

"They don't like the fence Uncle Pete," Hawk said.

"I don't care. They have to stay in there," Pete told him. He attempted to approach again and his nephew moved away. It angered him.

"Why?" Hawk asked, drunkenly. "Why do they have to stay in there?"

Pete glared at him. "Round them up and put them back."

"I'm no cowboy!" Hawk announced.

Everyone began to laugh.

"If I catch you…" Pete warned.

"You can't," Hawk told him.

Pete came stomping over to Stands Proud's house. "You better do something about him," he said. "I know he's got some problems but I can't have those horses running loose."

Stands Proud sighed. "I'm sorry Pete," he said. "I'll round them up for you. He's a little drunk right now."

"A little?" Pete asked. He looked at Khan. The old Japanese mans eyes were closed and he was leaning against the porch post. Pete shook his head.

"I made a crack about old ways stuff," Stands Proud said, "and he asked if I could ride old ways. Did you see him?"

"I saw him," Pete muttered quietly.

"I'll get the horses," Stands Proud promised. He could see his brother was embarrassed because he couldn't ride that way either. No one they knew could do it anymore.

"And you tell him that old ways shit is long gone," Pete said, glaring at Hawk. "He might be who they say he is but he's going to have to learn a few new ways now." He paused. "He used to do this when he was a kid. Did you know that?"

"No, I didn't," Stands Proud said.

"Sure, late at night, he'd sneak over and open the gate. Four years old, that little shit. In the morning, those horses would be out in the field. I'd see Hawk standing there, staring at them. I'd chase him off and he jumped back into his bedroom window."

"Why didn't you say anything?" Stands Proud asked.

"You weren't around," Pete said. "I told 'Nita. She said the boy couldn't help it. It wasn't his fault. But he's eighteen years old now, Stands Proud. This has to stop. I thought after all those years in the city; I wouldn't have a problem with him doing this."

"He remembers Pete," Stands Proud said quietly. "He remembers everything."

"Poor kid," Pete said softening.

"Yeah."

"I'm not trying to be hard on him but you know that field back there isn't rez land," Pete said. "Old Mr. Lawson is probably ringing the phone right now."

"I'll take care of it," Stands Proud promised.

Pete nodded and went back to his house. He went up onto his porch, looked over at Hawk and shook his head. He went inside. The screen door slammed shut.

Stands Proud looked at Hawk and saw the easy going smile was gone. He sat atop the horse, staring at the back field. Stands Proud sighed heavily and started over to his truck. Before he could open the door, Hawk bolted and charged into the back field. Stands Proud watched as his son expertly rode, cutting one way, then another and brought the horses together in a group. He moved them back into the corral and slid down from the black horse, hanging onto him, as if he needed the horse to stay on his own feet.

Hawk scowled and closed the gate. He saw the people from the rez had gathered to watch his latest weird stunt. Once again, he thought he'd provided the freak show. Didn't they have anything better to do? He wondered about it. When he saw Officer Shortwing's car pull into the yard next to Stands Proud's truck he muttered and swore under his breath.

"What's the problem Kent?" Stands Proud asked, facing the man.

Officer Shortwing closed the door to the patrol car and approached Stands Proud but his eyes were on Hawk. "I need to see your boy," he said.

"What for?" Stands Proud asked.

Hawk knew Shortwing had found another complaint. Maybe there was a mass murder in town. Whatever it was, Hawk accepted it was his fault. If it were anywhere in the area, it usually was. He stumbled through the field and over to the Tribal Police car. "What es it this time, eh?" he asked.

"There's been some vandalism to those bulldozers up on the construction sight," Officer Shortwing said. "Somebody took a few parts. The man who watches over that equipment said he saw you up there."

"I was there," Hawk said, "but I didn't touch the machines."

Stands Proud looked at Shortwing. "Get off his ass Kent," he warned. "Just because he was up there doesn't mean he vandalized those damn bulldozers." He was hoping Hawk hadn't but he wouldn't blame him if he had.

"Someone did," Shortwing announced, looking at Hawk through his sun glasses. The boy was wearing a pair of muddy pants, no shirt or shoes. "Where did you hide those parts young man?"

"I don't have them," Hawk said quietly.

"Well, you're coming with me until they show up," Shortwing said. "Put your hands on the car."

Hawk looked at Stands Proud. "If an ant crosses the road in a wrong direction here, I'll go in for it, eh?" He stumbled over to the car and put his hands on the hood of the car. He heard some angry yells and he raised his head. Coming down the reservation road were about twenty older guys, wearing black T-shirts and jackets with the same insignia on them.

"Shit," Shortwing muttered.

Hawk watched as they approached. He'd never met them and didn't know who they were. One of the men, who seemed to

190

be the leader of the rest, was carrying a metal piece of machinery in his hand.

"Three hundred years of dishonor!" the man said, holding the part up in his hand. "Three hundred years of lies, genocide against our people and destruction of our sacred lands!"

"Sunka Sapa," Shortwing stated.

"That's right," the man said, approaching him. "That's what they call me. Remember the name Shortwing because that's how you'll get the rest of those parts back. When the construction company agrees to talk with us, we'll hand them over."

"Those parts are worth…"

"What are our sacred lands worth to you Shortwing?" Sunka Sapa asked. "Are they worth these parts or your paycheck?"

"My personal feelings won't be brought into this," Officer Shortwing stated, "but you have no proof there was a burial ground on that ridge."

"There was," Hawk said. All the men looked at him. "It was to the right of where the cliff used to be." He lowered his gaze and stared hard at the white paint of the patrol car. His eyes blurred. "It was not meant to be a burial ground…but es what it turned into."

"You know about this?" Sunka Sapa asked, coming next to him and leaning down to hear the young man's words. He'd heard about Stands Proud's boy, everyone had, but he wasn't sure what to think.

"Yes," Hawk said.

"What happened there?" Sunka Sapa asked. "We know something did."

"It was a village of three hundred Lakota," Hawk told

191

him. "It was Dark Moon's village. They were on their way to the Bighorn Mountains. They were caught in that open space…and the blue coats surrounded them…the soldiers didn't say anything to the people," Hawk said softly. "They just…began killing them. They shot them down. The people ran and screamed… trying to get away but they couldn't…"

Officer Shortwing huffed out an annoyed breath. "This is getting ridiculous," he muttered.

Hawk stared at him, hard. "You don't believe me?" he asked in a low, deadly quiet tone. He could see that the man didn't. "Es old ways beliefs not to speak the names of the dead but maybe you don't believe that, eh?" Officer Shortwing refused to look at him. "It brings their spirits back to us," Hawk said. Still, Shortwing scowled at him. "Chief Dark Moon, Kangee, Sisika," Hawk said, looking at the Officer, "Walking Deer, Takes-The-Bear, Redboy, Shortwing…"

"That's enough!" Kent Shortwing snapped. His face reddened and he glared at the young man. "I said," he choked out, "that's enough."

It was quiet, reservation quiet, and the wind blew around them.

"Es why I went there the first time," Hawk said. "I went to that cliff and I saw no more reason to live. To my right were the people of my own village, killed when I was child. To my left were…the people who had gathered to dance, to bring back the old ways…they weren't hurting anyone. They hadn't done anything wrong…but they were killed too. I chose a place between them…hoping to join up with all of them in the spirit world."

Sunka Sapa nodded. His dark eyes glistened with a polished fury as he looked at Shortwing. "You tell that construction crew we want to talk," he said.

Officer Shortwing got into the patrol car, started the

engine and drove away.

Hawk backed up, stumbling.

"We'd like to talk to you too," Sunka Sapa said to Silver Hawk.

"Hiya," Hawk said, shaking his head. "Hiya." He turned and staggered away from them. "It's too late."

"Hawk knows where everything is," Sunka Sapa said, looking at Stands Proud, "Doesn't he?"

Stands Proud released a nervous sigh. He'd tried to stop the prophecy. He'd done everything he could to protect his son but it kept moving forward, like an old train engine, and every day it picked up more steam. His gaze settled upon the new warrior's face. "Yeah Sunka," he said, "he remembers."

Sunka Sapa stared at the young man who had walked into the back field. He stood there, alone in the high prairie grass, gazing at the Black Hills. "Will he ever talk to us?"

"I don't know," Stands Proud said. He turned and walked toward his son, taking off his denim jacket. When he reached Hawk, without a word, he draped the jacket over the boy's shoulders and took him into the house.

Chapter Twenty Two

Hawk sat at the kitchen table staring at his father and Rafa sitting in the living room. Rafa was mindlessly flipping through TV channels and Stands Proud was reading the newspaper. "You can go to bed," he told them both, in a loud voice. "I'm not sleeping, eh?"

They looked at him but went back to what they were doing.

Hawk knew Rafa was watching him because he'd been drinking whiskey and his friend was afraid he'd start looking for heroin. It had happened before. He still felt the strong cravings but he knew if he shot up, Khan would leave. He didn't know why Stands Proud was sitting up late. It wasn't like Hawk felt like running anywhere. He'd just come home and he was tired.

Stands Proud folded the paper and came into the kitchen. "You could try to sleep," he said gently.

"No," Hawk said.

"He can't sleep when he drinks like that," Rafa called out.

"Shut up in there," Hawk said, irritably.

"Here we go," Rafa mumbled.

"I told you to shut the hell up!" Hawk roared, standing up. He glared at Rafa, lying on the couch.

"Take it easy," Stands Proud said, quietly. "Everyone else is asleep."

"Everyone *was asleep*," Wolf muttered, coming down the hall.

"Are you saying I woke you up?" Hawk demanded, going around the kitchen table. "I didn't do anything."

Stands Proud's nerves rattled.

Rafa sat up on the couch.

Hawk noticed the shift, the change in the room. He glanced at them and looked at Wolf. "I didn't wake you up," he said angrily.

Wolf didn't want to say anything. How could he tell Hawk he'd gotten so used to all the trouble, all it took was hearing the sound of his voice…or a chair scraping on the floor to fast…or Stands Proud's footsteps going faster than they needed to be. "No," Wolf said quietly, "it wasn't you. I just can't sleep."

Hawk knew he was lying. "I'll go in my room," he said.

Stands Proud sighed heavily and watched him go down the hall. The door slammed shut.

"I'm going to move back in with Aunt Leah," Wolf said. He wanted to wait for a better time but a better time never arrived at this house.

Stands Proud turned around slowly and looked at his son. "I'm sorry," he said.

"No dad, it's not like that," Wolf said, "I liked what my life was like before. I talked to the coach and he said that if I come back, I can play next year."

"Well, I think you should go back to school," Stands Proud said, going into the living room. "I know how much you like to play basketball." He sat down in his chair and couldn't help but feel that he'd failed again, somewhere along the line.

"Listen," Wolf said, "it's not that I don't want to be with you or Hawk. I do. I didn't realize what I had until I met him again. I just…expected it. Basketball, Aunt Leah…everything." He paused reflectively. "And I used to be mad at you Dad, but I'm not mad anymore. I know what happened. I'm glad you're home and I'm glad Hawk's here too…but I don't think we can force everything into something that it never was."

Stands Proud nodded. "Okay son," he said. He couldn't say that he didn't see it coming. He felt as if he never had time to spend with Wolf. "You should go back to Leah. She did a fine job raising you."

"I feel like I let her down," Wolf said, "by quitting school and everything. I don't want her to feel like that. I want her to be proud of me."

"I understand son," Stands Proud told him. "It's all right."

"It's only three houses away," Wolf told him.

"It's all right," Stands Proud insisted.

"Ehhh…you'll still hear him screaming down there," Rafa muttered.

Wolf smirked at him.

Stands Proud smiled and shook his head. "How old are you Rafa? Shouldn't you be in school too?"

"Forget it," Rafa said. "I'm sixteen but I can't go to school, eh?"

"Why not?" Wolf asked.

"Because I'm allergic to teachers, principals hate me and they always need papers signed by the crack heads and I don't know where they are," Rafa stated.

"I'll sign papers for you," Stands Proud said.

"You would do that? You would be legally responsible for Rafael Gonzalez?" he asked.

"Yeah," Stands Proud said very slowly. "Sure. Why not?"

"You should go Rafa," Wolf said, grinning at him.

"Bah…there's a three day limit with me," Rafa informed them. "I'd be there three days and they'd throw me out."

"You've been here longer than three days," Stands Proud reminded him.

Rafa nodded. "Si, I have. Maybe there es hope for me, no? Maybe I'll start a new life. We give it a try, eh?"

"I'll come by in the morning and pick you up," Wolf said, walking over to the door.

"You're going…now?" Stands Proud asked.

"Yeah, I have to talk to Aunt Leah," Wolf said. "I'll see you tomorrow." He hesitantly stepped outside and closed the door, breathing a huge sigh of relief. He just couldn't do it anymore, he thought, not one more night of it.

"He can't stand it, eh?" Rafa said, reclining on the couch.

"I'm about ready to search for a hotel room myself," Stands Proud admitted. "How did do you do it?" he asked Rafa.

"I've known Cheetah since he moved into the apartment next to mine, eh?" Rafa said. "Thirteen years. Es a long time."

"It's even longer from the inside of a cell," Stands Proud told him.

Rafa nodded. "*Si, de verotas.* That's the real truth. The rest of the real truth es I owe him for many things, Senor. I know it looks like I put up with all his shit but es not the way it is." He sat up straight on the couch and looked at Stands Proud. "I was going with Angelina's sister when we were kids, eh twelve? Thirteen? No se. Any how, this sister was a bit loco. Why else would she like me? She was in my room, a little high…a lot drunk. She was messing around by the window. She fell." Rafa released a long, slow sigh. "My crack head mother calls the police and she tells them, I pushed her out the window. There were twelve of us kids and she was looking to get rid of me, eh? So, I went to Juvey. While I'm there, the whole family moved. Gone, understand? But I was un Caballero, eh? Cheetah came every day I was in there to visit me. He brought me things I was allowed to have, magazines to read, stuff to pass the time. I didn't push her. Cheetah knew I didn't. He didn't see it but he believed me. No one else did. Everyone blamed me for what happened...es why Angelina hates me." Rafa paused and shook his head. "Those guards knew he was *El Caudillo de Los Caballeros*. Every day they gave him a hard time, a real hard time. Once he came to a visit with his eye starting to turn black and blue, no? I tell him, don't come no more. He says a little black eye will stop me?" Rafa looked across the room at Stands Proud. "When I got out, he made sure I had a place to stay, something to eat and...someone to talk to."

"How long were you in there?" Stands Proud asked. He fully understood not having anyone visit, passing time and how the guards could give someone a hard time.

"A year," Rafa said. "Cheetah came for a whole year, eh? He didn't miss a day. And you know how much he don't like places like that. He did that for me. So eh...I'm putting up with nothing. There are no walls around him that you can see but I make sure every day, I'm there."

"You two are good friends," Stands Proud said. "You're what we call Kola. Two friends who will die for each other."

"Es right," Rafa told him. "De verotas."

They heard footsteps coming down the hall. Hawk came into the living room. He'd been in the shower. The fighting pants sagged on his hips and his hair was soaking wet. He had a towel around his shoulders and he was gripping the ends of it tightly.

Rafa looked up at him as Cheetah paced back and forth. "You sick?" he asked, knowing the cravings were always stronger after the whiskey started to wear off.

Hawk made himself sit down on the couch. He put his face in his hands, still not releasing the towel. "I don't want it Rafa."

"I know you don't," Rafa said.

"It'll mess up everything."

"Always does," Rafa agreed.

"I couldn't stay in the room."

"Es okay," Rafa said. "You can sit out here, eh? We'll talk until Khan wakes up. You'll be okay then, no?"

"A few more hours," Hawk told him. He visibly shook. He looked over at his father. "I'm sorry you're still awake."

"I'm not," Stands Proud said.

"Don't let me out the door okay?" he said. "If I go...I know I'll do it. I don't care what you do to me. Keep me here. I have to be here when Khan wakes up."

Khan heard Hawk talking in the living room. He left the bedroom, holding his aching head. He didn't bother to change and went out into the kitchen wearing a pair of fighting pants and an I LOVE NEW YORK t-shirt.

Stands Proud smiled when he saw the old man. "You don't miss a thing, do you Khan?" he asked.

"Old man need Hawk in one piece for training," Khan explained. "Must teach three more lessons." He poured a glass of cold tea from the refrigerator and came over to the couch. "Here," Khan said, handing Hawk the herb.

"Gracias," Hawk said quickly. He took the herb and drank the tea.

"What was that?" Stands Proud asked.

"Herb from China," Khan told him. "Big opium problem there. Not cure sickness but will help." He groaned. "Khan needs to find herb for big hung over head ache. Hawk get old man drunk. He try to get out of training today."

"I did not," Hawk said, wiping his face with the towel.

"Eh well Khan es here," Rafa said. "I'll get some sleep."

"No," Khan said. "Must beg Rafa to keep Hawk busy. Khan must rest aching head."

"Eh…okay," Rafa grinned.

Khan went back down the hall.

"Does that help?" Stands Proud asked Hawk.

"A little," Hawk said. "He's given it to me before."

"Why don't you teach me more drills, eh?" Rafa suggested. "When you do that you concentrate on the moves. It will help."

"I don't know," Hawk said.

"Let's go outside," Rafa suggested. "Es just getting light. You like that time of the morning, no?"

Hawk sighed. "I don't know Rafa."

"You get busy," Rafa told him. "You won't run. I know you won't."

Reluctantly, Hawk followed Rafa out the door. His head ached too but that was the least of his worries. If he shot up now, he knew he'd be throwing everything away. He knew what Khan wanted to pass on to him was very important. He would some how deal with what happened on the ridge but nothing was more important to him than being there for Khan. His mother had always been sick, it seemed, and Stands Proud wasn't there at all. Tassiano adopted him but had never been a father, only a dictator over his life. If anyone had raised him, it was Khan and Hawk would rather die than disappoint him.

Rafa went to the platform and lowered into a fighting stance.

"What was the last one we worked on?" Hawk asked.

"Number twelve," Rafa said.

"Do it," Hawk said. He watched as Rafa went through the

moves but stopped him part way through. "No, no," he said gently. "You're leg es coming around to low," he said. He stood next to Rafa. "Like this," he said, showing him the kick slowly.

"Es what I did," Rafa said.

"No," Hawk said. "You're leg was here…not here. Higher, Rafa. It needs to be higher."

"I'm too short," Rafa muttered.

Hawk grinned. "You're not," he said. "You're lazy. Higher."

Stands Proud watched them from the window. He knew Rafa would rather be lying on the couch watching TV and eating cake. He smiled at them as Hawk gently taught Rafa, with endless patience. He did seem to focus all of his energy in one place when it came to fighting or training, Stands Proud thought. Stands Proud saw Wolf coming down the road with his backpack and he had to smile. Then he realized Hawk didn't know Wolf had moved out and he didn't know Rafa was planning to go to school. Stands Proud moved to the screen door.

"No, no es all right," Hawk said, grinning at them. "I think es a good place for both of you." They laughed and he watched them walk away. He sighed, turned and went up onto the porch. Stands Proud was at the door. "Did you know?" he asked his father, "They are going to school?"

"Yeah, I knew," Stands Proud said, opening the door. "You could…" he began.

"Ah no…I'm finished with that, eh?"

"Hawk," Stands Proud said, "a good education is important."

"Did you read a 'How to be a Dad' book in prison or something?" Hawk asked him, walking into the kitchen.

Stands Proud followed him. "Yeah," he said dryly, "I did

but they didn't have the chapter on how to deal with a smart ass." He sat down in a kitchen chair. "You used to be the quiet one."

Hawk shrugged.

"You're smart," Stands Proud said. "You should go to school."

"I don't need to go."

"Why not? What would it hurt?" Stands Proud asked him. "How far did you go in school?"

Hawk gave a wicked laugh. "Oh…you…" He looked at his father with disbelief. "You think I quit, eh? You think because I was in a gang I left school?" He laughed again. "Ah no, this es unbelievable, eh?"

"You had to quit at some point," Stands Proud reasoned. "I know you and your brother started school in the same year."

"I'm done," Hawk said, leaning on the kitchen table with his palms down. "Es what I meant when I said, I'm finished with that. I went to public school in New York and then I had a private tutor at Tassiano Estates. My education was accelerated so that I could spend more time in the fighting arena."

"Accelerated?" Stands Proud asked. "Do you have a high school diploma?"

"Do you want to see it?" Hawk asked.

"Yeah, I missed a lot," Stands Proud said. "Fill me in." He watched as Hawk went down the hall and waited for him to come back. His son dropped a red folder on the table in front of him.

"Go ahead, look," Hawk said, "But before you do, I'll say this. No, I'm not going."

Stands Proud opened the folder and turned the papers over one by one. Each report told him his son Joseph Silver Hawk Argent was a straight A student. His reports from the tutor also gave an excellent mark for each subject. There was a high school diploma and Stands Proud found a white envelope in the back of the file from New York University. He looked at Hawk and then lowered his gaze, opening the letter and reading it. His son could have been in his second semester of college, right now. It was an academic scholarship. Stands Proud's arm dropped to the table and he stared at his son.

"I said, I'm not going," Hawk told him.

"Can I ask why?" Stands Proud inquired.

"There is nothing in that university," Hawk said, "has anything to do with who I am."

Stands Proud wanted to make an argument for that but he couldn't. He was beginning to wonder just how smart this son was.

"My old bones are probably in a university being studied and examined," Hawk said. "Do you know what would happen if they found out about me? If I have a desire to continue being treated as a freak, I'll keep it local. Ok?"

Stands Proud closed the red folder and handed it to him.

"Don't tell Wolf. *Pilamaya,*" Hawk said, and he went down the hall.

Chapter Twenty Three

Later that evening, Khan's hang over subsided. He felt as if he could get out of the bed and walk so he went to the kitchen. He found Hawk moving about and cooking supper. "I guess herbs helped you," Khan said.

"They did Khan," Hawk said, "Thank you." He smiled. Poor Khan looked like fifty miles of bad road. "I told you that whiskey was strong," he said.

"Next time Khan not share whiskey."

Hawk laughed.

"Where everybody at?" Khan asked, noticing the house was empty.

"Wolf moved back in with my Aunt Leah," Hawk said, stirring the pot, "and I think he and Rafa are up on the basketball court..." The phone rang. He picked it up. "Hola...eh hello?"

"Hello wise ass."

"Papa?" Hawk asked. "What's wrong? Why aren't you home?" He could hear music and loud voices in the background.

"I need a ride."

"Where are you?" Hawk asked.

"Broken Arrow."

"Your turn tonight, eh? Ok I'll come get you," Hawk said. He hung up the phone. "I have to pick up my father," Hawk said, grinning. "I think we're a bad influence Khan," he said, patting the old man's shoulder. "Eat," he suggested. "I'll be back soon."

Hawk went out into the yard. He could see his Uncle Pete inside the house, watching TV. Slowly, he crept over to the truck and crawled in behind the steering wheel. He smirked, turned the key, and pushed down hard on the gas. In the rear view mirror he saw his Uncle Pete come out of the house, yelling. Hawk laughed and turned the radio on in the truck. He flipped through the stations, sneering at the country music. Finally, he shut it off and drove in silence.

It didn't take long to get to the Broken Arrow but going inside of it was the hard part. The last time he was in the Broken Arrow, he watched a man being choked to death and it was Stands Proud who had done it. Hawk hoped his father would be in the parking lot waiting for him but he wasn't. As soon as he got out of the truck, Hawk felt people staring at him. He drew in a deep breath and exhaled slowly to steady his nerves. He walked over to the door, pulled it open and went inside.

"There he is," Buddy said in a loud voice. "Who's going to tell him?"

"Tell me what?" Hawk asked, looking at him.

"Hey, I didn't have anything to do with it man," Buddy said.

"With what?" Hawk demanded.

"Your old man's over there," another voice said.

Hawk looked and saw his father slumped in a booth, in a dark corner of the bar. The people got quieter as he walked over to Stands Proud. "Hey Papa…" he said. His heart sped up. "Papa?" he said in a louder voice. He slid into the booth and lifted Stands Proud's hat and saw that his face was bruised. There was a cut on his cheek. His father moaned. Blood came from the corner of his mouth. "Who did this?" Hawk yelled at the people. No one answered him. Hawk put his father's arm across his shoulder and pulled him to the edge of the seat. "Let's go, eh? I got you."

"Hey son," Stands Proud murmured.

"Who did this to you?"

"Walk son," Stands Proud warned him. "Just walk." Stands Proud stumbled from busted ribs and far too much whiskey.

"When I find out," Hawk warned everyone, "I'm coming back here, eh?" He hauled Stands Proud out into the parking lot. "Come on, I have Uncle Pete's truck. We'll get yours tomorrow."

Stands Proud groaned and used his last bit of strength to get up into the truck. He collapsed back against the seat and gasped sharply.

Hawk got in behind the wheel and started the truck. "I'm taking you home but I'm coming back here. I'll find out who did this to you."

"Let...it go," Stands Proud said.

"Who was it? Why did they do it?" Hawk demanded. "You're not going to tell me, are you?"

"Drive."

"I am driving," Hawk told him. He glared at the dark road ahead of them and glanced over at his father. "Are you ok Papa? I hope you're ok." Hawk swore when he didn't get an answer. He drove back to the reservation. When he pulled into the yard, the truck door flung open and Pete yanked him out of the truck. Hawk broke the hold Pete had on him and shoved him to the ground. He ran to the other side of the truck, with Pete coming right behind him.

"Shit," Pete muttered when Hawk opened the door and the light came on. "Who the hell were you fightin' now Stands Proud?"

"He called me from the Broken Arrow," Hawk said, taking his father's arm and putting it across his shoulders. "Sorry about taking your truck. I'll put gas in it tomorrow." He lifted his father from the truck.

"Don't worry about that," Pete said softly. "Come on, I'll

help you get him in the house. I never saw him take a beating like this. Hell Stands Proud, who did this?"

"I've been asking him that," Hawk said. "He won't say. KHAN! RAFA! Somebody get the door!" He started up the porch steps, hauling his father along with him.

Rafa pushed the screen door open. "Holy shit!" he uttered. "What the hell happened to him?"

"A fight," Hawk said, "I think. *No se.* He won't tell me." Hawk sat his father down on the couch and took off the big man's jacket. "Papa...I'm going to move you once more to lay you down, eh? Easy..."

"We going to take care of this, migo," Rafa told Hawk.

"You know it," Hawk said.

"No!" Stands Proud said. He clenched his teeth. "You... stay away...from there." He glared at Hawk. "You hear me?"

Hawk ignored him and began looking for wounds. A strong hand grabbed the front of his shirt and his father pulled him closer, face to face.

"You hear me?" Stands Proud asked sternly.

"Si Papa," Hawk said. "I hear you."

Khan came over with a wet cloth and handed it to Hawk.

"His ribs are broken," Hawk said, "at least two of them. I can't find anything else."

"I'm...ok," Stands Proud breathed out. He looked at Hawk. "Calm down."

Hawk wiped his father's face, wiping away the blood. "You can't ask me to be calm when I see this, eh?"

"Calm down," Stands Proud said. "I've been in...worse shape...getting thrown from...a horse."

"But you weren't thrown from a horse," Hawk said.

207

"Some one did this to you. I've seen you fight. It must have been a few of them, eh? How many? Four? Five?" he asked.

"Let it go," Stands Proud told him. "I don't want you...to fight. Ok?" He looked up at his son and put a hand on Hawk's face. "No more scars...for you. No more."

Hawk's vision blurred. "Do you want me to get Aunt Jolene?" he asked, in a throaty voice.

"No...just let me lay here awhile," Stands Proud said.

"Aunt Martha es close, I could get her," Hawk told him. "Why can't I do something to help you? Anything?"

"You want to help?" Stands Proud asked.

"Of course," Hawk said quickly.

"Go get Sunka," Stands Proud said.

"Where can I find him?" Hawk asked.

"The blue house...beside the Community Center," Stands Proud told him. "Ok?"

"Ok," Hawk said. He stood up. "Khan, will you look after him?"

"Yes, yes...Go Hawk," Khan said.

"*Venga conmigo Rafa*," Hawk said. "*Vamanos.*"

They left the house together and walked together down the reservation road.

"They beat him bad, eh?" Rafa said angrily.

"Si," Hawk said. "I don't care what he says. They won't get away with it. I know he doesn't want me to fight but I can't let this go. I can't do it. He'll have to understand that, no?"

"Es right," Rafa said, agreeing with him.

They walked up to the door of the green house and knocked. An angry black dog jumped against the door, scratching. Hawk moved back and waited. Sunka appeared and moved the beast.

"Hey Hawk," Sunka said, a little surprised. "Come in."

"No, I can't," Hawk said. "I need you to come with me. My father asked to see you now, eh? Es important."

"He got beat up," Rafa told Sunka.

"By who?" Sunka asked, grabbing his jacket from a hook.

"He's not saying," Hawk told him. He was glad Sunka Sapa came outside right away and began walking with them. "He was at the Broken Arrow, es all I know," Hawk added.

Sunka nodded. He glanced over at Hawk every now and then as they walked. He was hoping the kid would come around but not like this. Hawk was moving at a fast, furious pace and he was extremely pissed off.

"Don't start that shit tonight," Hawk warned, "I'm not in the mood."

"What shit?" Sunka asked.

"Looking at me as if you're watching a damn spirit, eh? I can make myself real enough for you," Hawk said, in a threatening voice. He grabbed the door to the house and opened it. He followed Sunka and Rafa inside.

"Oh man," Sunka groaned, seeing Stands Proud. He halted in his steps.

"Khan…" Stands Proud said. "Take Rafa and Hawk in the other…room."

"I'm not a child, eh?" Hawk protested.

"Go," Stands Proud said.

"You listen to father," Khan told Hawk. "You must show respect. Come."

Reluctantly, Hawk followed Khan and Rafa into the

kitchen but he scowled. "He's going to tell Sunka but he won't tell me?"

"Not every fight is your fight," Khan said. "Never borrow trouble. You not have enough?"

Hawk sat at the kitchen table and watched as Sunka knelt down beside the couch. Sunka nodded a few times and talked to his father. Hawk glanced at Rafa. Rafael was seething with rage. Rafa caught his glance and they nodded. They'd find out who did this.

Chapter Twenty Four

"You not focus," Khan told Hawk.

Hawk sighed and stood up from the fighting stance. "I can't. I'm worried about my father."

"You not worry about father," Khan said. "He have broken ribs. He go to clinic. Stands Proud fine." Khan paused. "You worry about revenge."

"He wants me to stay out of it? How can I?" Hawk asked.

"You must respect wishes of father," Khan said to him. "If you do not show respect, you do not honor your father." He paused and came forward. "To fight is something *you* want, not something father wants you to do."

"I know," Hawk said quietly. "He doesn't want me involved. That was pretty obvious when he called in Sunka and told me to go in the kitchen."

"Your pride is hurt," Khan said.

Hawk sighed and looked away. "I guess. What makes him think Sunka can handle this better than I could? I've been in a lot of fights. I've defended a lot of people."

"Too late to defend Stands Proud," Khan told him. "Ribs already broken."

"I don't know why he went there," Hawk muttered. "He's been doing really well since he got out of prison. When I was a kid, he was always drunk except for days when we went to a Pow Wow."

"Only Stands Proud know this," Khan said.

Hawk sighed heavily.

"Turn," Khan said.

Hawk looked at him. "Khan I…" His voice faltered. He reluctantly turned around and stood with his back to Khan. He waited for the push, the shove that would cause Don Antone's voice to echo in his head. When Khan's hand shoved into his back, he stumbled forward. The silence stunned him. Khan pushed him again. Slowly, Hawk turned around.

"What you hear?" Khan asked.

Hawk stared at him. "Nothing," he whispered.

"What you see?"

"Only Khan," Hawk told him.

Khan smiled and nodded.

"It's gone…" Hawk said, surprised. "But how?"

"Strike with right arm," Khan told him.

Hawk threw a punch toward Khan. The old man caught his wrist. The rage was gone. His skin didn't burn from Khan's touch. A chuckle escaped him. He placed his other hand gently over the old man's. "Thank you," he said.

Khan smiled at him. "You better now. Hawk in control. Not Don Antone," he said.

"I didn't think I'd ever get it back," Hawk said. "I thought I lost it forever. He told me it would happen that way, eh?"

"Come," Khan said. "Sit with Khan."

They walked over to the porch steps and sat down.

"Don Antone fill up half of Hawk that was empty," Khan told him. "That half no longer empty. You very sure who you are now. Hawk is home. Family here."

"Yeah but…I still feel like I don't belong here," Hawk told Khan. "I don't fit."

"You not belong here."

Hawk's heart sank a little. "Great," he said, bitterly.

"This reservation," Khan explained, "Never good place for Hawk. You fight to stay here. It can never work. In first life time, you have great freedom. It taken from you. In second life time, freedom taken again. Your spirit free, like wind. It fights against confinement. You come here to make father happy. You come to make grandfather and rest of people happy but you suffer."

"Es true Khan," Hawk said, "but without my people, what am I?"

"A warrior without his people," Khan agreed, "is a lost warrior but a warrior not true to himself is lost and broken man. You not fight for anybody if Hawk loses heart. You become machine. Hawk fight for no reason but to fight. No purpose but to survive."

"Es what Tassiano did to me," Hawk said quietly.

Khan nodded. "Many years Tassiano take away all things important to Hawk, leave boy with nothing. He no longer proud of who he is. He ashamed. He become like machine. Tassiano turn machine on, fight. Turn off, Hawk sit and wait for next fight. No sense to fight every day. Other things to do in this life time." Khan smiled at him. "Find pretty girl and be happy."

Hawk grinned and laughed. "Maybe," he said.

"You bring wife to Okinawa," Khan said, "to see old man."

Hawk's smile faded. He lowered his gaze and stared at the ground. "You're leaving," he said hoarsely.

"Khan must return to homeland," he said.

Hawk felt the lump growing in his throat. He turned his face away so the old man wouldn't see the tears welling in his eyes.

"Hawk know everything now," Khan told him. "You carry ancient wisdom of seventeen generations Khan family warriors. Some day you pass on to son."

"Khan…" Hawk said, looking at him. He couldn't help it that tears had escaped from his eyes.

"I cannot stay," Khan said gently. "One day, you come to Okinawa. You very welcome there."

Hawk swallowed, hard. He nodded. "Were you really going to take me to Okinawa when I was a kid?"

"Yes," Khan said. "First time Don Antone whip boy. Khan made plans to take boy away. Khan hide boy and never return."

"Why didn't you?" Hawk asked.

"Khan set aside own wishes, very hard thing to do," Khan explained, "Khan knew one day warrior must be returned to his people. Khan knew people in city depend on boy, mother depend on boy. Not so easy to take him away."

"I'm glad you decided to stay with me at Don Antone's," Hawk said.

"No decision to make," Khan said. His eyes glistened with tears. "Khan see boy. Khan's heart full again." He patted the young man's knee. "Come. We'll make tea."

Hawk nodded and stood up. "Wait…" he said. "What about the three lessons?" he asked.

"Ehhhh…" Khan said, smiling at him, "No lessons. Khan teach Hawk everything in New York. Khan spend more time with Hawk this way."

Hawk smiled. "You're kidding. Khan you never lied to me."

"Not big lie," Khan said. He looked up at Hawk. "You

not need lessons. You master long time."

Hawk raised his eyebrows and grinned at the old man. "Best quality?"

"Very best quality," Khan told him.

Chapter Twenty Four

When Hawk returned from the airport, he found his father sitting upright in the recliner. There were stark white bandages wrapped around his chest. His face was still swollen and bruised. Hawk didn't know what to say to him and started into the kitchen.

"Hawk," Stands Proud said, "I want to talk to you."

Hawk turned and looked at him. "I'm not going to do anything if that's what you're worried about, eh? And I'll try to convince Rafa to stay out of it, too."

"Come in and sit down," Stands Proud said.

Hawk wondered about the serious tone in his father's voice. He'd only heard it once or twice. Still, it bothered him. He wasn't used to it. He walked over and sat down on the couch. "Did I do something wrong?" he asked.

"No," Stands Proud said softly. "You didn't do anything wrong." The adams apple quivered in his throat and he swallowed, hard. "I think you should go back to New York," he said.

Hawk stared at him. "What?"

"You should take Rafa and go back to New York," Stands Proud said. "You have money. You're smart enough. You'll be okay."

He was so angry, he couldn't speak. Hawk's eyes filled with tears all over again. He'd just taken Khan to the airport and now his own father was throwing him out. His chest arose and fell as his anger simmered in silence.

"I watched you with your friends," Stands Proud went on. "You're happy with them. You're not happy here."

"This has nothing to do with my friends," Hawk said in a

low quiet voice. "You don't want me here."

"You're right," Stands Proud told him. "This isn't working out. Wolf figured it out. He went back to Leah's."

"Wolf is wrong," Hawk said angrily.

"He had the sense to know when to call it quits," Stands Proud said.

"Es that what this is, eh?" Hawk stood up and paced. "You're quitting. Nothing has changed. You couldn't do it before either. You went off to rodeo and left Mama here to do everything!"

"This has nothing to do with that."

"The hell it doesn't," Hawk told him. He flipped his long hair over his shoulder and stopped pacing. He stood in front of his father. "You always quit," he said.

"Call it what you want to," Stands Proud said quietly, "but you don't belong here."

"No, I don't. I never did," Hawk retorted. "I hate this place. I can't stand being here every day but I came here because you wanted me to...and now, you're throwing me out?"

"You'll get by," Stands Proud said.

Hawk glared at him and started to storm off but something caught him and held him still. He stood with his back to his father and braced one hand against the wall. After he managed to calm the anger, everything fell into place. "You're trying to protect me from something," he said. Hawk turned around. His father didn't say anything. "You don't want me to leave."

Stands Proud forced his voice to remain steady. "I said, you don't belong here. You know you don't. Take your things and your friend and go back to New York."

Hawk backed up and stood in front of Stands Proud. "Who did this to you?" he asked. "Tell me Papa."

217

"It's not your business."

"It was because of me, wasn't it?" Hawk asked him. "It has everything to do with me and you won't tell me." He saw his father's dark eyes flicker and he knew he'd found the truth. "I'm not running Papa."

"Oh?" Stands Proud inquired sarcastically, "now you're going to stop running?"

Hawk glared at him. "Insults won't help you."

"Listen wiset ass I was never cut out to be a father," Stands Proud told him. "You're right about me, ok? I fucked it up from day one. I drank. I disappeared for months at a time. I was never here for you or your mother. What made you think that all of a sudden, I'd get it right?" He tore his gaze away from his son's face. "Now get out of here," he muttered. "Go back to New York."

"No," Hawk said firmly.

"Or go follow Khan." Stands Proud said. "Go to Okinawa. You like that old man. He likes you. You'll get along fine."

"I'm not going anywhere," Hawk said, "at least, not right now. When your ribs are healed if you still want me to leave, I'll go."

Stands Proud's eyes clouded with tears. "Why are you such a stubborn little bastard?" he whispered hoarsely.

"I think I inherited that from somewhere, eh?"

Stands Proud raised his hand and covered his eyes for a moment. Suddenly, he slammed his arm down on the chair and glared at Hawk. "I'm telling you to leave! Don't you have any sense, boy?" he yelled.

"I have enough sense to know you're trying to get me out of they way, eh?" Hawk said calmly.

"You can't stay here!" Stands Proud roared. He winced from the sharp pains shooting inside of his chest.

"Eh well," Hawk sneered. "I'm staying. Who ever did this to you might come after you again and I'm not leaving you here like this. You can't protect yourself."

"I spent thirteen years in prison," Stands Proud seethed, "with the worst this society has to offer. I don't need a little piss ant like you protecting me."

Hawk laughed. "Piss ant," he said. He shook his head. "Es a good one Papa but I'm not going." He walked over to the couch and reclined back against the seat, watching his father's face a mixture of anger and sorrow colliding.

"You have to go," Stands Proud said.

"Why?" Hawk asked.

Stands Proud closed his eyes and leaned his head back. "They'll never stop," he said quietly. "It's never going to stop."

"What isn't going to stop, eh?"

"The stares, the whispers and all the god damn talk."

Hawk swallowed, hard. "I know that." He was right. It had been about him. His father's pain, his broken ribs…were because of him.

"I can only take so much," Stands Proud said.

"I know that too," Hawk said.

"I stopped at the Broken Arrow to pick up a few of those barbeque sandwiches Lindy makes," Stands Proud said. "I know you boys used to like those. I knew I'd hear a few things when I went in there. I haven't been there since I got out…"

Hawk's breathing slowed to a quiet pace. He left his head back, against the seat and watched his father talking. Stands Proud's head was back too but his eyes were closed.

"They made a few comments," Stands Proud said. "Not all of them. Some people stood up for you…the others…well, you know how they are. I got the sandwiches and went out into the parking lot. That's when I saw they were waiting by the truck…" He paused for a few moments. "Now I guess I could've walked away…and if they were from the rez, I probably would have." He drew in a breath and gently let it out. "You got trouble Hawk," Stands Proud warned, "the kind you can't fight around here."

"Who was it?" Hawk asked him.

"Six or seven white boys," Stands Proud said, raising his head. "I did everything I could to get in the truck. They said a few things. They pushed…"

"What were they saying?" Hawk asked, sitting upright.

"They said they didn't like fags," Stands Proud said, quietly.

"Ah…" Hawk said. He looked away from his father's face and stared at the wall until it blurred.

"Injuns, spics and fags," Stands Proud said. "I let the words slide until one of those little pricks mentioned you by name. After that, it was one swing after another and the dust flew. They said you'd better not step off the rez or they'll get you."

"Es that right?" Hawk asked roughly.

"You can't live here like that Hawk," Stands Proud said. "I asked Sunka and the others to look after you but they can't be there all the time. You don't want have to fight every time you leave the reservation. Those white boys will never quit. Their fathers are the same. It's always been that way." Stands Proud swallowed, hard. "No son, I don't want you to go but I know you can't stay."

"I can fight six or seven easily," Hawk said.

"I'm trying to tell you, there are always more behind them," Stands Proud said. "You should know this by now."

"So eh…you think I should go?"

"Yeah."

"What about the prophecy? The people?"

"The hell with it," Stands Proud said angrily. "Save your own ass."

He smirked. "I did that once," he said, "it didn't work out too well."

"Listen, you don't like it here," Stands Proud said. "Why put up with that shit? You're more like your mother's people anyway. I saw that when your friends were here. You have her eyes. Her laughter," he said. "I was only thinking of your Lakota blood. You should be where people accept you. Even the people here…they stare at you like you're some kind of…"

"Freak?" Hawk asked, smirking. He laughed. "Eh well, I am. I don't know of anyone else who came back. It has to be strange for them knowing I'm here." He paused and sighed. "I'll think about it Papa but I won't be forced to leave. I won't be forced to stay on the rez either."

"I was afraid that's what you'd say," Stands Proud said, softly. "If you leave now son, you'll avoid the heart ache."

"Will I?" Hawk asked. "I thought es what would happen the last time. I thought if I jumped from that cliff…it would be over. It doesn't end Papa. Old ways belief, one circle with no beginning and no end. Some how we go on, eh?"

"You've been through enough," Stands Proud said.

"Apparently, there's more I have to go through," Hawk told him. "I'll decide where I'll live and what to do, eh? I spent most of my life being controlled by one man. I don't know how much longer I'll be here…but I know who es in control from now

221

on, eh?"

"Be careful with that too," Stands Proud advised. "There's really only one in control of all things."

"Wakan Tanka, the Great Mystery," Hawk told him. "I know that too."

"You're a smart kid," Stands Proud said.

"I spent a lifetime and a half here, eh? I'd better know something by now," Hawk said, grinning. "Don't worry. Everything will be all right."

Chapter Twenty Five

"Sunka said they're having a gathering at the Community Center tonight," Stands Proud told Hawk. "I think we should go."

"Ehh...I don't know."

"I'd like to get out too," Stands Proud said. "I'm tired of being in the house."

Hawk nodded. "I don't feel going," he said.

"I think it'll be ok," Stands Proud encouraged him. "You'll be on the rez."

"I'm not worried about being on or off the rez," Hawk told him, pointedly. He glanced at Stands Proud. "You want me to talk to Sunka."

"I know better than to try and force you into anything."

"I don't know," Hawk said, quietly.

"Your brother and Rafa are going," Stands Proud said, "and your aunts have been calling every day asking about you. Pete's not asking though," Stands Proud teased, "he's glad you're in the house."

Hawk smirked. "I bet he is."

"Let's go," Stands Proud suggested.

"You're not trying to force me, eh?"

Stands Proud grinned at him.

"Okay," Hawk said. "Give me a few minutes. I'll be ready." He went down the hall and into his room to get clean clothes, showered and dressed. When he got back to the living room, he saw his father was ready and waiting for him. "You

223

really want to go, eh?"

"I'm looking forward to it," Stands Proud said. He got up slowly from the couch, holding his chest. The ache was still there but it wasn't as bad.

"Where is Rafa?" Hawk asked.

"They're already over there," Stands Proud said. He picked up his denim jacket and walked to the door. He looked at his son. "Do you own any clothes that aren't black?" he asked.

Hawk raised his brows. "Do you have any that aren't cowboy?"

Stands Proud chuckled. "Come on," he said. He tossed him the keys. "You drive."

They went outside, got into the truck and Hawk drove them to the center. He parked the truck and got out. His Aunt Jolene saw him and smiled. He said hello to her and waited for Stands Proud to come around the truck.

As soon as they got inside, a group of men greeted Stands Proud and began talking to him. Hawk knew who they were now. They'd been coming by the house. He realized that his father was a part of this group and that Sunka Sapa seemed to be leading it. He also noticed that when Stands Proud said something, Sunka got real quiet and listened. They tried to include Hawk in their discussions but he wasn't ready to talk. It wasn't that he didn't want to. He'd open his mouth to tell them about something that happened but his heart couldn't form the words.

Hawk found an empty chair and sat down. He listened to the drum and watched the people dance. Rafa and Wolf were busy flirting and talking to the girls. His uncles and his grandfather said hello to him when they came in. His aunts were in the kitchen with the rest of the women, preparing the meal. Hawk noticed how busy they were, scurrying about. There were a lot of people in the center to feed. He got up and walked across the floor, opened the kitchen door and went inside. When the women stopped working and got quiet, he grinned.

"You lost nephew?" Jolene asked, putting a bag of potatoes on the counter.

"Of course he is," Leah added, smiling at him. "Everyone knows the men sit out there talking and wait for the food."

Hawk smiled. He took off his long sleeve black shirt, leaving the white muscle T-shirt on and picked up a knife. They stared at him. "I'm going to help," he announced.

"Oh," Jolene said. She looked at the rest of the women.

"Good," Martha said, "You can peel half of these potatoes." She pushed most of the potatoes to his side of the table.

The women laughed.

"Muchas gracias, mi Tia," Hawk said, smiling at her, "for giving me *half*."

"Yeah hey," Leah added, "When you're done with those, I need help with the fry bread."

Hawk smiled and politely nodded. "I asked for this, eh?" He started cutting the potatoes and winked at his Aunt Martha.

"Do you want an apron?" Lindy Whitehorse asked.

Hawk smiled, "Thank you but no. I will catch enough hell for this, eh?"

"Why aren't you out there?" Jolene asked.

"Nothing to do out there but sit, talk and wait for the food," he said. "All the hard work es being done in here."

"Finally, an honest man," Leah announced.

They cheered.

Hawk laughed. He saw Suzy come in with her mother,

Carol, and he lowered his gaze, concentrating on peeling the potatoes.

"We have a new kitchen helper," Martha announced.

Carol studied him.

A few seconds passed. It was too quiet for him. Hawk raised his gaze and looked over at her.

"You're the one aren't you?" she asked.

"The one?" Hawk asked.

"The one who gave my daughter, Carrie, the bandana at the clinic," Carol said. She moved closer to him. "You're Stands Proud's son. The one from New York?"

"Es the one," Hawk admitted. He saw her coming to embrace him and he laid the knife down on the table. He wrapped his arms around her. She began to cry. She clung to him and sobbed. "Es all right," he said softly. "Es all right now."

"Thank you for being nice to Carrie," she said, looking up at him.

Hawk nodded. He smiled sheepishly and pulled another bandana from his pocket and handed it to her.

She laughed a little and took it from him, wiping her tears away. "Thank you," Carol said again.

"*De nada*...eh you're welcome," Hawk said. He picked up the knife and went back to peeling the potatoes.

The women smiled at him and went back to work.

"You like to cook," Jolene said to him. "I can tell."

"Si, I do," Hawk admitted.

"Did you cook *before*," Martha said, "or did you sit around and wait for your wives to feed you."

Hawk gave a hearty laugh.

"Well?" Leah inquired. "You're in here with us. You have to tell."

"I did not have *wives*," Hawk told them, smiling.

"Bah…you had at least one," Leah insisted.

"Ehhhh…." Hawk finished peeling the potatoes and began to cut them into pieces. He smirked. "I cooked," he said.

"You didn't," Martha said, not believing him.

"I did," he told her. "When I was in the village, my mother prepared the meals but I was away a lot on war parties or hunting. We had to eat."

"You didn't tell us about the wife," Lindy piped in.

Hawk picked up the pot of potatoes and carried it to the stove. "No, I didn't," he said, lighting the flame. "Es very sad story," he told them, "and I didn't bring enough bandanas."

"We won't cry," Leah said.

"I know you won't Aunt Leah," Hawk said, knowing her character, "but they will, eh?"

"We'll try not to," Martha said.

"Too much crying es not good, eh?" Hawk told them. He walked over to where Leah was mixing the fry bread dough and he started to help her.

"We promise not to cry," Lindy told him.

"But eh…I might," Hawk said.

They smiled at him.

"Okay you're off the hook for now," Leah told him. "We can't have you crying in the fry bread. What ever you're feeling goes in there. Did you know that?"

"No, I didn't," Hawk said.

"That's right," Leah said. "You weren't on the

reservation, were you?"

"No," Hawk said. "I was in the hills."

"It must have been beautiful then," Leah said.

"Ah it was," Hawk told her. He described the way the land was before, including every detail. He told them how he rode for miles through an endless prairie and talked about the buffalo. Hawk mixed the fry bread and told them the story of how it was long ago. His story was interrupted by loud laughter coming from the main room. Hawk saw Luke and Tommy Eagle Chase pointing and laughing at him.

"You don't have to stay in here," Jolene said, gently. "We're almost done."

"Es all right," Hawk said, taking his hands out of the dough.

"That Luke," Martha said, "now that boy is dumb. He's coming back for more even after you taught him a lesson."

"I didn't teach him anything," Hawk said, quietly. "I only made him angrier and I hit him too hard. I lost control of everything that night."

"They've been giving you a hard time," Leah said. "I'm glad you knocked him on his ass. He's needed that for a long time."

"That's the truth," Lindy said.

"It doesn't justify what I did," Hawk told them. He saw Luke and Tommy coming closer to the kitchen and he sighed heavily. "Stands Proud wanted me to come tonight but I think I'm going to have to leave, eh?" He started for the back door of the kitchen.

"Where are you going?" Leah asked.

"To the house," Hawk told her. He saw her eyes flash. "Aunt Leah," he said, walking over to her. "They're going to start something. I don't want that to happen. The only thing I can do is…"

"Run out the back door?" Leah inquired.

Hawk looked at her. "I don't want to fight."

"Even if you weren't here," Martha said, "they'd be starting something. They always do."

"You want me to stay," Hawk said quietly.

The women all began to talk at once.

"Ok," Hawk said. "I'll stay." He smiled at them and carried the tray of dough over to the stove.

"Good," Jolene said. "Can you reach that pan up there?"

"Who put that way up there?" Martha complained, looking at the tray on the very top shelf.

"I'll get it," Hawk said. He walked over and stepped up on a chair. He took the tray and handed it down to his Aunt Jolene. He heard Rafa's voice and he looked into the main room. Rafa was saying something to Tommy. He stepped down off the chair. "Excuse me, Carol," he said, going past her. He pushed on the kitchen door and went straight to Rafa's side. "Rafa, forget this, eh?" Hawk said. "*Vamanos.*"

"He needs to shut up," Rafa said, pointing at Tommy.

"Not in here Rafa, por favor," Hawk said. "Let it go."

"Do you know what he's saying?"

"I don't care," Hawk said. "There are little kids here tonight. Enough of this." He gently attempted to move his friend back, away from Tommy and Luke. "Let them talk. It doesn't matter."

"They're not getting away with this," Rafa scowled.

"Ok," Hawk said, "but we can't fight in here, eh?" He turned to see that Luke and Tommy had gone elsewhere.

"If we were on Salcida," Rafa told him, "you'd never let anybody talk like that."

"We're not on Salcida Rafa," Hawk reminded him. "This is different."

"Why?"

"It just is," Hawk said, quietly.

"You let them get away with too much, eh?" Rafa accused.

"I didn't let them get away with anything," Hawk argued. "Luke was in the hospital after I beat him, eh? And he's still doing this? There's something wrong with him Rafa."

Rafa muttered angrily and walked away.

Chapter Twenty Six

By the end of the night, all the men had something to say about him being in the kitchen with the women, even Stands Proud, but Hawk didn't care. He didn't want to go to the social anyway. He liked being in the kitchen. It reminded him of when he was small and Mama used to work for catering companies. She would set him on a stool in the corner and all the women would fuss over him. The men could say what they wanted as far as he was concerned, but the women still fussed over him that way and he liked it.

The next morning, Stands Proud still made an occasional wise crack. He'd wanted Hawk to sit with the men and talk. It was important for him to get to know them. He watched as Hawk rolled his eyes, gathered his wallet and the truck keys. "Where are you going?" Stands Proud asked.

"I'm going to the grocery store, eh? We need food. Don't worry; I think es a job for a man, no? I'll be hunting and gathering in several aisles," Hawk muttered.

"I'll go with you," Stands Proud offered. The grocery store was in town. "You might need some help."

"No, no. Por favor, you stay here. Ok?"

"Son, I was just teasing you about being with the women," Stands Proud said.

"I don't care about that, eh? But I can do this alone," Hawk told him. He went out onto the porch and down the steps. He'd spent too much time with his father lately, he thought, because he was ready to punch him in the mouth.

He drove to the grocery store and parked the truck in the lot. Hawk knew Stands Proud was worried about him coming into town but with the training he had, Hawk wasn't concerned at

231

all. It was a regular day at the grocery store, people coming in and out, putting groceries in their cars, and stopping now and then to talk to each other. Hawk got a cart and began to go through the aisles, picking up the food he needed to cook with.

"Hey Hawk," Lindy Whitehorse called out. "How are you?"

Hawk smiled and looked up from reading the label on a jar of picante sauce. "Hi Lindy. You're not working today?" he asked.

"Oh we needed a few things. Tom's watching the place," Lindy said, coming over to him. "Is Stands Proud with you?"

"No, I left him at the house."

"Ah," she said. "Are you having any trouble?"

"No, no…I can't decide whether to get this or not," Hawk said, he put the sauce back on the shelf. "I think I'll make my own."

Lindy smiled at him. "No Hawk, I mean with the ones who were in the parking lot at the Broken Arrow."

"Oh, them?" Hawk shrugged. "No, I haven't seen anyone."

"You be careful," she said. "It can get kind of rough in town but I guess you've had it that way since you got here. I know the men were giving you a bad time about being in the kitchen. You really helped us out a lot."

"I'm glad I could help," he said. "I didn't want to be in the way."

"Oh no, you weren't in the way at all," she patted his arm. "I'll see you later. Ok?"

"Ok," Hawk said. He finished the shopping, went through the check out and loaded the truck. He saw Lindy in the parking lot and he waved, smiling at her. He saw the first one coming when he started for the door of the truck. Hawk backed up and watched the white boy about his age, walking toward him.

"What are you doing in town fag?" the boy demanded.

Hawk moved to where there was more open space. The others came out from behind the cars. He counted six. One with a baseball bat. He almost smirked, watching how mean they tried to look.

"You were told to stay on the rez injun," another one snarled.

"Are you sure this is him? It might be the other one."

"No, Wolf's in school."

Hawk watched them closely. They seemed hesitant. It was broad daylight but there were no police, only a parking lot full of people who had begun to gather to see a fight.

"Leave him alone you thugs!" Lindy's voice called out.

The one carrying the bat drew it backward and aimed for his legs. Hawk jumped over it, spun and lowered into a fighting stance. They rushed at him in an unorganized attack. He tossed them aside as they came, throwing their bodies away from him but not striking to leave any serious damage. A few got back up and tried again. In a few seconds, he'd changed their minds. Hawk remained in the fighting stance and watched as they ran away from the truck, scratched and bruised. He heard Lindy laughing as he stood upright. He smiled at her, waved, and he got into the truck and drove home.

"Lindy called," Stands Proud said, as Hawk came into the house. Hawk put the groceries on the table and began to put them away. "She said you had some trouble in town."

"I took care of it," Hawk said quietly.

"What did they say?" Stands Proud asked.

"I don't know," Hawk said. "I don't listen to what's being

said when I fight. I was watching their shoulders to see who was going to swing first and keeping an eye on where they were standing so I could judge their distance from me."

Stands Proud stared at him. "Oh," he said. "She said they didn't give you too much trouble."

"Eh…" Hawk said, putting the milk in the refrigerator. He shut the door. "Not much," he said. "I didn't hurt anyone."

"I didn't say you did, son," Stands Proud said, "but there will be more next time."

Hawk shrugged. He looked in the bottom of the bag. "Eh, I forgot to get butter," he said.

Stands Proud smirked. "They didn't bother you at all, did they?"

Hawk looked at him. His father's face was still bruised and broken ribs always caused a lot of pain. "Eh…well…" he began.

Stands Proud laughed. "It's ok son. I've got two bad habits when I fight. I'm usually too drunk to walk and I always hear what's being said." Stands Proud went into the living room and sat down, smiling.

Hawk picked the keys up from the table. "I'm going to the Trading Post to get butter," he said. "I need it for tonight, eh?"

Stands Proud grinned and waved him off. He picked up the newspaper and began to read.

Hawk got in the truck and drove down the road. He went into the Trading Post and said hello to Leah. She was behind the counter. His Aunt Leah was a very beautiful woman. She was tall, thin and had long legs. She always wore her hair loose and it fell to the waist of her jeans. He wondered why there was no man with her, until he realized sometimes she was just plain mean to them. "Aunt Leah, where's the butter?" Hawk asked.

"Over there," she said, pointing to the refrigerated case. "We usually try to keep it in a cold place," she snickered.

Hawk smiled at her. When his back was to her, he rolled his eyes. He found the butter and brought it to the counter.

"I heard you were in town," she said, grinning.

"Si, I was," he said. He wondered if Lindy called everyone from the parking lot on her cell phone. "How are you today?" he asked, trying to change the subject.

"I'm fine," Leah said. "Lindy said there were six of them and one had a baseball bat."

Hawk smiled and looked down at the butter on the counter. She hadn't even picked it up. "Si, there were six. They tried to jump me," he said, "but it eh…didn't work out so well for them."

Leah smiled. "That's what I heard nephew," she said, proudly.

Hawk glanced at the butter again. "I'd like to get this into a cold place, eh?"

She laughed. "Okay Silver Hawk," she said. "I guess it's not a big deal to you but it's a very big deal when we go into town and have trouble with those assholes."

"You've had trouble before?"

"Yeah hey," Leah said, ringing up the butter. "They target different people from time to time but the target's always an Indian, always from the rez." She put the butter in a small bag. "Thanks," she said, smiling at him.

Hawk looked at her. Leah rarely wore a full smile. "For what?"

"For throwing them all over the parking lot like a handful of confetti," Leah said, smiling and leaning on the counter. She leaned over and kissed his cheek.

"I didn't do anything," Hawk told her. "It wasn't even a fight, eh?"

She laughed.

Hawk grinned shyly and walked over to the door. "I couldn't fight them Aunt Leah, they fell down too fast." He could hear her laughter as he stepped out onto the porch of the Trading Post. He saw Luke Eagle Chaser standing across the road, watching him. Hawk could see the bulge from the gun under the boy's shirt. He'd taunted Luke before, saying Luke wouldn't shoot the gun, but the more Hawk got to know Luke he was less sure of it. Luke didn't move as Hawk opened the door of the truck. When Hawk drove off, he kept an eye on Luke in the rear view mirror. Luke was standing completely still and staring in his direction.

Late in the afternoon, Hawk was bored because he had nothing to do. Stands Proud fell asleep on the couch and it was too quiet inside the house. He wandered outside. It was still too early for anyone to be home from school. The only person who was around was his Uncle Pete. Pete was underneath of a car trying to fix it. Hawk walked over and stood there. "Need any help?" he asked.

"The only thing you know about cars is how to steal them," Pete's muffled voice said, from under the car.

Hawk laughed. "Es not true."

"Don't you steal anything while I'm under here either," Pete warned.

"Uncle Pete, I borrowed your things, eh? I didn't steal them."

"Don't touch anything."

Hawk smiled as Pete came out from under the car. Pete was Stands Proud's younger brother. They shared a few similar features but Pete had a long jagged scar on the side of his face

236

that no one talked about. Pete stood up and examined him with a look. "I didn't touch anything Uncle Pete, honest," Hawk said, trying to convince him.

"You should know better than to steal something of an Indian," Pete muttered. He went over to the tool box and dropped the wrench in.

"Eh…an Indian stealing from another Indian es called a raid, no?"

Pete's muscles bulged on his stocky frame as he stared at his nephew. "Don't you have anything else to do?" he asked. "Where'd your China man go?"

"Khan es Japanese," Hawk told him, "and no, I don't have anything to do."

"Go jump around for a while, do those fancy kicks."

Hawk grinned and looked away. "I did that this morning."

"What's the old man doing?"

"He's asleep," Hawk told him. He followed Pete and looked at the engine underneath the hood. Pete glanced at him. Hawk shrugged.

"Why aren't you in school?" Pete inquired.

"I'm finished with that," Hawk said. "I mean…I have a diploma."

"You graduated already?"

"Si."

"See what?"

"Yes, I graduated," Hawk said. He watched as Pete worked on the engine of the car.

"Lindy said you whooped ass on those white boys this morning," Pete said.

Hawk sighed and stood upright. "Did she call you too?"

"No, Lindy called Leah, Leah called your dad and your dad called me," Pete told him. "You better be more careful," he warned.

"I didn't hurt them. I just defended myself, eh?"

"You pissed them off is what you did. It'll get worse now," Pete said.

"They don't even know how to fight," Hawk said.

Pete stood up from underneath the hood. He tapped the jagged scar on his cheek with a screw driver. "Where do you think this came from?" he asked.

"Those boys?" Hawk asked weakly.

"No, not those boys. There are more people behind them than you realize," Pete said. "This isn't anything new just because you rolled onto the rez. This has been going on as long as I can remember *hoksila.*"

"Who's behind them?" Hawk asked.

"The whole town," Pete said.

"Why?"

"Why?" Pete asked roughly. "Because they're white and we're not. That's why." He lowered and went back under the hood. "You should've left when your dad told you to."

"You knew about that?" Hawk asked.

"Everyone knows about it," Pete said. "Once they decide they're going to get you, they'll get you and don't think all that fancy fighting is going to save your ass. Trust me; they increase in number and strength real fast."

"Why did they cut you?" Hawk asked.

Pete stood up again. "Are you listening to me at all?" he asked. "Nothing has changed Silver Hawk," he said very plainly.

"We're here on a reserved land and they got everything else around it. You see that field back there between here and the Paha Sapa? That's not ours anymore. Why do you think I yell at you? That bastard Mr. Lawson calls every time he sees my horses out there. He says they're ruining his field."

"I didn't know," Hawk said quietly.

"Listen, if you're going to stay here you better get caught up on things quick," Pete advised. "The old ways are gone. This is a new time we're living in. The only thing that remains the same is that we're Indian. That's all."

Hawk nodded and walked away. He didn't like the way his Uncle raised his voice and he didn't like what the man said either.

"They'll come after you harder now," Pete called out.

Hawk walked over to the porch and sat down on the step. He looked up on the hillside and saw Luke standing by the basketball court staring at him. Hawk stood up and started walking toward him. Luke disappeared, fast.

Chapter Twenty Seven

Hawk went up to the basketball court and sat in the bleachers. From that spot, he could out over the reservation. The trucks and cars came and went from the Trading Post. The school bus came down the road. His Aunt Martha returned from working at the clinic. She seemed ok but tired. A group of men gathered in front of the Trading Post and walked over to Sunka's house. Hawk sighed, wondering if it had anything to do with what he'd done in town. He knew he'd hear about it soon enough. Hawk heard footsteps on the asphalt and he turned around.

"Hello Hawk," Bruce said, smiling. "Enjoying your little vacation?"

Hawk stood up, staring at him. "Where did you come from?" he asked. He couldn't believe he hadn't seen Bruce until he was this close, too close.

"Don't be so nervous kid. I just came for a visit," Bruce said. He took a long drag from his cigarette. "So, this is where you've been hiding. A little on the desolate side, isn't it?"

"What do you want?" Hawk asked, cautiously coming down from the bleachers and onto the asphalt.

"Have you been fighting any matches?"

"No."

"I didn't think so. I'd have heard about it if you were," Bruce said. "There's an arena being held not too far from here. You interested?"

"No, I'm not."

Bruce laughed. "Some how I knew you'd say that," he said.

"Look Bruce, I don't want anything to do with that anymore." Hawk scowled at him. "You can just go, eh?"

"Go?" Bruce laughed again. "No, I don't think so. I don't think you understand the situation here, kid. Let me explain it to you. I've got a few of our old friends waiting off the next exit, down the Interstate. So…if you start any shit with me, you've been warned. Understand?"

Hawk gave a frustrated sigh. This wasn't happening, he told himself, it wasn't. He ran a hand nervously through his long black hair.

"Are your dad's ribs healed up yet?" Bruce asked.

Hawk looked at him.

Bruce smiled. "Isn't it amazing? With the right amount of cash, you can purchase anything in this world, kid. You'd know that if you hadn't given away all of Don Antone's money." He took another drag from the cigarette, blew the smoke into the air and watched the kid's face. "Hell kid, you could have bought your freedom."

"I have my freedom," Hawk said, quietly.

Bruce laughed. "You took down the head of the Tassiano organization; I'll give you that much credit but the body is still fully functional. Do you understand what I'm saying to you?"

"You're full of shit Bruce," Hawk said angrily.

"Am I?" Bruce asked, smiling at him. "The east coast was a little crowded since you gave all of Don Antone's business to Gambriotti but this is the land of opportunity, isn't it?" He grinned. "You put about a hundred of us out of work, kid. We're just looking for a way back, a way to raise some serious cash. And guess who came to mind?"

Hawk swallowed, hard. He stepped back, away from Bruce. "I can't fight anymore. I hurt my leg and I suck at it." He shrugged. "Sorry."

Bruce laughed. "Nice try kid," he said. "We know Khan was here. You re-trained yourself. How convenient is that?" Bruce drew his head slowly back and forth, smiling at him. "You should know better than to lie to me, Hawk," he said.

"What do you want?" Hawk asked, anxiously. He looked down the road. Wolf, Rafa and Suzy would be coming any minute.

"Let's go," Bruce said.

"What?"

"I said, let's go," Bruce told him. He dropped the cigarette butt on the asphalt and ground it out with his shoe. "You're coming with me."

"Ah no I'm not," Hawk said, backing up.

"Go ahead. Run you little fuck," Bruce said, "and dear old dad will get more than a few busted ribs." He paused. "Your whole family lives here, right? Your brother, aunts, uncles…your grandfather." Bruce laughed and pointed a finger at Hawk. "You fucked up," he said. "Your head must have been twisted on ass backwards when you left the city. You led me straight to your entire family."

"I can get some of the business back Bruce," Hawk said quickly, "I can…"

"Let's go," Bruce said, lowering his voice.

Hawk saw Wolf, Rafa and Suzy coming and he knew he had no time left. He didn't want Bruce anywhere near them. "Okay," he said. "All right, I'll go with you." He walked down the hillside with Bruce. The man was right, he'd screwed up. If Tassiano's men came to the rez with their guns, in no time at all, a lot of people would be hurt. "Shit," he muttered as he got into the car.

"Well, there's your brother," Bruce said, starting the engine, "and that shit bag Rafa. Who's the girl?"

242

"Leave them out of this," Hawk said. "I'll do anything you want, just leave them alone."

Bruce drove slowly past the three teenagers, crawling past Wolf, Rafa and Suzy.

"Come on Bruce," Hawk said, nervously. "You don't need them for anything. You got me."

"Yeah I do," Bruce said, looking over and smiling at him. "Don't I?" He saw the kid in the middle of the road with a gun aimed straight at the windshield of the car. Bruce floored the gas pedal and the kid's body slammed off the front end and rolled to the side of the road.

Hawk gasped sharply and turned to see Luke lying motionless in the grass. He lowered his face into his hand.

"Who the fuck was that?" Bruce muttered, swerving the car onto the highway.

Hawk's entire body shook. "Damn you Bruce," he whispered.

"What the fuck?" Bruce demanded. He shook his head and swore loudly. "You fuckin' Indians man. You fuckin' Indians are crazy."

The car sped down the road, the tires spraying dust until it reached the highway. Bruce raced to the next exit. A truck was parked on the side of the road with more of Tassiano's men, armed and waiting. They opened the back of the truck.

"Get in," Bruce ordered.

Cheetah felt the sweat trickling down the back of his neck. He knew once he got inside of the truck, the door would be locked.

"I said," Bruce repeated, "get in."

Cheetah climbed up into the truck and backed up. He watched as the men laughed and closed the doors. The lock slammed into place. It was dark. There was nothing else inside of it except for him. He sat down as the truck began to move, listening to the tires humming beneath the truck, as it traveled down the Interstate. There was nothing he could do. The men knew him well enough to know there were things he could not fight against, stun guns, a gun aimed at him from a distance and the pinch of a needle filled with heroin. They also knew he would do anything to protect the people he loved and they saw that as his weakness.

As he sat in the corner, on the floor of the truck, Hawk tried not to think. He didn't want to think about what Rafa thought when he saw Bruce. He didn't want to wonder what Stands Proud had said. He definitely wanted to erase from his mind the sight of Luke Eagle Chaser's body rolling over the hood of the car and falling, limp, to the ground.

When the door was opened, Hawk couldn't guess how long he'd been in the truck or how far he'd gone. He had no idea where he was. He stood up and walked from the back of the truck, to the edge, where the men were waiting. The bright fluorescent lights nearly blinded him as he stood there.

"Bring him down here," a voice said.

"Get down Hawk," Bruce ordered.

Hawk jumped from the truck and landed on his feet. He was surrounded by men in suits and beyond them; he could see that he was inside of a warehouse. The men were armed. Some of them he knew but many more of them, he didn't.

"So, this is Hawk," a man said, stepping forward. "Tassiano's best fighter."

Hawk watched the man circle around him slowly. The man was only about five years older than he was, tall; broad shouldered and appeared to be strong. He wore a suit, covered by a long black overcoat. His hair was jet black and his piercing blue eyes examined Hawk as he walked around him.

244

"Twenty five," the man said stopping and looking over at Bruce.

"Thirty," Bruce said. "Trust me, you'll get it back. You've seen him fight."

Hawk looked at Bruce, and then at the man. They were negotiating a price for him. He was being sold! His chest began to rise and fall. He looked around, looking for a way to run. There wasn't one. They'd expected his reaction and the guns were out from beneath their suit jackets and in their hands, ready to fire.

"Does he have any wounds?" the man asked.

"Take off your coat and your shirt kid," Bruce said.

Hawk glared at Bruce.

"Do it," Bruce warned. "I can always go back to that reservation. Don't force my hand Hawk."

Hawk looked at the man who was apparently buying him. He slowly removed the trench coat and dropped it on the cement floor. Silently, he pulled the white muscle T-shirt up over his head and stood with it dangling from his fingertips. His anger smoldered inside of him like hot molten lava waiting to erupt.

"Don Antone beat the hell out of him, didn't he?" the man said, studying the scars.

"Hawk can be difficult to handle," Bruce said, giving an explanation, "but properly motivated, he'll be ten times worth the investment."

The man approached Hawk and looked into his eyes. "Are you worth thirty million dollars?" the man asked.

Hawk's rage increased. His breathing quickened. "No," he said.

A slow smile came to the man's lips.

The men laughed.

"How much are you worth?" the man inquired. He tilted his head slightly and rubbed his chin with a finger, waiting for the young man's reaction.

"I've been shot four times, whipped seven times and stabbed twice," Hawk told him. "I'm not worth shit."

The men laughed again.

The man smiled. "Thirty five," he said. He shrugged. "I like his attitude," the man joked. The warehouse filled with laughter.

"Sold," Bruce said.

Hawk looked over at Bruce, seething with fury. "I'll find you," he promised. He felt a sharp jab of a needle into his arm. He grabbed his arm and turned. The faces of the men began to blur and he felt himself slipping away, falling into darkness.

When Hawk awoke, he found he was lying on a white tile floor. Around him were walls that appeared to be glass. He could see a few men in suits watching him and nodding. One of the men took a cell phone from his pocket but Hawk couldn't hear what he was saying. He looked down and found he was wearing a clean pair of fighting pants. His long black hair was still damp but not brushed. He had no memory of what happened after Bruce had sold him.

The man who had bought him, his new owner, came into the room with the other men. Hawk watched him as he came toward the see through wall and pressed a button on a panel. "How are you feeling?" the man asked.

Hawk tore his gaze away from the man and stared at the floor.

"Are you hungry?"

Hawk ignored him. The man went away. It wasn't long before the isolation of the room began to drive him crazy. The walls weren't glass. He found this out by delivering a powerful high front kick to one of them and discovering the wall would not break. He began to pace back and forth. The man came back. Hawk stopped and turned, looking directly at him.

"If I let you out of there," the man said, "will you calm down?" He waited for the young man to speak. He hadn't uttered a single word since he'd been brought from the warehouse. "Hawk, no harm will come to you if you can calm down and control yourself."

Hawk nodded his head.

"Do you want to come out?" the man asked.

"Yes," Hawk said. The man motioned to the others and they pressed a few buttons, a code, into another panel. A door he didn't know was there slid open.

"Come out," the man said.

Hesitantly, Hawk left the isolation room.

"Follow me," the man told him.

Hawk walked behind the man and the other men surrounded him on all sides. He discovered that the isolation room was a part of a large richly decorated house. The lush emerald green carpet felt odd beneath his bare feet. He followed the man into another room where a table had been set.

"Please, sit down," the man said.

Hawk slowly pulled out the chair at the head of the table and sat down.

The man laughed and sat down at Hawk's right. "I usually sit there," he said, smiling, "but considering your fight record, I don't think I'll argue with you over a chair." He motioned with his hand. "Bring the food, please." He looked at the young man. "My name is Richard," he said. "Richard Dean." He paused but received no response. "What do you prefer to be called?" he asked.

"What difference does it make?" Hawk asked. "I'm a piece of property to you. Call me whatever you want."

Richard Dean smiled and straightened his shoulders. "All right, I'll call you Harry or maybe Charlie."

Hawk sneered at him.

The man smiled. "Listen, I'm well aware of how you were treated at Tassiano Estates. You will not be treated in that manner under my..."

"Ownership?" Hawk inquired.

"True," Richard stated, "but I am *not* Don Antone."

"I don't care who you are," Hawk told him, turning his face away.

"But I care very much about who you are," Richard said. "You've only been taken down three times in the past nine years, is that true?"

"Yes," Hawk told him.

Richard nodded. "You're considered a master of martial arts and you know several other forms of fighting as well?"

"Yes."

The food was brought to the table and served. Hawk looked at the food but he wasn't able to eat it. Again, he looked away.

"Is something wrong with your food?" Richard asked. "Would you like something else?"

"No, I can't eat."

"Why not?" Richard asked. "It's been three days. You must be hungry."

"Three days?" Hawk asked. He thought he'd only been there for a night. Memory, time and everything else was a blur in his mind.

"The sedative was strong but you slept longer than I anticipated," Richard said. "You must've been very tired."

"Eh well…" Hawk said quietly. "I…I don't eat much. I get sick a lot. I think you wasted your money."

"I don't think so," Richard said. "Eat whatever you can. You should try to eat some thing." He ate and watched the young man. "I suppose I wouldn't feel very good if I were bought or sold," he said.

Hawk's eyes met and held Richard Dean's gaze. "Why are you doing this?" he asked.

"I don't understand what you mean," Richard said. He stopped eating and gave the young man his full attention.

"You don't have to be kind to someone you own," Hawk stated.

"Would you have rather stayed in the hands of Tassiano's men?" Richard inquired.

"I'd rather…go home," Hawk said. He swallowed, hard and lowered his chin. He hadn't wanted to feel any emotion. He'd tried to remain numb to it all and when his eyes filled with tears, he became angry at himself.

"A fighter with your skill, of your caliber, is virtually non-existent," Richard said. "There is one fighter in the Philippine Islands who is coming very close…"

"I don't care," Hawk said.

"If you don't care about fighting, why did you invite Khan of Okinawa to come and stay with you at the reservation?" Richard asked. "You must have some feeling for the sport of it?"

"Not in the arena," Hawk told him.

"That's understandable," Richard said. "How do you feel about it otherwise?"

"I feel I've been forced to do too much of it."

Richard suppressed a smile. "I see," he said gently. "Hawk, if I may call you that, I'm not involved in the organized crime syndicate or any other criminal activities…"

"Who are you?" Hawk asked, interrupting him.

"I told you," the man said, "My name is Richard Dean. I'm not surprised that you don't know who I am. I tried to talk with you several times. Don Antone went to great lengths to keep you away from any one who might be interested in your abilities. I've seen you fight but I've never able to speak with you which is why, when I heard Bruce Muldone was accepting offers, I made one of my own." He paused and looked at the young man. "I've seen what you can do under threats and intimidation. I am very curious to find out how you would fight if you were not oppressed in such a violent manner."

"I wouldn't," Hawk said. "I hate to fight."

Richard laughed. "You're joking." He leaned back in the chair and smiled. "You can't be telling the truth."

"I never liked it." The man started laughing again and Hawk stared at him.

"Well," Richard said, grinning. "This joke is on me then, isn't it? I just wasted thirty five million dollars. I hope my father stays in Greece for a long time." He paused and explained. "I'm very interested in the underground fighting arenas but only to watch the fighters." He reached into the pocket of his suit coat and laid an envelope on the table.

"What es that?" Hawk asked.

"Your plane ticket home," Richard said. "If you don't want to fight, or as you've said, hate to fight…you're not what I'm looking for." He saw the confusion in Hawk's eyes. "I bought you, yes, but that was the only way to get you from Bruce. I'm not holding you against your will."

"What about the room?" Hawk asked.

"Well, they told me that you might run," Richard said, "and I wanted to be able to talk to you first. Also, that room is rather interesting. It was a kind of a test."

"A test?" Hawk asked him.

"Yes," Richard admitted. "Those walls are built to record any pressure from the inside. When you kicked the wall I was able to measure the force of the kick. It was rather impressive. But mostly, I didn't want you to run off. I'm sorry if you were uncomfortable."

"What about them?" Hawk asked, looking at the armed men.

"Are you kidding? They've been with me since I was three years old," Richard said. "They aren't guarding you, Hawk. They're my body guards, good friends as well."

"You're not going to make me stay?" Hawk asked.

Richard smiled. "No, I told you I'm not Don Antone," he said. "I was hoping that you would *want* to fight. I wanted to see how well you'd do if you were actually able to do it with some heart." He paused. "That's the only thing missing when you fight Silver Hawk. You're heart isn't in it. I understand why…it's just never been there."

Hawk laid his hand on the plane ticket. "What about your thirty five million dollars?" he asked.

Richard shrugged and grinned. "My father will chew my ass for a few months but it will be forgotten. Look at it this way; you won't have to worry about Tassiano's goon squad anymore. Now you have a new owner who can't make you fight. Hell, I'm afraid to ask for my chair back."

Hawk smirked. "I can leave if I want?" he asked, still not entirely convinced.

"Sure but I…" Richard hesitated. "Sure. You can go whenever you're ready. I'd like to hear about Khan though and those fights with Belerignio. I heard the two of you are friends."

"We still are," Hawk said, "but I haven't seen him in a while."

"And you're Indian, right? Sioux Indian?" Richard asked.

"Teton Oglala, Lakota," Hawk told him. He paused then quietly asked, "What do you do?"

"Me?" Richard smiled. "I uh…well; I travel and waste my father's money." He grinned. "I have a few interests. I travel. I like the races…horses or cars…and the fights."

"You're bored as hell," Hawk remarked.

"Yes, I'm bored as hell," Richard admitted, "Why else would I pay my body guards extra to act like thugs and take me into a dangerous situation with known criminals to buy a human being. Yes, Hawk, I'm bored as hell." He grinned and looked at Hawk. "I heard you gave away Don Antone's money."

"Es right, I did."

"Good for you," Richard said, "because money is nothing but a comfortable prison." He raised the wine glass, and then drank from it.

Chapter Twenty Eight

The next morning, Hawk called Stands Proud and told his father that he was in Aspen, Colorado and that he was okay. He explained the situation the best he could, reassuring Stands Proud that he wasn't in any danger. He learned that Luke was alive and that he was wanted for questioning but no were charges filed. When Stands Proud asked him about coming home, Hawk said he would come as soon as he could. After he hung up the phone, he went across the hall and told Richard he could stay for a few days.

"Great," Richard said. "I'm dying to hear what Khan is really like. I've only seen him standing on the sidelines with you. I've never seen him fight. Is he as great as they claim he is?"

Hawk smiled. "Better," he said. He told Richard about doing the fourteenth drill on the roof top and how well Khan did it. "He's amazing."

Richard nodded. "Come on," he said. "I want to show you something." He led Hawk down the hall, down the stairs and through another room. "I have this entire room filled with pictures of old fighters, new ones and some other things I think you might like."

Hawk stepped into the room and his gaze traveled over the walls. There were ancient swords and knives mounted above small plaques, telling where the item was acquired. He saw the large black and white photo of Khan and he smiled. Then his gazed focused on something he'd never seen before, a photo of him spinning in mid-air before delivering a double kick. Hawk stared at it.

"I took that photo," Richard said. "I hope you don't mind."

Hawk didn't know what to say. He studied the position of his feet, legs and where his arms and hands were held. "Es perfect," he whispered.

"What?" Richard asked.

Hawk moved closer to the photograph. "The kick…es perfect."

Richard laughed. "Sure it is. It's you."

"But I…" Hawk paused. "I've never seen myself fighting."

"No?" Richard asked, grinning. "You'll really like this." He pushed a few buttons and an image appeared on a huge screen on the wall. "Remember this fight?" he asked.

Hawk stared, hard at the screen. He fought twenty men that night and he was moving with an acquired precision, kicking, blocking and taking the men down. He moved closer. Every move was perfect. The fight was over. He'd won but Don Antone angrily crossed the floor and backhanded him across the face. Hawk turned away from the screen and closed his eyes.

"I…I'm sorry," Richard said. "I let that run too long. I…"

"Es all right," Hawk said quietly.

Silence wedged into the room and swelled between them.

"You fought without a single mistake that night," Richard said. "Why did he hit you?"

"Run the tape back," Hawk said. "Go ahead, es all right. I'll show you. Ok. There. Right there. Es why?"

"What? I don't see anything."

"I talked to the emcee," Hawk said. "I wasn't allowed to talk to anyone." Again, he watched as he fought in the arena that night. His gaze returned to the photograph on the wall.

"Does the picture bother you?" Richard asked.

"Es old ways belief that if someone takes your image, they capture your soul," Hawk told him.

"Really?" Richard asked. "Well if I got it, I'll keep it here and take care of it. I won't do anything weird with it," he joked. He saw that Hawk was very serious. "Do you believe that?"

"I don't know," Hawk said, honestly.

"You can have it," Richard said, "just in case. When you're ready to leave I'll have it wrapped for you."

Hawk gave him a surprised look. "You're giving it to me?"

"Sure," Richard smirked. "I spend a lot of time in this house alone. I'm not comfortable with the idea that your soul might be wandering around loose in here."

Hawk laughed at him. "I should tell you a few other stories about me some time," he teased. He looked at the photograph again.

"You keep looking at that picture as if you're seeing something you don't believe," Richard stated.

"Es the kick…es perfect," Hawk said again.

"All of your kicks are," Richard told him.

"They had to be," Hawk said, "but es all together different doing it and looking at it, frozen, like this."

"Well, I can't fight at all," Richard said, "but I know what it's supposed to look like and you're right, that is perfect."

"Eh…how much do you know about fighting?" Hawk asked him.

"I just like to watch it," Richard said.

"What were you planning on doing with me?" Hawk inquired.

"Hell, I wouldn't have to know, would I?" Richard said. "I'd just finance everything until you're career took off…and you could do it, if you wanted to."

"To make more money?"

"If that's what you want," Richard said. "Fuck money. I'm a billionaire's son, Hawk. I don't need anything and I certainly don't want any more of it."

"What would you get from it?" Hawk asked.

"Freedom," Richard said. "I get to witness freedom."

"Freedom?"

"Look at that picture," Richard said, pointing at it. He moved closer to it. "You are free at this moment. No one is around you. No one is bothering you. No one can. You're flying through the air. You are completely free."

Hawk rolled his eyes. "I wasn't free," he said, "You should give your money away. Es doing terrible things to you."

Richard laughed. "I do give a lot of it away," he said, "but dad is so good at finding more of it. I tried to run away a few times. You can't really…when you have six body guards."

Hawk laughed. "You just wanted to travel and have me fight, eh?"

"Yeah," Richard said. "There's not a lot of excitement in my life. I thought maybe we could go to the fights, drink and carry on pretty much all over the world."

Hawk smiled. "Ah," he said. "Good business plan, Mr. New Owner."

Richard laughed and shrugged.

"For one thing," Hawk said, "the fighting and drinking does not work out so well for me, eh? I can do it. I win but it makes me very sick and throw up all night." He paused. "If I would've said yes, where would this first fight be?"

"Actually, I thought we'd go to the Philippine Islands," Richard said, "and check out this new fighter. He's damn good. But you hate to fight…"

Hawk shrugged. "I've only lost one fight in the past four years," he said. "Maybe I wouldn't have to fight so much, eh? It would be over quick enough."

Richard looked at him. "Are you saying…you'll go?"

"One or two," Hawk told him. "I want to find out something for myself."

"Yeah? What's that?"

Hawk looked at the picture of him in mid-air. "I want to find out if there es total freedom in that moment."

"I guess you didn't feel that way when you fought for Don Antone," Richard said, quietly. "What was that moment about for you? What were you feeling?"

"Fear," Hawk stated.

"Fear?" Richard asked.

"Fear of failure," Hawk said, still looking at the photograph. "Failure is unacceptable."

Chapter Twenty Nine

"The fights are tonight in Manila," Richard explained as they traveled through the airport, "but I have a place here in Northern Palawan. Is that all right?"

"Es fine," Hawk said. Traveling with Richard was different and much more pleasant than when he was taken to the Philippine Islands with Don Antone. He had always been brought in by private jet just before the matches and taken away as soon as they were over. He'd never been allowed to see the islands.

It was hot and the tropical air blew from the China Sea. There were many native people in the streets, vendors and tourists.

"I like it here," Richard said, smiling. He led Hawk down to the shoreline. "We'll reach my place faster by boat," he said. They boarded and he noticed Hawk wasn't saying much. "Is something wrong?"

"No," Hawk said. He felt the wind blowing through his hair and the sun on his face. "I've never seen this," he said.

"You've been to the Philippines hundreds of times," Richard said.

"Not like this," Hawk told him.

"You can see my place from here," Richard said, pointing out a beach house on the near by island. "It's very primitive, a shack really, but I like it." He tossed his pack over his shoulder and climbed out. He was wearing an aqua green barong tagalong shirt, the traditional shirt of the islands. The wind tousled his hair about and he was smiling.

Hawk nodded and waited for the boat to slowly dock at the shoreline. He heard some people chattering behind him and he turned. They were pointing at him and talking. They didn't have to whisper because he didn't know what they were saying. He smirked.

"They recognize you," Richard said, grinning. "I bet you could collect a hundred girls tonight."

Hawk laughed and got off the boat. "Do you want me to fight, eh?"

"Of course," Richard said, "but we could go to the clubs before hand."

Hawk smiled and came to a halt, standing in the white sand. "You are a terrible owner," he said. "You eh, shouldn't let your fighter near women before a fight."

"Oh," Richard said, shyly. He smiled. "You're right."

Hawk laughed and they walked up to the beach house. "If you want to go to a club, pick up some women or something you can. I can prepare for the fights alone, eh?"

"I don't have any use for…" Richard's voice faltered.

Hawk looked at him. He saw the flash of embarrassment in Richard's clear blue eyes. "Are you gay?" Hawk asked. He'd had suspicions but he wasn't sure.

"Yes," Richard said, quietly. When Hawk didn't say anything Richard sighed. "I should've told you."

"I'm not," Hawk said hoarsely.

"I know," Richard said.

"How did you know?" Hawk asked, watching him.

"I uh…asked a few people," Richard admitted. He released a nervous sigh and tried not to look at Hawk. Hawk had an exotic appearance which was very appealing to him. His flowing dark hair, tan skin and finely chiseled features were, well, Richard thought, perfect. What Richard found most attractive and intriguing was Hawk's intense gaze and his unusual dark eyes.

259

"Hell, you're..." Richard began softly, "Uh well, never mind. If you want to leave, I'll understand."

Hawk smirked. He started to laugh. "You're…interested in me?"

Richard sighed and smirked. "I'm sorry," he said, "I'm sure that makes you uncomfortable." He paused then added, "I'm not like Antonio. I'm gay. I don't know what was wrong with Antonio. Rape is rape."

Hawk nodded silently. Everyone, it seemed, had read the papers or saw it on the news. Young boy brutally raped repeatedly, Hawk thought, and forced to engage in sexual activities with various men. He felt his stomach roll and felt like he'd be sick.

Richard saw Hawk's entire face change, drain of color, emotion and his beautiful eyes grew cold. "I'm sorry," Richard said, hoarsely. "I…I shouldn't have said anything." Hawk seemed to be elsewhere, not hearing him or acknowledging the rest of the world. "Hawk?"

Hawk turned his head and looked at Richard. "Es all right," he said, quietly.

"No it's not," Richard said. He walked toward the beach house. "A long time ago, some boys I was with found out I was gay." He glanced at Hawk, "I was beaten very badly. I still have nightmares because of it," he said. He walked up onto the porch and stood in front of the door. "If you want to leave because I'm gay," Richard stated, "and that makes you uncomfortable, I understand."

Hawk could still hear Luke and Tommy Eagle Chaser taunting him. Hey fag, they had said, where you going fag? Luke wanted to kill him because he suspected Hawk might be gay. He leaned against the house. "Are you going to hit on me?" Hawk asked, rather bluntly.

Richard grinned and opened the door. "I'll try not to," he

said.

Hawk laughed at him and followed him into the beach house. "Good because I have to concentrate very hard to win the fights, eh?"

"You'll stay then?" Richard asked.

"I told you I'd fight for you," Hawk said. "Es what I'm going to do."

"Don't do it for me," Richard told him. "That's not the point. I want you to fight because *you* want it."

Hawk nodded with understanding. There were fights, a very, very long time ago that he went into with all of his heart. In this life time, he'd never experienced that feeling, not even with Los Caballeros.

"I can get you anything you want," Richard said. "Is there anything you need to be ready for tonight?"

"No, eh…just a hard flat surface with a lot of space," Hawk said, "and a pair of boots, light weight with steel toes."

"There's a deck in the back of the house," Richard told him, "I'll have the boots delivered. Anything else?"

Hawk shook his head. "No, es fine." He noticed the house was empty. "Where are your body guards?"

"At the clubs," Richard said. "I always send them there. If my father knew, he'd be furious but I hate being guarded constantly."

"Why do you need them?" Hawk asked.

"When I was little, my father was afraid I'd be kidnapped for ransom," Richard said. "I guess he still thinks that now even though I'm twenty four. I understand, I mean, I can't fight for shit."

"Do you want me to teach you to defend yourself?" Hawk asked. "I am a master. I'm qualified to teach."

Richard smiled and his face flushed. "Thanks but...I don't think so."

"Ah..." Hawk said, with a smirk. He walked to the back of the house and moved a curtain away from a sliding glass door. There was an expansive wooden deck connecting to the house and meeting up with the sand of the beach.

"Will that be okay?"

"Perfect," Hawk said.

"Take any room you want," Richard said, flopping down on the couch.

Hawk looked over at him. "What are you going to do?" he asked.

"Sleep," Richard said.

Hawk laughed again. "You are a horrible owner," he said. "Don't you care at all if I win?"

"If you lose, you lose," Richard said, tiredly. "It's never about the end result, is it? Life is about the journey of getting there." He closed his eyes and folded his arms over his chest. "Winning would be nice though," he added.

"I'll see what I can do," Hawk told him, smiling. He laughed and went out onto the back deck while his new owner completely ignored him and soon fell fast asleep. Hawk began going through the drills, one after another, under the heat of the sun and the gentle breeze from the sea cooled his skin. He didn't mind doing the drills outside. In fact, he'd begun to prefer it. For too many years Hawk had been kept in the training room. The only time Tassiano put him in the courtyard was if it were snowing or raining, to strengthen his obedience, he was told. But here, with the sun shining and the palm trees swaying around him, the drills took on more rhythm moving with the earth and not apart from it. Hawk heard a horrendous scream full of pain from inside the house. He slid the door open quickly and went inside.

He saw Richard sitting upright on the couch, with his face buried in his hands. Hawk swallowed, hard and turned his face away.

Richard gave a weary glance over his shoulder but didn't speak.

"Are you all right?" Hawk asked, in a raspy voice.

"Yeah," Richard said quietly. "I'm sorry."

Hawk walked into the living room and sat down in a chair. He didn't say anything but decided to sit there until Richard stopped shaking.

"I can't control that," Richard said. "It's the nightmares... the scream scares the hell out of everyone who stays with me. I can't do anything about it."

Hawk nodded and sighed. "Do you have any neighbors close by?" he asked.

"Why?"

"Because eh…the sounds coming from here tonight might seem…odd."

Richard looked at him.

"I have nightmares too," Hawk told him.

"I can understand why you would," Richard said. "Do you scream?"

Hawk smirked and tried to hide it with a hand.

A small smile came to Richard's lips. "No," he said, "there aren't any neighbors close by."

"Es good," Hawk said. A laugh escaped him.

"I'll say," Richard agreed. Nervously, he got up and went into the kitchen. "Are you hungry yet?" he asked.

"No," Hawk told him. "I'll eat later, after the match." He shook his head. His new owner tried to set him up with women and fill his stomach before the fights. It was strikingly clear that Richard Dean didn't know shit about managing a fighter. Hawk wasn't sure but he began to think Richard paid thirty five million dollars to gain a friend. Richard's cell phone never rang. He didn't call anyone, either, Hawk noticed. Except for the body guards, it seemed as if Richard were completely alone and isolated from the rest world.

Richard came into the room with a huge piece of pineapple cake on a china plate. "Do you want some of this? It's very good."

Hawk threw his head back and laughed, hard.

Chapter Thirty

They entered the arena together. Richard Dean was wearing another traditional shirt and a pair of khaki pants. The heat of the islands made suits completely stifling and uncomfortable. It was acceptable to show up at formal events dressed this way and Richard was glad. Hawk wore the new steel toed boots, a pair of black fighting pants and a black muscle T-shirt. His long black hair was in a single braid down his back.

"Do you know what to do?" Hawk asked Richard.

"I have no clue," Richard said, turning and looking at the massive swarm of people around him.

"See that table over there?" Hawk asked, pointing it out. "Enter me in as many fights as you can and bet on me to win. I'll take care of the rest."

"How many times do you want to fight?" Richard asked.

Hawk stared at him. He'd never heard that question before. "Richard," he said, "I don't know how to answer that, eh? I can fight eight times, perfectly. After that, you might see something a little bit off. You decide."

"Okay," Richard said. He went over to the table.

Hawk stood in the arena, completely unguarded, and he felt lost.

"Hey Hawk!" a familiar voice called out. The young Japanese boy approached him. "Remember me?"

Hawk hesitated and then he realized there was no one to stop him from speaking. He smiled at the boy. "Hey Kenji, how are you?"

"Very good," he said. "I hope I'm not fighting you today. I want to win."

Hawk laughed. "I hope you do well," he said.

"I know you will," Kenji assured him. "I'm glad you're here. Why are you talking to me?"

"Because I can," Hawk said, "and because I've wanted to for a long time but I wasn't allowed. I'm not with Don Antone anymore."

"You have a new manager?" Kenji asked.

"I do," Hawk told him. Suddenly, people surrounded him and tried to talk with him. They asked questions and moved in closer. Hawk was surprised and flattered but the crush of the spectators wasn't something he'd ever experienced. There were too many of them, he thought. What could they all want?

"Hey!" Richards's voice called out. "Back up people, leave him alone! Don't step on those thirty five million dollar toes of his! Let's go…give him some air." He gently moved people away from Hawk. "We're going to have to find a better place for you to stand," Richard said.

"They heard me talking to Kenji," Hawk explained. "I don't know what happened."

Richard smiled. "You have no idea how many people are dying to talk with you," he said. "You're very popular, especially here. The native people believe you're more of a spirit than human. They fear it but they love it."

"What?" Hawk asked. He stopped short. "What did you say?"

"These people," Richard explained, "have a story going around that some how you're connected to a spirit world, an after life type of place and that some how you are still in this world also. I know it sounds crazy but a lot of the people, especially the kids, think of you as…some kind of supernatural hero."

"Why do they believe this?" Hawk asked.

"Well," Richard explained, "the native people claim that when you fight... something strange happens, a shift of some sort, and they see..." Richard's voice trailed off and went flat. "This sounds dumb. I'm sorry."

"No," Hawk said, "tell me. What do they see?"

"An old warrior," Richard said. "You're a hero to them. They're local villagers, islanders...they don't have much, just their stories. I guess they've made you one of them."

Hawk turned and looked at the crowd of spectators. The native people smiled and waved to him. They were chanting something in their language. "Do you understand them? What are they saying?"

"American warrior. Silver Hawk," Richard translated.

Hawk smiled, surprised. He raised his left arm and waved. They cheered and jumped up and down. Quietly and unannounced, he was suddenly filled with a great desire to win.

"Listen," Richard said, "we do have one small problem."

"What problem?" Hawk asked, looking at him.

"This isn't an underground match," Richard said. "They're still placing bets and all but they have a rule about those boots you're wearing."

"I'll take them off," Hawk said.

"I don't have any other shoes," Richard said. "I could try to find a pair."

"Es all right."

"The floor is hard but most of the fighting is on mats."

"Richard, es all right," Hawk assured him. "I can do this. Don Antone never let me wear shoes when I was training. I can fight bare foot." He paused. "If es not underground...what match is this?"

267

Richard gave him a weak grin. "Um…well…" he began. "It's the…"

"Yes?" Hawk asked him, urging him to speak.

"A World Champion Martial Arts competition," Richard said, quietly. "If you don't want to…"

"They're fighting for points and scoring?" Hawk asked, concerned. "Richard I don't know how to do that, eh? I'm an underground fighter."

"You know the difference between the styles," Richard said. "If they call Karate, fight Karate. If they call Jeet Kune Do…do that." He shrugged.

Hawk laughed at him. "Richard, you suck as an owner," he stated. "I could lose this, badly. I don't know anything about tournament fighting."

"Look, it's relatively the same," Richard told him, "just don't break any bones."

Hawk released a loud groan of frustration. "Richard!" he exclaimed, "I can't do this." He saw Kenji walking toward the locker room. Hawk ran after him and stopped the fourteen year old. "Kenji please, I need a favor," he said.

"Ok," Kenji said, smiling. "What can I do for you Hawk?"

"Tell me about tournament fighting," Hawk said.

"What about it?"

"Everything," Hawk said.

Kenji smiled. He nodded and began to speak. He talked about the matches, the points and how they were scored. Kenji recited the rules and explained what could and what could not be done. Finally, he drew in a deep breath and sighed. "That is tournament fighting."

"Thank you Kenji," Hawk said.

"Good luck to you Hawk," Kenji said to him.

"I'll need it. I've never done this before," Hawk admitted. "I'm used to underground fighting."

"You will win," Kenji told him. "You are the best fighter here."

"Thanks Kenji," Hawk said, appreciatively. He noticed all the other fighters were wearing their best Karate and other fighting attire. He stuck out like a coyote among a flock of chickens and the judges had already noticed it. "Eh…well…" Hawk said slowly. The chant from the crowd caught his attention again. The native people didn't seem to care. They waved and smiled at him.

"Here," Richard said, handing Hawk a piece of paper. "Maybe this will help."

"Tournament rules," Hawk read, as they walked to the first competition. "Thanks Richard," he said dryly. "Five point loss for injury of opponent," he read, "five point loss for excessive force against opponent. If you use sweeps and takedowns you must know how safely drop your opponent?" Hawk stopped in his tracks. "This is a very bad idea."

"The underground fights are a little bit rougher," Richard agreed.

"A little bit?" Hawk asked. He lowered his voice and spoke quietly to Richard. "Friend, listen to me, eh? I was trained to fight so I could stand up when there es blood on the floor."

"Okay, so you'll have to tone it down a bit," Richard advised.

Hawk sighed. They reached the area where the first competition was to take place. All the fighters were wearing head gear, a mouth piece and other protective equipment. They also wore immaculate uniforms from their Martial Arts schools with patches on their shoulders and, Hawk did not fail to notice, they

269

were wearing the various colored belts they had received.

Richard looked at Hawk and sighed. "Okay, so we have a few problems."

"I don't even have shoes, Richard," Hawk told him.

"Let me talk to the judges," Richard said.

Hawk tried to pretend he wasn't there when Richard went over to the judges to explain their situation. He looked around nonchalantly and waited.

"Okay," Richard said. "They said as the gear is optional but you have to sign a form to release them of any injury you sustain. I told them your luggage was lost going through customs."

"I won't go into this on a lie, eh?" Hawk walked over to the judges. He was embarrassed and humiliated. "Excuse me," he said quietly. They looked up at him. "My friend doesn't mean any disrespect for the arts. He's very unfamiliar with tournaments. I am also. I don't have any gear," Hawk said. "I don't even have shoes but I would like to seek your permission to fight here today."

The judges exchanged glances and talked among themselves.

"Why do you wish to fight in this tournament?" One judge asked.

"It was a mistake," Hawk admitted. "I didn't know it was a tournament. I would go away and not bother you except...I want to see if I have the heart to do this. I've never fought in a real tournament. I've only been in illegal fights, nothing honorable. I want to see if I have the heart for it and if I can find my honor again."

The judges talked among themselves again and the first judge nodded. "You may fight," he said. "Sign this form." His gaze leveled with Hawk's. "Read and understand the rules," he advised.

"Thank you," Hawk said. He leaned over, took the pen into his hand and signed 'Joseph Silver Hawk Argent' on the form. He gave it to the judge.

"You may join the circle, Silver Hawk," the judge said.

Hawk went to stand with the other fighters. He didn't know them at all. They stared at him and began to whisper until the first match was called. He watched each match as it took place. At the end of each match, the judges held up a score from the number two for very bad to a number ten for excellent. So far, the highest scores were eights. He was very nervous when he was called to fight. Hawk bowed to the judges, and then took his place inside the circle. He lowered into a fighting stance.

His opponent came at him hard, with a high front kick. Hawk used a downward block, spun the opponent and delivered a punch to his back. His bare feet had not moved. The opponent tried again and again to punch and kick. Hawk used self defense only and blocked every move. Finally, he took one step and threw a high side sweep into his opponents shoulder, knocking the man sideways. Hawk moved gracefully and broke the man's fall to the matt. The fight ended. He turned and bowed to the judges.

The judges stared at him. Slowly, they began to turn the score cards over. Hawk received a straight line of tens, all excellent scores.

A cheer arose from the crowd and Richard let out a loud victory cry.

Hawk wondered what the fuss was about. He bowed again to the judges and went over to Richard. "Something es wrong, eh?" he said. "I didn't do anything."

"You won," Richard told him, smiling. "You'll go to the next round."

"Okay," Hawk said. He entered each competition

advancing to the final rounds thinking he could have eaten a big piece of that pineapple cake. But as he advanced the competition grew fiercer. Some of his opponents became angry and lost points for bad sportsmanship. One was disqualified for kicking him in the head. Hawk had managed to control the force he used and he didn't get angry at all. More importantly, he decided, he had done very well without breaking any bones.

The native people in the crowd were very happy, cheering him on. They repeated the chant for him over and over again.

"You're in the finals," Richard announced. "You might find this more interesting."

Hawk hoped so but he didn't say that. "Are you sure these are the best in the world?" he asked.

"You had to go through the first five rounds of matches," Richard said, reading from a piece of paper. "All of the best fighters are to meet in the center arena. It says here that four are chosen from the five hundred who have been fighting today. You must be one of the four!" Richard said, excitedly.

"Must be," Hawk stated. He saw the other finalists and stopped dead in his tracks.

"This is unbelievable," Richard uttered. "There's Khan!" he exclaimed. "Khan of Okinawa! And isn't that Belerignio?"

"Ah shit," Hawk uttered. "Ah no," he moaned. They saw him and smiled. He walked over and embraced Khan. He looked at Frank and laughed. "The two of you are finalists here?" he asked.

"This is Khan's title for seven years," Khan informed him.

"He wins every year," Frank said, smiling. "How are ya kid?"

"I'm ok," Hawk said. "This es Richard. He brought me here, eh? I'm doing all right, I guess."

272

"You doing better than all right," Khan told him. "Hello Richard."

"Hi," Richard said, staring at him.

"I can't fight you Khan," Hawk said. "I'll forfeit."

"You fight," Khan said, "in here or on the street. Old man kick your ass."

Hawk laughed. "Ok, I'll fight. I'm having trouble adjusting my kicks to the force they use."

"It's a lot different than the arena," Frank agreed, "but you can do it. You're going to lose against me so don't worry, you won't have to fight Khan."

Hawk laughed. He looked over at the fourth finalist. "Who es he?"

"He's the fighter I was telling you about," Richard said. "He's good."

"He bad news," Khan warned. "Be careful. He cheat his way to this circle."

"How do you cheat at this?" Hawk asked.

"You new to tournament fighting," Khan told him. "Watch his hands. You must be faster."

"What's his name?" Hawk asked.

"Khan," the old man stated.

Hawk saw the sadness in the old man's eyes.

"He nephew," Khan said, "bring much dishonor to family. You must be careful. You carry honor of Khan Family. You American Warrior. This nephew will try to bring harm to you."

"In other words kid," Frank Belerignio said, "He hates you because Khan trained you and not him."

"He's angry," Hawk said quietly.

273

"Very," Frank agreed. "What are you doing here anyway? You never fought a tournament in your life."

"It was my mistake," Richard told them. "We didn't know this was the World Championship. I thought it was just another underground fight."

Frank laughed, hard. He reached over and rubbed Hawk's head, boyishly. "You're a finalist for the best in the world, and you came in here by accident?" He laughed again.

Khan smiled. "He best quality. He fight anywhere."

"Any place, any time," Hawk added.

"What's your score so far?" Frank inquired. He took the paper out of Richard's hand. "Is this right?" he asked.

"Oh yes, it's very accurate," Richard said. "I've been careful with it."

Frank smirked and handed the paper to Khan.

"What es wrong with it, eh? I know I suck at this," Hawk said. "You don't have to rub it in."

Frank smiled at him. "You're second, you little shit. Khan's first. You past me up by twenty points."

"I didn't. How could I? I haven't been doing anything," Hawk said.

"I guess you won't have to fight me," Frank said, "or him." He nodded toward Khan's nephew.

Hawk looked at Khan. "You mean I…have to fight you?"

"Khan is first place," the old man stated. "First place long time."

A man came to the center of the arena with a microphone. "We will now conduct the final round for the Martial Arts World Championships. Standing in the center arena are the four finalists from today's event. With the top score, Khan of Okinawa,

Japan!"

The crowd cheered and Hawk cheered with them, smiling and clapping his hands.

"The second highest score belongs to Joseph Silver Hawk Argent of the Lakota Nation, United States of America!"

More thunderous cheering erupted. The native people yelled and called out to him. Hawk laughed.

"The third highest score of the day, Franco Bellerignio, New York, United States of America!"

"Bah," Hawk said, sneering playfully at him. "You don't live in New York."

Frank laughed. "I don't live anywhere kid."

"And our fourth finalist of the day, Sai Khan, Shanghai, China!" the man announced. "Our first match, Sai Khan and Franco Bellerignio!"

"Good luck Frank," Hawk said. He watched as Frank faced Khan's nephew and they began the first phase of the fight. The fighting was tougher now, full contact, but still scored on the point system.

"You see hands?" Khan asked Hawk.

"I see them," Hawk said. As Sai Khan moved, he was throwing discreet illegal punches hard, into Frank's chest. Frank was doing very well at blocking most of them but still, Hawk knew it wasn't allowed.

Frank retaliated with a high front kick, knocking Sai backward and away from him. He jumped, spun and swept Sai's legs from beneath him and dropped him to the mat. Frank turned and bowed to the judges.

The judges turned over their score cards. Frank received straight nines.

Hawk smiled and clapped his hands together. He felt

something stinging his right arm, saw the blood, looked up and saw Sai's angry face. Before he knew exactly what had happened, Frank grabbed Sai and pulled him away, taking the knife out of his hand.

Hawk stared down at his bloody arm. He'd been cut. It was a long cut from shoulder to elbow. People rushed over to him. He raised his head and stared as Sai Khan was escorted from the arena.

"Shit!" Frank swore loudly.

"I didn't see him," Hawk uttered. "I didn't…"

"He not supposed to have knife!" Khan yelled angrily.

"How bad is it kid?" Frank asked. "Jesus…"

Hawk stood still while the medics came and attended to his arm. They pressed hard to stop the bleeding, glued and taped the cut together. When it was over, his arm was wrapped in thick white bandages. He could barely move it.

"This is terrible," the emcee said. "You were second place."

"Am I being thrown out?" Hawk asked. "I didn't do anything."

The emcee looked at him. "Are you going to fight?"

"Es what I came here for," Hawk said. "I don't need this arm." It grew quiet around him then Frank's hearty laughter broke loose.

Khan smiled.

The emcee gave him and odd look. He walked over to the judges table.

"It wasn't my fault," Hawk said fiercely.

"They know it wasn't your fault kid," Frank said. "I think they're trying to decide whether or not you should continue. The biggest injuries so far were a busted rib and a bloody nose. Sai cut you pretty deep."

"That is a bad cut," Richard told him.

"I've had worse," Hawk said. He waited until the emcee returned.

"The judges agreed to allow you to fight," the emcee stated.

Hawk nodded. He looked over at Khan. The old man smiled at him. Hawk didn't want to fight Khan but he knew he had no choice. Khan would never allow him to forfeit the match. If Hawk chose to do that, he would disappoint his former teacher.

They were called to the center of the floor.

They bowed to each other and to the judges.

Hawk faced Khan and he swallowed, hard, feeling a lump growing in his throat. Instead of throwing the first punch, Hawk moved forward and wrapped his arms around the old man.

The entire room fell silent.

Hawk backed up somberly and bowed again, while Khan stood straight and tall. When Khan bowed in return to him, he felt honored. Khan came after him quickly, throwing several devastating blows. Hawk blocked efficiently and powerfully, as he'd been taught. He stopped every punch, and brought each kick to a sudden halt. He reacted instinctively. It was like breathing, easy and natural. Hawk refused to use a sweep. He declined to take Khan down to the matt. He stood and fought in a self defensive manner without attack…and his bare feet never moved an inch forward or backward.

They fought the full length of the match with neither of them falling to the floor. They bowed to each other, turned and bowed to the judges.

Hawk watched as they turned over the scorecards for

277

Khan. He received all tens and one nine. Hawk smiled at him. He waited for a few moments for his own score. The cards flipped over quickly, all tens. He drew in a breath and stared. Khan hugged him and smiled. Hawk was frozen, unable to move breath or think.

"You best quality," Khan said, smiling. "You beat old man!"

Frank laughed and congratulated him. "You did it kid! World Champion!"

The emcee announced it to the crowd and they went crazy, yelling and cheering but Hawk was stunned. Finally, he smiled. He laughed as they handed him the belt and the trophy. The news reporters flashed the cameras. Hawk posed with the Championship belt draped over his wounded arm and with his good arm across Khan's shoulders. Beside him stood Richard Dean and off to the side, in a more low profile place but still very proud was Franco Bellerignio. The picture was printed in newspapers all over the world.

Chapter Thirty One

Stands Proud sat down in the recliner and put the newspaper on his lap. He opened it and the sports section fell out onto the floor. He saw the photo and started to smile, slowly retrieving it. American Warrior, the headline read, Silver Hawk. It said his son was the Martial Arts Champion of the World. Stands Proud smiled at the picture of his son, standing with Khan. The phone rang and he picked it up, "Hello…yes, Jolene. I'm looking at it right now. He said he'd come home as soon as he could. I guess this is what he was up to," Stands Proud said. Someone was knocking at the door. Stands Proud got up with the phone in his hand. Leah was on the other side of the screen door, showing him the newspaper. "Come over," he told Jolene. "Leah is here already."

They started arriving at the Argent home in the morning and the gathering continued well into the night. They read pieces of the story aloud and talked about Silver Hawk. There was a big discussion on the story of the local islanders who somehow knew who Hawk was. The women cooked in the kitchen. They missed their 'helper' and talked about how good his fry bread was.

In Northern Palawan on the Philippine Islands, Hawk, Khan, Frank and Richard shared an evening meal, quietly, in the beach house together. They laughed and talked, sharing stories and enjoying each others company. Franco Bellerignio was the first to leave, having to exit the islands in a hurry due to the nature of his profession. He was the one who had carried out the hit on Don Antone Tassiano. He never stayed anywhere for long but he promised to visit the kid on the rez, soon. Khan said he had to return to Okinawa and he was very glad it was Hawk who now carried 'his' title.

They had been gone for hours. There was a full moon in the night sky over the China Sea. Hawk stood on the deck in front of the house. In the distance, he could hear the gulls crying out and the gentle ocean waves lapping at the shore. In this one day, he thought, he had recovered his pride, honor and dignity. Everything that had been stripped away had been restored, given back to him, and he was finally satisfied.

Richard came out onto the deck, smiling. "You look happy."

"I am," Hawk said. He looked over at Richard. "Thank you."

"For what? Being a lousy owner? The whole thing was one big mistake," Richard said, laughing.

Hawk grinned, "Ah, everything happens for a reason."

"Your arm is bleeding," Richard said, seeing the blood seeping through the gauze. "Does it hurt?"

"No," Hawk said, slowly. "Not so much."

Richard listened to the gentle lull of the water. "I guess you'll go home now," he said, looking intently at Hawk's face.

"Mmm hmmm," Hawk said. "I have a cabin in the Black Hills. I'm going to live there. I don't belong on the reservation, never have, but I do like those hills." He looked over at Richard. "You can visit some time if you want."

"I will," Richard said.

"Sorry I can't allow you to 'own' me anymore," Hawk said, teasing him. "You're so bad at it something has to be done about this."

Richard laughed. "Hey, I was able to go in there and get you from Bruce. I think I did all right. You believed it. I must've been a little scary."

"You were very scary to me," Hawk said. "I thought it

was starting all over again. It turned out to be the exact opposite." He paused. "I owe you Richard Dean."

"You don't owe me anything," Richard said, smiling, "unless you have thirty five million dollars I can give to my father…I'm kidding. Actually, I made a lot of money today. You did too."

Hawk nodded.

Richard watched as the night wind blew Hawk's long black hair over his shoulders. He noticed the way the moonlight glistened in Hawk's dark eyes and he smiled. "You're beautiful," he said softly.

Hawk laughed and leaned on the railing.

"You are," Richard insisted. He smiled as Hawk fell silent and he felt a slight rejection coming. "Very well then. I'm going to drink myself into oblivion," he stated. "Care to join me?" He handed Hawk a beer and opened one for himself.

Hawk grinned. He opened the can and drank from it.

"So the story I read in the newspaper, about the girlfriend," Richard said gently. "That was true?"

"Yeah," Hawk said softly. "I was with her for a few years."

"Were you in love with her?"

"I…thought I was but…"

"But what?" Richard asked.

"I've always known there should be something more…I mean…" he stammered. "I don't think I can love anyone."

"Why do you say that?"

"They never touch me."

"What do you mean they never touch you?" Richard asked, watching him.

"I mean, when anyone touched me," Hawk admitted, "their hands were like fire, burning my skin. It got so bad that any time someone put a hand on me, I turned to fight them. I even broke my best friend's arm because he tried to grab me, to stop me from fighting someone else." He paused and absently rubbed the wood of the railing with his fingertips. "Es why Khan came to the reservation. It wasn't just a visit. It was because I was out of control."

"When someone touched you...it hurt?"

"Yes," he said quietly.

"What about before?"

"Before?" Hawk asked him. He lifted the beer can to his lips, drank and swallowed. "There was no 'before'."

"What do you mean?"

"I mean," Hawk explained, "the first time I had sex I was forced into it." He glanced at Richard and looked away.

Richard watched him closely. "And now? Does it hurt now?"

"I don't know," Hawk said quietly. He hadn't let anyone close to him in a while. There was a nervous silence between them. He saw Richard's hand moving toward his face in the darkness. He grabbed Richard's wrist and his own chest began to arise and fall with anguish. "Don't," he whispered. "Don't do this."

"I won't hurt you," Richard promised.

Hawk glared at him.

"You don't want to know."

"I don't want *you* to know," Hawk said angrily. He expected the hurt look in Richard's eyes but he hadn't expected it to cause him pain as well. He released Richard's wrist and turned his face away. "Damn it Richard...just leave me alone."

"Are you going to be alone forever? Why are you doing this to yourself?"

Hawk lifted his head and looked directly into Richard's eyes. "I killed the last man I had sex with," he said coldly.

Richard faltered and stepped back. "Antonio?"

"Yes Antonio!" Hawk said with annoyance, "I was only a kid when they started…" Hawk's voice stopped short, choked off by his rage. He grasped the railing with both hands as if to hold himself still, to keep from hitting something…anything. "No one touches me," he said again. "No one."

"You killed him?" Richard asked quietly.

"He came into the vault with me," Hawk said slowly, "and I was still in chains. He wanted my hands 'cuffed in front of me and he released them from the waist chain so I could…" His eyes burned with angry tears and he blinked them away. "He always told me what to do…and I did it. It was easier to do this than to be taken to the wall and whipped, eh? I didn't fight. I never fought. I let him do whatever he wanted and I didn't refuse anything he asked for. In the morning…I put my arms around his neck and I…I choked him to death." Hawk saw Richard's hand slowly coming toward his face again and he closed his eyes. "You…are crazy," he said, taking deep breaths and trying to steady himself.

"I won't hurt you," Richard said.

Hawk felt the warmth of Richard's hand on his cheek. He released a breath of anguish and sorrow. "Damn you," he whispered.

"Does that hurt?" Richard asked gently.

"No," Hawk admitted. He stood up straight, released the railing and blinked the tears from his eyes. They cascaded over his face. "Damn it Richard…why? Why are you doing this?"

"I don't want you to be alone," Richard said. He was

283

surprised when Hawk's arm came across his shoulders and pulled him closer. He was warm and he smelled of smoke and leather.

"But I'm not alone," Hawk whispered hoarsely.

The next morning they flew back to Colorado and Hawk used some of the fighting money to buy a car, a high gloss black 1969 Mustang. Richard gave him the picture that he'd promised and invited him to come and stay anytime he wanted. Hawk told him that he would and he encouraged Richard to visit the Black Hills. Hawk put the large photograph, framed and wrapped, in the backseat of the car. As he got behind the steering wheel, he realized that he hadn't gone anywhere alone in this life time. When he was small, he was with his mother and his family. As he grew, he walked with Los Caballeros on Salcida. And then, there was Don Antone where he was constantly guarded.

Hawk drew in a deep breath and exhaled. It was nearly summer time, a warm spring day. He started the car and put the roof down. He smiled as he put on his sun glasses and started down the driveway. When he reached the highway, the wind blew through his hair and his heart lifted inside of his chest. He thought of the moment Richard had photographed and decided, yes, that was freedom. But this freedom, he thought, of being on the road, moving down the highway and knowing that he was headed back to his homeland…this, he knew, was true freedom. He knew who he was, where he belonged and Silver Hawk was going home.

Chapter Thirty Two

Hawk arrived home late at night. There was a small lamp on in the living room and it cast a path of dim light from the front door, onto the porch. He walked quietly up the steps, carrying the picture. Through the screen door, he could see his father sleeping in the recliner. The picture from the newspaper had been framed and hung on the wall beside him. Hawk smiled as he closed the door, quietly. He leaned the larger photograph against the wall and crossed the floor.

Stands Proud had seemed to age in the past month and Hawk felt responsible for it. Perhaps his father had been careless in his younger days but he was trying hard now. Could they ever make up for lost time? Would they? Hawk wasn't sure but time, he knew, moved along. And there was a time for forgiveness. Hawk lowered to one knee beside his father's chair and very carefully placed his hand over his father's.

Hawk watched as Stands Proud stirred and he began to smile. "Ate'," he said in Lakota. "Ma' ate. I'm home." Stands Proud opened his eyes. Hawk knew his father was wondering if it was real or a dream. Hawk's smile grew.

Stands Proud smiled at him. "You found your way back," he said.

"Hau, I did." As his father arose from the chair, Hawk slowly stood upright. He felt taller and somehow stronger than what he'd been when he left. He put his arm across his father's shoulders, gently. "I'm going to stay," he told Stands Proud. His father's arms tightened around him.

Stands Proud's hand touched the white bandage of the wounded arm. "You're hurt again, Cetan."

"It will heal." Hawk backed up and looked at his father. "Are you all right? I'm sorry if I worried you."

Stands Proud nodded. "I was very worried," he admitted, "and afraid for you. All I knew was one of Tassiano's men came and took you away." He settled back into his chair, tiredly.

Hawk sat down on the couch. "It was Bruce," he said. "They took me to Colorado and eh…" He looked away from his father.

"Did they hurt you again?" Stands Proud asked.

"No Papa…I was sold on the black market." Hawk told him. He started to smile and Stands Proud gave him a strange look. "The man who bought me turned out to be a good person. He has admired my fighting skills for a very long time. His name is Richard Dean. He had no intention of holding me against my will."

"That's good," Stands Proud said quietly.

"Yeah," Hawk breathed out and nodded. "Anyway, I was going to come home but I felt I should stay with him a while. He entered me in a fight. We thought it was an underground fight, an illegal one." Hawk looked over at the newspaper photo and smiled wide. "It wasn't."

Stands Proud laughed. He pointed to the picture. "You did that by accident?" he asked.

"Yeah," Hawk admitted. He laughed. He thought of the larger photo and how perfect it was. Don Antone had adopted him and demanded perfection. Stands Proud, he realized, never made any such demands. Stands Proud, his true father, had always accepted him no matter who he was or what he'd done. "I have a gift for you," Hawk said, standing up. He walked over to the large photo, stood it in the center of the room and tore the brown wrapping paper away from it. Hawk smiled at the look on his father's face.

Stands Proud chuckled, in a very pleased manner. "You're flying," he said.

Hawk laughed and nodded.

"What about the old ways belief?" Stands Proud asked him, knowing this son clung to tradition and would not give it up easily.

"If my soul es captured here," Hawk told him, "then I will give it to you and place it in your care. From tonight on, I'll never be far away from it." He paused. "I'm going to live in the hills, Papa, in my old cabin."

Stands Proud released a sigh of satisfaction and contentment. His vision blurred and he found he couldn't speak.

"I belong here," Hawk told him. "I am a part of all that is here, the prairie, the wind…the laughter of the people…and even in their tears. I can't be away from them or from you anymore."

Stands Proud arose to his feet once again and embraced his son. "Welcome home Silver Hawk," he said, in a muffled voice.

Rafa came stumbled sleepily down the hallway, rubbing his eyes. "I knew it!" he exclaimed. "I knew I heard you, eh?" He ran forward and grabbed his old friend roughly.

Hawk laughed and cringed with pain at the same time. "Ow, ow, ow!" he yelped, "Rafa! My arm!"

"Oh sorry," Rafa said, letting go. "Dios mio…how bad is that?" He saw the blood seeping through the gauze.

"Another scar," Hawk told him, smiling. "How are you?"

"Ok, you know? The same," Rafa said. "I'm still in school. They didn't throw me out yet, so I guess that's good, eh?"

"Si, muy bueno," Hawk said.

"You," Rafa said, waking up, "you're a World Champion now? You're famous."

Hawk laughed. "It was a mistake Rafa," he said. "It was terrible really," he said. "It was a tournament with rules and regulations. I was bored to tears, eh? But I did ok." He shook his head. "I had to fight Khan. I didn't want to."

"You beat Khan?"

"The judges gave me a better score," Hawk said. "Khan said he was tired anyway. He had the title for seven years. He said I did him a favor."

"Everyone es talking about it," Rafa told him. "Your brother es bragging to anyone who will listen to him."

Hawk smiled. "He's bragging? He's not angry?" Wolf had always been jealous of everything Hawk had done.

"You'll hear him," Rafa told Hawk. "He never shuts up, eh?"

"How is he?" Hawk asked Rafa and Stands Proud. "How is Wolf? Is he all right?"

"Wolf is fine," Wolf said, coming in the front door. "Wolf is just very tired from being woken up again by his younger brother."

Hawk smiled and embraced him. "How did you know I was here?"

"I had a feeling," Wolf muttered. He rubbed his upper arm. "Why don't you take some pain medicine once in a while?"

Hawk laughed. "Quit fooling with me," he said. "You can't feel this."

Wolf smirked. "You think?" He walked over and plopped down onto the couch. "Your right leg hurts too, the one that was broken before."

Hawk looked at him. There was a pain in his lower right leg where the bone had never set right.

"And I don't know what you were doing last night," Wolf

said tiredly, rubbing his face, "but that was really weird, ok?"

Hawk stared at him. As identical twins, Wolf had never had a connection to him but somehow, it was there now. "Do… you know what I was doing?" he asked.

"No but I felt it," Wolf told him.

Rafa leaned closer to Hawk and whispered, "He's been like this," Rafa said. "Es kind of freaky, eh?"

Hawk smiled and tilted his head, amused. He crossed his arms over his chest. "Wolf?" he said.

"Hmmmm?" Wolf asked, raising his head and giving his brother a dazed stare.

"You're weird," Hawk said. He threw his head back and laughed, hard.

LaVergne, TN USA
22 April 2010
180215LV00002B/65/P